Critical Acclaim for *Mara*

Mara by Lisette van de Heg is in many ways a pleasant surprise.

[...] You are pulled into the story and sympathize intensely with the injustice done to main character, Mara. Lisette van de Heg is a promise, that will hopefully write many more beautiful books.

– EO (Evangelische Omroep)

The descriptions of [Mara's] feelings are magnificent.

– De Waarheidsvriend

Abuse of power of a protestant spiritual leader did [in the novel's time] not necessarily harm vulnerable children in boarding-schools, but their lust was aimed mainly at vulnerable women. Lisette van de Heg dared to portray such a young woman and to show the poignant consequences of sexual abuse. She knows how to do this credibly and without giving cheap solutions, [...] a spirited book by a committed author with unmistakable talent.

– Lydeke van Beek, Protestant.nl

Author Lisette van de Heg has drawn the main character with great emphatic ability. Mara is the victim of abuse and has been brainwashed completely by the culprit. It is Mara's own fault. God is very far away. God belongs to the perpetrator, who calls the abuse a punishment from God. This spiritual destruction is an added crime besides the abuse of crossing physical borders. Van de Heg is able to narrate very visually, without verbiage. She has written a credible, hopeful novel about life after abuse.

– Martha Aalbers, Nederlands Dagblad

The main character of this story goes on through a credible growth and the author does not easily brush off the major questions of life. [...] Her novel holds the reader's breathless attention thanks to an excellent build up of tension in the story, the smooth wording and an exact character drawing.

– Enny de Bruijn, Reformatorisch Dagblad

Mara

Library and Archives Canada Cataloguing in Publication

Heg, Lisette van de, 1983-
[Mara. English]
    Mara / Lisette van de Heg ; Inge van Delft.

Translation of: Mara.
Issued in print and electronic formats.
ISBN 978-1-77161-001-8 (pbk.).--ISBN 978-1-77161-002-5 (html).--
ISBN 978-1-77161-003-2 (pdf)

    I. Delft, Inge van, translator II. Title. III. Title: Mara. English.

PT5882.18.E3M3713 2014   839.313'7   C2013-908670-6
                                                   C2013-908671-4

Pubished by Mosaic Press, Oakville, Ontario, Canada, 2014.
Distributed in the United States by Bookmasters (www.bookmasters.com).
Distributed in the U.K. by Gazelle Book Services (www.gazellebookservices.co.uk).

MOSAIC PRESS, Publishers
Copyright © 2014, Lisette van de Heg.
Originally published by Uitgeverij Vuurbaak/Plateau, Barneveld, The Netherlands.
English language translation copyright © 2014, Inge van Delft

Printed and bound in Canada.
Cover design by Eric Normann.
Cover photo by Samantha Villagran (http://www.freeimages.com/profile/sammylee)
ISBN   Paperback 978-1-77161-001-8
              ePub 978-1-77161-002-5
              ePDF 978-1-77161-003-2

We acknowledge the financial support
of the Government of Canada through the
Canada Book Fund (CBF) for
this project.

Nous reconnaissons l'aide financière du
gouvernement du Canada par l'entremise
du Fonds du livre du Canada (FLC) pour
ce projet.

 Canadian   Patrimoine
Heritage   canadien

Canadä

Mosaic Press gratefully acknowledges the assistance of the OMDC (Ontario Media Development Corporation) in support of our publishing program.

MOSAIC PRESS
1252 Speers Road, Units 1 & 2
Oakville, Ontario L6L 5N9
phone: (905) 825-2130
info@mosaic-press.com

www.mosaic-press.com

Mara

Lisette van de Heg

Translated by Inge van Delft

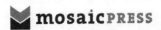

Other titles by Lisette van de Heg

Noor, 2011

Sub Rosa, 2012

Later, 2014

For more information on the author, please visit:
http://www.lisettevandeheg.nl/

*'He heals the brokenhearted
and binds up their wounds.'*

(Psalm 147:3)

I

It was still pitch black outside when it was time to leave. I had not been able to sleep at all. Slowly I dressed myself for the journey that lay ahead. I would have to dress warm for this cold, dreary night. With every layer of clothing I added another protective barrier for my body. Then I pressed my hand against the cold glass of my bedroom window as I looked out one last time. The heavens were weeping.

My mother, however, did not shed a tear. She still refused to even look at me and did not speak a word. I reached for her, hugged her and I hoped for a word, a gesture, a kiss. But there was nothing. She was like carved marble, devoid of any emotion. At last I kissed her on the cheek and let go of her. I clenched my teeth and turned away from her to pick up my suitcases.

I didn't take much with me. Just my clothes, a wedding picture of my parents (for years I had kept this hidden away), some writing paper and a pen. Nothing but small items, and I realized that my existence was so insignificant that I could pack it up in a couple of plain suitcases.

I opened the door and stepped out into the rain with my suitcases in hand, and a travel bag hanging off my shoulder. I started to walk and did not look back, for I knew the Reverend would be following me. The sound of footsteps behind me confirmed this. He would accompany me on the first part of my journey.

He did not speak a word. We walked the path around the manse, through the gate, into Hooghe Breet Street, past the little white church, toward Harbour Street. Our footsteps echoed loudly in the dark, deserted street. It would not be this quiet in Harbor Street. Fishermen would already be hard at work there, and just about ready to set sail.

I shivered when a few raindrops fell in my neck. The silence between us was broken only by the sound of our echoing footsteps and the rain pouring down from the rooftops beside us. The silence was like a humming sound in my ears. It grew louder and louder to the point where I wanted to cover my ears with my hands and shut everything out. But I could not. I had two suitcases to carry. So I just waited for his words of admonition. But still no words broke the silence. I took a deep breath of relief when I saw, in the distance, the first flickers of hurricane lanterns. People. Voices. Noise.

One last time I glanced back over my shoulder, to the past, and I wished my mother were there behind me, loving, as she used to be. But she was not there and I turned again to look ahead of me. There, in front of me, was my future. My mother would no longer be a part of it. I had come to realize that much. My mother had chosen him, and nothing could change that.

Finally he broke the silence, and also my thoughts of mother, with his commanding words.

'Give me your suitcases, Maria.'

Of course, we had to keep up appearances. Outward appearances were always so important to him. He was always concerned of what others would perceive.

'Here you are.' I had to stop myself from dropping the suitcases right there and simply keep walking. Instead, I stopped, and handed him the suitcases. Even though I was wearing gloves, I shuddered when our hands briefly touched. I looked down at the ground and waited for him to start walking again. There was only a short distance left to go.

When we came to the end of Harbor Street, the smell of seawater and fish welcomed us. Also the sounds of men shouting, chains rattling and here and there a starting engine drifted our way. These

were the sounds that would accompany me on my journey. I obediently followed the Reverend as he walked up to a cutter bearing
the name 'Coby'.

'Good mornin', Rev'rend!'

'Pieters.' The Reverend nodded slightly, but his shoulders
tensed, and I could tell that the thick local dialect annoyed him. I
never did find out why he had agreed to accept the call to preach in
this distant corner of the country. He could not possibly have expected to find educated people living and working here?

'Mornin', Maria.'

'Good morning, Pieters.' My voice was no more than a whisper,
but Pieters did not seem to notice. He gestured for us to come
aboard and he took the suitcases from the Reverend. He showed
me the hatch and started to open it, but I shook my head. I preferred to stay on deck despite the rain. Below it would be dark and
stuffy, stifling and lonely. Pieters chatted with the Reverend while
pointing me toward a place in the center of the cutter where I
could take a seat, in between the barrels, which normally would
transport the cutter's catch of mussels. I ignored the conversation,
and strolled along past the barrels, toward the bow. Canal water
lightly sprayed upwards and mingled with the continual rain.

'I am leaving now, Maria. Take good care of your aunt.' I had
not heard him approach me and I started. Playing the part of a loving father he leaned toward me and kissed my cheek. At the same
time he hissed a vicious word in my ear. I shuddered and couldn't
hide it from him. He remained very close to me and smiled down
at me.

'You know it's true,' he whispered. 'You're no better than
Helène.'

His breath singed my skin and I wanted to get away from him,
but there was no room. There was only the rail. And the canal. An
impossible possibility since I couldn't swim. My eyes searched for
Pieters, but he was busy and didn't concern himself with us. I did
not want to breathe in the smell of the Reverend, and tried to hold
my breath.

Finally the Reverend took a small step back, and with relieve I
breathed more freely. He kept staring at me intently and expec-

tantly, until I realized what he was waiting for.

'Goodbye, Father.' The words came out of my mouth, but had lost all meaning. Still, he nodded approvingly.

The Reverend left the cutter, turned and raised his hand in a quick salutation. 'Goodbye, Pieters. You'll take good care of her?'

'Yeah, Rev'rend.' Pieters raised his hand in response, without giving the Reverend another look. At the same time he winked at me. 'What's he thinkin'! Of course I'll look after ya!'

I smiled, grateful for his indignation. Then I turned and looked out over the water in front of me. Look forward now. There's nothing left behind me. There was no loved one waving me off from the quay. There were no sweet memories to cherish.

The innocent white of the little church I left behind had long ago become a tarnished yellow for me. Eventually it was even stained with desperate-black. Time and time again I would visit the church, Sunday after Sunday. Every time I walked up to the church entrance I'd look up and hope that the fish-shaped wind dial would tumble down and shatter into a thousand pieces, every fragment small enough to be crushed by my feet. It never happened.

I knew that the little white steeple of the church towered proudly over the surrounding houses, but I refused to look at that accusing finger again. That's where he was in contact with his God. That's where he received permission to do what he did. That's where he was the obedient servant.

I would now return to the house of my youth, back to the woods and meadows. I remembered Grandpa and Grandma. And Aunt Be. My thoughts briefly recalled the shadowy figure that remained in my memory of the person waiting for me at the end of my journey. I had not seen her for 10 years and now I was expected to share a home with her, confined like a recluse.

A boy of about 14 years old presented himself to Pieters, and this seemed to indicate that the whole crew was accounted for. The cutter was only a small one and one young hand sufficed. The anchor was raised and we cast off. I remained at the bow and held on to the rail. My jaws were clenched tight as my skin caught the last tears the rain was shedding. I had a lump in my throat and a child in my belly, but my eyes remained dry. I was leaving the village

9

with the white church, the Reverend, and the woman who used to be my mother, and I did not look back. But his words haunted me, and I slid back into the past while the fishing boat brought me to my first destination.

I was skipping along, holding my mother's hand. The two braided pigtails in my hair kept falling softly on my shoulders, a feeling I enjoyed. Sometimes I would purposely shake my head from left to right as hard as I could, just to make the pigtails fly in a circle through the air around my head. But not now, now I let them fall softly. With each skip a soft flop, flop.

'They'll fall off, you know,' Mother said. She smiled and gave my hair a tug. Her smile was friendly and reminded me of Grandma and Auntie Be, who still lived on the farm. Their mouths were all the same, I thought.

We arrived at the market and Mother pulled me along past the stalls. She stopped at the vegetable stall and selected some nice red apples. I pulled on the sleeve of her dress.

'Why don't we pick apples from a tree?'

'We don't have an orchard here, sweetie, so I have to buy apples now.'

I nodded and thought of our new house with the little garden. Mother was right, there was no orchard. Mother bargained with the salesman about the apples and vegetables. In the end they agreed on a price. All the while I kept holding her hand, but I let my eyes roam freely.

The next stall was a fishmonger's. I stared at the man behind the table. He wore a white apron, and he shouted continually while he'd grab a fish from the pile with one hand, and cut its head off with the other. I shuddered, but kept watching, intrigued by his appearance, his handiwork and especially his voice. His voice was so loud, I was convinced that the whole village could hear him. This man would for sure make an excellent preacher. Everyone in church would be able to hear him.

Suddenly the fishmonger smiled and nodded straight at me, and with a quick movement he tossed something in my direction. Before I knew what had happened I felt something cold slap against my face. I screamed, loud and shrill. I touched my nose but couldn't feel anything unusual. The man's bellowing laughter made people turn their heads. Mother, worriedly, lowered herself down to my level, and asked me what was wrong. I didn't know and looked down with embarrassment. Then I noticed something lying on my wooden shoe, and again I shrieked. I jumped to make the thing slip off. Mother started and pulled me close to her. I trembled, and held on to her tightly. Gradually I calmed down, and when mother rose I heard a woman's voice.

'I saw what happened. He threw that starfish at her and it hit her in on the nose.'

Beside us stood a woman, holding a little boy by the hand. Her hair was red and her nose was red, her eyes were green and her dress was green. In her hand she held up the very thing that only a moment earlier had been lying on my feet.

'Go ahead, you can touch it,' she said to me. 'It can't hurt you, it's only a starfish.' She smiled, and I tentatively reached out my hand to take the thing from her. Then suddenly my mother pulled my hand away.

'How dare you! I may be new in this village, but I know who you are. Stay away from my daughter!'

Mother took my hand and squeezed it so hard it hurt, but before I could protest she had dragged me along. She pulled my arm so hard, I had to run to keep up with her. Mother hurried me along through the streets, not stopping at any of the other stalls, back to the manse.

'What is it, Mother, why are we walking so fast?' I whimpered. My foot got caught in the pavement and I tripped. I would have fallen, had Mother not held my hand so tightly.

Finally she slowed down, and in the end she stood still. Her cheeks were flushed and her eyes still burned with anger, but when she looked at me I saw that her eyes slowly softened.

'Oh sweetie, I didn't mean to hurt you. It was…' Mother swallowed, and for a moment she closed her eyes. 'That woman from the market is a very bad woman, Maria. I did not want her to talk to you. Will you remember that? You are not ever allowed to talk to her, or to that boy. They are bad people, very, very bad.'

Mother looked at me gravely, and I nodded obediently. *I nodded so hard that my pigtails made small flops. Not nice ones. Serious, harsh little flops.*

Pieters' voice brought me out of my reveries and I turned to face him. I realized that he was shouting at his deck hand, not me. The boy jumped around the deck with great agility and followed every order Pieters shouted at him.

The rain had stopped and I wiped my face with my sleeve. My woolen coat had kept me mostly dry, but the water felt cold on my cheeks. I shivered and wondered how long it would take us to reach our destination.

Pieters and the boy were working hard, and I turned away. Just look forward now. From now on I must only look forward. My fingers tightened around the wet rail, and I stared into the water as the cutter was gliding over it. Again the idea surfaced that this water could be the solution for all my troubles. It would mean the end of everything I now had to deal with. I would disappear into the depth and nobody would ever see me again. Nobody would miss me.

I shook my head and straightened up. Just look forward. The past no longer mattered. Today was the first day of my new life.

2

Vlissingen. The last time I had been here, I had been a little girl with a new father. The wedding celebrations had just come to an end, and we had been full of plans for the future and were eagerly anticipating the journey ahead to 'our new congregation'. I had trustfully nestled my hand in Mother's hand. She had smiled at me, and I had known that everything would be all right. I had a new father! I had been so excited when we had first arrived at the harbour and I had seen all the boats. Seagulls had circled in the air above us shrieking at each other. I had held my head back, with my mouth open in thrilled delight. I had pointed with my finger and laughed out loud, until his voice harshly had cut through my enthusiasm.

'Come along. Now.'

His hand had taken mine and I had obediently followed him. I had looked up to him, smiling. My new father was going to bring me to a new life. He would care for us, and Mother would no longer be sad and full of grieve because my real father was dead.

Vlissingen. It was as if memories of happier days had been waiting here for me all these years. As if the water was an invisible barrier between here and there, between the past and the present. As soon as we sailed into the harbour I could hear the shrill shriek of a seag-

13

ull and I looked up. I wanted to be as free as that bird. Maybe this was my chance. The corners of my mouth curled into a smile and I moved my tongue, ready to shriek just like that seagull. Then I noticed Pieters watching me and I contained myself. I walked back to the centre of the deck. My suitcases were still there and I picked them up. With my luggage in hand I watched how Pieters maneuvered the cutter to the quayside.

The minister had refused to arrange for a chaperone. He had also forbidden my mother to travel with me and she had accepted that.

'Your daughter will manage just fine, whichever way.'

Mother had nodded with her lips tightly closed. I could not only see, but also feel the anger that for weeks now had been wrapped around her like a cloak. At first I had asked her about it.

'You make me angry, Maria.'

'But Mother…'

'No, Maria, enough has been said…' her voice faltered as she turned away from me. Her shoulders square in rejection.

After that I had tried to sooth her with my actions. I performed every task without complaint. I looked for extra chores and brought home some candy as a treat, paid for with my own savings. All I hoped for was her arm around me, but she dispelled that hope so lightly.

'Don't bother, Maria.'

In the end I stopped looking at her with hopeful expectation, for I couldn't expect anything from her anymore.

'That's where ya have to be, Maria!' Pieters walked over and stood beside me. He shouted, even though he stood close to me, and he pointed at the other side of a busy street.

'That building there. Will ya need help?'

I shook my head. I knew that he wanted to drop me off as soon as possible, so he would be able to continue and make the most of his workday. He kindly helped me with my suitcases, and he placed them on the quayside for me.

'Thank you very much, Pieters.' I shook his hand, slung the strap of the bag over my shoulder, took the two suitcases in my hands and started to walk.

The building I headed for was large and tall. From the outside it looked regal, with ornamental relief, a small tower, and stained glass windows. I could hardly believe I would be allowed to just walk in.

I chose the middle one of three tall entrance doors, and I followed other travelers, who all purposefully found their way. To the left and to the right I saw waiting areas, and I saw a sign that pointed out the royal waiting area. Not a place for me. I ended up at a ticket booth by simply following the travelers ahead of me. I kept a little distance and put the suitcases down beside me on the floor.

I pulled the travel bag off my shoulder and unfastened the button, all the while trying to stay calm and look like a seasoned traveler. But my breath came fast and my fingers trembled when I took hold of the notebook in which I had written all the details of my journey. I had borrowed the grocer's train timetable and had carefully copied everything, down to the abbreviation of each station's name. That is how afraid I was to end up in the wrong place. I quickly found the right page and checked the list of train station, which I actually knew by heart by now. All I had to do was buy a train ticket. How hard could this be?

I slapped the notebook shut and put it back into my bag. Then I lifted up my suitcases and joined the line-up.

Most of the people ahead of me, I thought, were working class, judging by their clothing. They were clearly used to traveling, casually chatting amongst themselves while the line slowly moved up. Behind me new passengers joined the line. They also seemed to enjoy themselves just fine.

Each time another person's turn came up, I would pick up my suitcases, move one single step closer toward the ticket booth, and place the suitcases back down, one on either side of me. Bend, lift, step, put back down. Simple movements, but my fingers trembled more and more, and I started to transpire as I came closer and closer to the ticket booth.

The Reverend had given me enough money, but not for my sake. It was all for the sake of appearances. Auntie was not to think that I had been sent away uncared for.

'You will buy yourself a second class ticket.'

I had nodded my head. Of course, appearances were worth a lot. I would be traveling second class, and if possible even in a women's-only car. Although, the grocer had told me that they didn't always have those anymore.

Finally it was my turn.

The man at the booth yawned good and long behind his hand and he blinked his eyes a number of times.

'Good morning Miss, how can I help you.'

'I would like to buy a train ticket.'

'I figured that. Where to?'

'To Velp, sir.'

'What class?'

'Second class, please.'

The man pulled a green pad of paper toward him and he started to write quickly. He looked up for a minute.

'One passenger?'

'Yes, sir.'

He lay down his pen and put a stamp on the paper.

'That will be seven guilders and fifty five cents, Miss.'

I took my little wallet from the bag and fumbled in the coin compartment. I was looking for three two-and-a-half guilder coins and a ten cent piece to give to the man, but I let the ten cent coin slip and it rolled onto the floor. I bent down to pick it up, but I could not get a grip on the smooth round coin. I imagined that the people behind me would come forward and walk around me. Someone would take my place at the booth.

Finally I got a hold of the coin and I stood up. The people behind me were still patiently waiting and I paid the clerk.

'There you are, sir.' I knew my cheeks were flaming red and I felt a drop of sweat on my nose. I quickly put the money in the container on the ticket counter, then wiped my nose with my sleeve.

The man put my train ticket in a similar container on his side. Then he gave the contraption a twist and I got my ticket and he got the money. After another twist I got my change.

'Could you tell me where I should go, sir?' I leaned slightly closer to get his attention, since by now already he was looking over my shoulder for the next passenger.

He pointed briefly with his hand, then waved me on.

'Platform two, can't miss it. Next!'

Without a word of thanks I stepped back, and first placed my wallet and ticket in my bag. Then I looked around me. There were several groups of passengers all moving in different directions. I grabbed my suitcases and returned into the hall that I had crossed earlier on. I looked around me, searching, until I found the sign that I had noticed on my way in.

Platform two. An arrow pointed me into the right direction and I saw on the clock beside the sign, that I had plenty of time. Nevertheless, I walked as quickly as I could to the platform. Better to be early than late.

'Ticket, Miss.'

A man stopped me before I could enter the platform and he stretched his hand out toward me. I looked at him, not understanding, until I noticed the ticket punch in his other hand. I quickly found my ticket and handed it to him.

'Here you are.' My voice trembled. I looked left when I heard a warning whistle, a short sound followed by a longer one. Then I saw a train slowly roll into the station accompanied by a lot of hissing and smoke. If that was my train I had to hurry.

I looked back at the man who calmly took the train ticket and punched a hole in it with his ticket punch. Everything went slowly. With his thumb he pointed back over his shoulder toward the train which stood still by now. Then he returned the ticket to me. I quickly folded it in half and stuffed it into my wallet. Once again I grabbed my luggage and I walked onto the platform, struggling with the shoulder bag that almost slipped off, and the two suitcases that kept bumping into my legs, hindering me in my clumsy walk toward the train.

On the platform I let a porter help me and I watched how he dragged the suitcases to the baggage car. The smell of oil and soot, blown onto the platform with the train's arrival, made me nauseous and I was relieved that someone else took my luggage so I didn't need to carry them anymore. I gratefully gave the porter a good tip and he in turn kindly pointed me to the right passenger car.

'If you look for a seat now, you will probably still find one by a window.'

He touched his hat and disappeared, in search of a new passenger.

I decided to follow his advice and got on the passenger car he had pointed out. In the first empty car I looked for a window seat. Exhausted, I slumped down with the bag still hanging off my shoulder. I closed my eyes and breathed deeply in and out.

Then I pulled the bag onto my lap.

I realized I was exhausted, drained.

In my mind's eye I saw my mother's face and his. The two of them together, like a cold and impenetrable front. Again I wondered to myself what had happened to the woman my mother once had been. When had he consumed all her spirit and snuffed out the light in her eyes? *Had* he done that?

At first, when we had just moved into the manse, my mother had been just like I always knew her. We went exploring together through the spacious house and I helped her keeping the rooms clean. When we were finished with our work, she would prepare tea and we would have a cup of tea together. On a rug on the floor sometimes, in one of the rooms of our new home. We'd be having a picnic, Mother would say, and we would pretend we were outside, in one of the fields surrounding the farm.

'We'll invite Auntie Be and Grandma for a visit,' she told me. That same evening she suggested it to the Reverend. I stood beside her and squeezed my hands in excitement. Full of expectation I smiled up at the man in black, who was my new father, and I listened while my mother offered her suggestion.

'No.'

The answer was short and clear. It left no room for questions, doubt or hope. I looked at my mother, expecting her to try once more, but she gave me a sad smile and shook her head.

I missed Grandma and Auntie Be, and Mother missed them too. I knew that, because she had told me, but she never talked about it again in the Reverend's presence, and I also kept quiet about it. When word arrived that Grandma had died, Mother cried for many long days, but we did not make the journey to her funeral. Mother turned pale and quiet, and I silently looked on.

3

'May I sit here, my dear?'
I flinched and opened my eyes to find myself face to face with an old nun.

No, I'd rather you didn't. 'Yes, of course.' I moved over a little and pulled back the shoulder bag, which was about to slip off my lap.

'Would you like the window seat?' I asked to be polite.

'No, no, I'm quite alright here.' She let herself drop on the seat beside me and groaned a bit as her joints protested.

'Old and falling apart.' She laughed as she looked at me, but I just held on to my bag tighter and moved another half an inch closer to the window.

'I'm Sister Olivia.' My hope for a peaceful train ride dissipated when she offered me her hand. Carefully I took her old hand in mine, and before I could remove my hand, I could feel the brittle bones move under my fingers.

'Maria Klomp.' I was silent again and looked outside where it was awfully busy now. Not much time could have passed between the moment I got on the train and when I dozed off, but there were noticeably more people now. It was as if everyone had been hiding away in little holes for the right moment to appear.

When finally the train departed, I watched, with dry eyes, how Vlissingen station disappeared. I did not waste any thoughts on my own village, family, or the villagers. It was bad enough that I would have to carry that part of my life around with me the months ahead. I felt cursed, and I quietly cursed my past. Maybe after doing that I would be able to bury and forget.

'So, where are you going to, if I may ask?' The old nun again. Couldn't she go sit somewhere else?

I quickly told her that I had a long journey to make, all the way to Velp. To my amazement she smiled joyfully as I spoke.

'How wonderful, my dear. Our Dear Lord must have put you in my path. I am on my way to Velp, as well. We can travel together. O, how wonderful! I really dislike traveling you know.' Her wrinkles folded and unfolded while she spoke, and a few white hairs on her chin moved up and down.

'I seriously doubt that your Dear Lord had anything to do with that,' I said sullenly. I did not at all like the idea that God would still concern himself with my life, and the words slipped out of my mouth before I could stop them.

'Oh.' She was quiet and did not ask anymore, but instead she took her rosary and started to mumble softly.

I felt ashamed of what I had said, and I looked out of the window at the passing scenery. The silence I had wanted so badly was now no longer pleasant, as I was responsible for it because of my harsh words. After a few minutes, I could no longer hold back an apology.

'I am sorry, Sister Olivia. I should not have said that.' If I had felt free to do so, I would have explained to her why I did not believe that her Dear Lord had anything to do with it. I remained silent however, for I knew she would not be interested in hearing my explanations. Mother always said that an excuse consisted of the excuse, not an explanation.

The old nun smiled at me and she placed her hand gently on mine. I immediately wanted to pull my hand back, but I held back and merely made a fist of my hand.

'It's all right. We won't talk about it anymore, good?'

Thankfully, she removed her hand when I nodded in response. I wiped my hand on my skirt and then hid my hands in the pockets of my cloak. Safe underneath the fabric they were untouchable.

The train jerked slightly. It made me jostle in my seat and I brushed her shoulder when she moved as well. The train started to slow down and once again I heard the shrieking whistle. I quickly looked out the window, curious to find out what was going on, but I saw nothing but a thick cloud of steam floating along beside us.

'It will be a while yet before we stop. The train starts to slow down at least ten minutes ahead of time. You can easily sit back for a while yet. Middelburg is quite a nice city. Do you know it?'

I shook my head. 'No, I have never been far from home.'

'And what about this big journey you're undertaking now? You are brave, Maria Klomp.' The nun clasped her hands together in her lap. 'I've never enjoyed traveling much myself. The only reason I'm on this journey is because a good friend of mine needs me.' She winked at me, and I smiled vaguely at her. I have never been able to wink and every time I've tried to I was laughed at, so years ago I decided to respond to winks with a smile.

'What brings you so far from home, Maria?'

I wanted to say something in response, but didn't know what. I was still thinking about it when a sudden wave of nausea came over me. Terrified I looked around me, not knowing what to do.

'Are you all right, my dear?' With a concerned expression the nun sat up and patted me lightly on the back. 'Travel sickness, of course. Some people have that.' She stood and reached over me to open the window. 'Some fresh air will do you good.'

I nodded, but knew it wasn't true. I had simply forgotten to have a bite to eat and now my empty stomach was protesting.

Sister Olivia sat down again with creaking knees and a light moan. I raised my head toward the window, trying to catch as much fresh air as possible in the hope it would help. I breathed in and out slowly and deeply. After a few moments the horrible feeling seemed to fade and I quickly searched in my bag for a sandwich. The first bite was horrible, as usual, but I knew I would be feeling better soon if I had some food in me.

I had completely forgotten about the nun, when she started to speak again.

'I was wrong, apparently.'

With the napkin that I had brought along, I wiped the breadcrumbs from my mouth. I had no idea what she meant and looked at her expectantly.

'My conclusion, travel sickness,' she clarified. 'For you are after all... '

Suddenly she stopped, looked me in the eyes, then glanced at my stomach, then my ring finger on the left hand. When she found nothing there, she checked the ring finger on my right hand.

'I'm sorry, I'm talking way too much again, so silly.' She swallowed with difficulty. 'Of course it is travel sickness that's bothering you.' Her sparkling eyes turned dull and she avoided my eyes.

This stranger's confusion somehow reminded me of how my mother had turned away from me. All of a sudden I wanted to talk, explain, beg for understanding. But of course I kept my lips sealed and again I looked out the window. I could see a few houses now and I could feel the train slowing down more and more. Finally it stopped at a station that was less imposing to me than the earlier station in Vlissingen, even though the building was large. There were no impressive ornaments, frames or decorations here.

But the nun did not remain silent. She brushed my sleeve and said 'Don't worry about it, my dear. Don't mind this silly old nun. It's the greatest curse of my life that I've never learned to tame my tongue. The holy apostle St. James says it so beautifully in his letter and I have tried so often to do something about it...' She was quiet for a moment and seemed lost in thought. 'Please forgive me for jumping to the wrong conclusion.'

She was silent now and I realized that she expected a response from me, the loose, pregnant, unmarried young woman. I swallowed and wanted to reply, but no sound wanted to pass my lips. In the end I managed to produce a light whisper.

'That's good.'

My mother would have smacked me on the back of my head, had she heard me speak that way. It was rude, and could barely pass for an acceptance of apology, but Sister Olivia visibly relaxed and crossed herself. Then she looked heavenward and muttered a thankful prayer. She picked up her rosary again and mumbled to herself.

I silently watched her and straightened up in my seat, my back firmly pressed against the back of the seat. I reminded myself that with every station we passed today we were another step closer.

The rest of the journey, all the way to Roosendaal, we traveled in silence. This time the silence was not uncomfortable. I gazed out of the window and let the world pass by. Some of the pressure weighing me down slipped off my shoulders with every tree we passed, every pasture, every town and station. It wasn't until we approached Roosendaal that we picked up our conversation again. Sister Olivia had nodded off and was softly snoring beside me. I gently nudged her elbow to wake her.

'O, my goodness, we're at Roosendaal already?' she exclaimed. 'Time flies when you're asleep. Thank you for waking me up, Maria Klomp, if it wasn't for you I would have missed my station. Would you mind if we continued our journey together?'

This time she asked me, without referring to her Dear Lord, and I nodded gratefully, because I would be in need of her help. When we finally were seated on the train bound for Arnhem, I was so very grateful for Sister Olivia's company that I opened up somewhat.

'I would never have made it without your help!'

It had been Sister Olivia who had made sure that my suitcases were loaded on the right train, she was the one who had navigated us through the station to the correct platform, and she had been the one who had located our train. I simply had blindly followed her, and had gratefully accepted every bit of help.

The train we were on now was much like the earlier train, with this difference that I had the feeling this train had recently been cleaned. The scent of soft soap hung in the air and it reminded me of when I still lived on the farm. I had often helped Mother to wash the kitchen floor. We would crouch on our knees and Mother would give me a brush. I used to watch her carefully and tried to copy her. When we finished, with our knees wet and our hands slippery with soap, we would look at each other and smile contentedly. Even in the days of the influenza, when Father died, just like Grandpa and many other people we knew, we could still laugh at these moments. When did laughter disappear from our home? How could that have happened? Was it the farm? Had our laughter stayed behind on the farm the day we left? Maybe I would rediscover happiness when I returned to the farm? I shut my eyes tightly and tried to remember what the farm looked like. After our move

my homesickness had lasted such a long time that I had not expected to forget any details ever, but now, as I tried to recollect and
form a picture in my mind, many details remained blurry.

The train rocked gently and made me nudge Sister Olivia again
who, I couldn't blame her, had fallen asleep already. The sudden
movement awoke her with a start and her eyes veered toward me
immediately.

'Traveling is a rather monotonous endeavour, isn't it?' she said
and she dejectedly regarded the scenery of the passing farmers
fields over my shoulder.

I nodded, but did not respond. Instead, I bent down to grab my
bag in search of another sandwich to settle down my stomach,
which was starting to act up again. Sister Olivia quietly looked on
while I ate. I had the impression that her face was stuck inside the
black and white coif she was wearing.

'Is that not very uncomfortable?' The words were out of my
mouth before I realized it and I shocked myself. I could feel my
cheeks turn hot. I quickly took another bite to hide my embarrassment.

'This coif, you mean? Oh, no, you get used to it. At first it feels
a bit odd, but after a while you don't notice it anymore.'

'To me it seems lonely and difficult to be a nun,' I said when my
mouth was empty again.

'It was, sometimes.' Sister Olivia gazed dreamily of to the side
and then started to smile. 'But I have received so many blessings in
return.'

I nodded and thought of what her life must be like. Maybe it
was a nice thing to live in a monastery. No doubt, a place with only
women must be better than any place. No male body to struggle
with in loneliness, no shame, no fear.

'Why did you become a nun?'

It seemed that Sister Olivia did not hear my question, because
she quietly stared over my shoulder out the window and gently
rocked back and forth with the rhythm of the train. Then finally
she answered.

'It seemed like the best thing to do.'

She looked at me for a moment and I saw in her eyes a glow of sadness, which took me by surprise.

'I did not go for the right reasons, Maria, although I didn't know it at the time. No, when I made my vows I was a young girl and I could not think of any other solution. It was an escape, really.'

She smiled vaguely.

'It's a good thing that Mother Superior never knew this. She was a tough one. Are you considering something similar, Maria?'

Her sudden, straightforward question startled me and I quickly turned my face to the window. It was as if Sister Olivia had read my mind. While I looked away, I gave her a safe answer.

'I am a Protestant.'

'Well, well!' Sister Olivia laughed and clapped her hands. 'Who would have thought? And all this time I thought... Your name is Maria after all...' She clapped her hands together again and laughed cheerfully. A Protestant girl and a Catholic nun, well, well. This just goes to show that nothing will thwart our Dear Lord's plans.'

I nodded, but did not say that I disagreed. Her Dear Lord was no longer concerned with my life. Maybe it was even part of his cruel joke to bring the two of us together.

The journey was monotonous and the nun, once again, fell asleep. I on the other hand took extreme care to stay awake, because the idea of being transported to an unknown and unwanted destination seemed awfully frightening to me. As we approached Arnhem, the landscape seemed to beckon me, as if I were welcomed home. The day had begun with rain, but now the rain had stopped and was replaced by blue skies and big cumulus clouds. Rays of sunlight dropped down from between the clouds like golden chains. They touched the earth and gave it a warm glow. I noticed a pair of geese keeping watch beside a narrow stream and I smiled when they bravely stood their ground despite the racket of the passing train. Along the train track stood some beautiful farmhouses and I spotted a single laundry line weighed down with whites. It reminded me of Grandma's laundry day. Mondays were always laundry day. Whoever owned this line apparently did not bother with Grandma's traditions.

I wondered, would Auntie still keep to the old weekly schedule? There had been a specific time for everything, although I could not recall what exactly happened when. So many of my memories had either blurred or completely disappeared. Would I even be able to recognize Auntie when I finally would arrive in Velp? I felt anxious and closed my eyes in an attempt to recall what Auntie looked like, but I could not remember anything about her except for her Sunday bonnet. How was I supposed to find her in such a large train station? During our journey I had noticed passengers at all the different stations, all so confident and focused. They would take their luggage, greet their loved ones and walk out of the station laughing, talking, sometimes in silence, holding hands. How would I ever be able to recognize her amongst all those people? I bent down to grab my bag and placed it in my lap. I clenched the leather handles of the bag so tightly that the colour drained from my fingers, as I tried to remember my Auntie whom I had not seen in ten years. However hard I tried, I could recall nothing except for the bonnet.

'We're almost there, Maria.'

I did not respond.

Sister Olivia seemed to sense that something had changed in the last few minutes, for she placed her old hands over mine. Again I had to restrain myself and I held my fingers tightly together so she would not notice that I wanted nothing more than to pull my hands away from her well-meaning touch.

'What are you afraid of?'

While I considered this question, her old hands seemed to compel my fingers to be calm, and slowly my hands relaxed. Finally I whispered, 'Everything'. *How would Auntie respond? Would she welcome me or take me under her roof grudgingly?*

'Will there be someone waiting for you?'

'Yes, but…' *I haven't seen her for years. I've no idea who she is anymore.*

'Is it a family member, or a stranger?' Sister Olivia persisted.

'Family, my aunt.' *Who, I'm sure, is not at all eager to receive an unmarried, pregnant niece.*

'Listen, I'll stay with you until you and your aunt have found each other.'

'Thank you very much.'

She did not ask for any more information and I did not volunteer any, but her kind words made me feel better. I was not alone. The old nun would stay with me until I had to face my aunt. Would she smile and embrace me? Or was she like the Reverend, outwardly kind, friendly in the train station, within earshot of others, but on the inside harsh and ugly?

The train slowed down and I knew we were approaching Arnhem Station. One more transfer and then we would reach our destination. After the long journey behind us, this last little stretch to Velp wasn't much. Once again we found a seat together at a window. We were both tired and stared out window in silence. Much too soon the train stopped again.

For the last time, I helped Sister Olivia step out of the train, and one last time she made sure we found our suitcases. Then, there we were, standing at the end of our journey, our luggage standing between us. I looked about me, searching, but I did not really know what to do or what to expect. Then I saw her.

'Auntie Be, here I am!' I called out to her, despite the doubt I felt. But the woman who was walking along the train and looked hesitantly into each compartment, looked up and smiled. For a moment I forgot about my anxiety and I moved towards her, but as we approached each other I felt tense and I stood still, uncertain. So this was it, my destination. All of a sudden I wanted to turn around and run away, to a place where nobody would see me and no one could find me.

'Maria, is it really you? Of course it is, you look like Anna.' She grabbed both my hands and looked at me with a kind smile. It made her round cheeks even rounder, and they seemed to almost touch her eyelashes.

I stared back at her, but could not speak a word. In my mind images of Mother and Auntie whirled around until they blended into one. They looked very much alike indeed. Auntie Be was several years older than Mother, but I thought she looked much younger. She had a sparkle in her eyes and crows' feet around her mouth. She was so very different from Mother. It was as if I was looking at a lively version of my mother. As if my mother herself was nothing but a portrait on a canvas. The colors were perfect and all the details were right, but the life, the sparkle could not be captured in the canvas.

Of course there were differences too. Mother was a slight woman, and now that I saw Auntie, I realized that Mother was also a pale woman. A woman with soft hands, who always stayed in doors. Not Auntie. She had a healthy color on her cheeks, and the hands that were holding mine were calloused and strong. With a shock I realized that Mother's hands used to feel the same way. Strong, damaged and rough, but also warm and friendly. Strong enough to hold me up when I fell.

Auntie Be took my arm and pulled me toward my suitcases. Sister Olivia was still there, waiting. She had a smile on her face and she nodded encouragingly toward me. I introduced her to my aunt and they chatted for a little while.

'Goodbye, my dear.' The time had come to say our farewells. The nun embraced me and I smelled her peppermint-scented breath, and I could feel how her stiff nun's coif rubbed my hair. I would never forget the last time my mother embraced me that way.

It was the winter of the year I turned twelve, a very cold winter. There was a layer of ice in the ditches and I wanted to go skating so badly. Nobody had forbidden me to do so, but I was well aware that it was only because I had not asked for permission. I knew that if I wanted to go skating, I had to do it in secret. Late in the afternoon I sneaked out of the house and met up with Aleide, the church's caretaker's wife. I had convinced her that I had permission to go and she had promised me the use of her granddaughter's skates. She arrived at the agreed location on time, but did not have the time to stay and watch.

'You'll be careful now, won't you? Where is your mother?' I just nodded and mumbled a vague excuse, but Aleide paid no notice to it in her haste. She returned home and I tied on the skates. It had been a long time since I had skated last. It had been on the farm, but I did not want to think about that. Now, as the day was drawing to a close and twilight set in, it was just me on the ice and no one else. I was as free as a bird!

I'll never forget the sudden sound of ice cracking and the icy cold of the water. From one moment to the next the ice gave way under my feet and I was soaked. I managed, with much difficulty, to climb out of the icy water and I stood shivering and dripping at the edge of the water. Then it dawned on me that I would have to confess my secret. There was no way I could get away with this unnoticed. Despite the cold, which took hold of my whole body, I took my time walking home. I had slung the skates over my shoulders, laces tied together, and while I considered what might happen as a result of my ice skating escapade, the skates seemed to weigh more and more with each step I took.

I arrived in our street and headed for the manse. There was still light in the study and I grew hopeful. Would there be a chance that I could deceive him? Maybe, if Mother cooperated. I took the back door and opened it as quietly as I possibly could. It wasn't quietly enough though. Mother had heard me and was at the back door within moments. She reprimanded me softly and at the same time hugged me so tight. She pulled me into the kitchen and had me sit close to the stove where it was nice and warm. Then she stripped me down and wrapped me into a thick blanket. She held me tight again and pulled me onto her lap. She talked in soft whispers, worriedly enquiring if I was all right. Then she was silent and I quietly sat with her, listening to her heartbeat underneath my ear, pressed against her bosom. I savored her warm embrace. I had missed her so much. At that moment I was absolutely convinced that all would turn out well. *Nothing was further from the truth.*

'Will I see you again sometime?' The words left my mouth like a fleeting breath, but the nun had understood and embraced me once more. 'Maybe. If it is our Dear Lord's will. Maybe.'

She let go and turned to leave. It seemed as if saying goodbye was not easy for her either. I looked at the slender woman wearing her black habit and I pretended to smile. It was better this way. It's no good placing too much value on relationships.

The nun embraced me yet again and I could feel how she slipped something into my pocket. She whispered a quick 'all the best to you' in my ear and that was that.

My silent 'goodbye' accompanied her as she walked away. I watched her as she walked toward another nun, younger, who welcomed her warmly. I kept watching until my view was blocked by a group of people assembling beside one of the trains.

I checked my pocket and found a small, tightly folded piece of paper. I unfolded it and saw her name and address. Sister Olivia's home was in Amsterdam. What strange combination of circumstances had brought us together that day?

4

'Come along, Maria. You must be so tired.' Auntie broke the silence and I quickly replaced the piece of paper in my pocket. I would keep it safe, although I suspected I would never see Sister Olivia again. I might write to her.

Auntie picked up my suitcases, and all I needed to carry was my bag. I felt guilty to let her carry my cases but I didn't offer to take them from her. The sleepless night and the exhausting journey had taken their toll and I feared I would collapse, suitcases and all, if I were to carry them. We left the crowded station hall where people kept coming and going. Auntie lead the way, checking often to make sure I kept up.

'The wagon is just a little ways further. You think you can make it?' My exhaustion must have been obvious to her, but I nodded, determined to follow. We followed a busy road to a large square and arrived at Auntie's wagon. A large brown dog sat beside the wagon and it walked up with wagging tail to greet Auntie. She hoisted the suitcases over the side of the wagon while the dog circled at her legs. It didn't seem to bother her at all and she deftly avoided the dog each time. She took the bag from me and threw it also into the back of the wagon. Then she called the dog and motioned me to come closer.

She took my hand and held it at the dog's nose. 'This is Maria. You'll have to be kind to her.'

When the dog gave a short bark, I quickly pulled my hand away from his nose and I stroked him between the ears.

'Shall we go?' Auntie asked. I nodded gratefully. The sooner the better, I thought. I knew we would have quite a ride ahead of us yet with the wagon. I walked around to the other side and climbed on. Auntie was seated already and patted the seat beside her invitingly. The dog jumped on the wagon and found a spot with the luggage, and we could depart. The city was crowded and Auntie seemed to need all her attention to drive. My thoughts moved on ahead, towards the farm of my youth and the new life that awaited me.

As we approached the farm I started to wonder what it was exactly that my mother – or the Reverend for that matter - had written in the letter to Auntie. If had been the Reverend, I could well guess what kind of a letter it was: your sister's daughter has lost her virginity to some bum and is now expecting a bastard. We want her to live with you for now. Period.

I could hardly imagine that Mother had written the letter. She had not written any in all these years because the Reverend did not allow her to have contact with her sister. But if she had written this time, I could not begin to imagine what the letter would be about. What did she know of it after all?

'Do you think you can tell me what the matter is, or would you rather not talk about it?'

I carefully considered her words. So carefully that, had they been objects I would have taken them in my hands and looked at them from every angle to see where the catches were and what possibilities there were. I was silent for a long time as I considered her question. She allowed me the freedom to not discuss it, an easy way out. I wouldn't have to talk about my current sad circumstances. On the other hand, if I did answer her, I would find out exactly what she knew about my situation. I realized that this would either make me feel more at ease with her, or the complete opposite. How did Auntie see me? As an innocent child? As a careless young woman? As an innocent virgin?

A deep pothole in the road made me bounce up and I came down hard on the wooden seat. For a moment I wondered to myself if maybe that would solve my problem right there. A miscarriage would suit me fine, but surely the Reverend's god wouldn't be *that* gracious. In the end I asked her my question.

'What did the letter say?'

Auntie did not need to ask me which letter I was talking about, that was obvious. She nodded in acknowledgement and clucked her tongue at the horse before she looked at me.

'I will give you the letter when we get home, then you can read it for yourself.'

She would give me the letter?

At home this kind of openness would be unthinkable. At home they would never involve me in any adult matters. 'Are you sure about that?'

'Of course. I don't mind telling you, if you would prefer that, but I may forget something or say something the wrong way. If you read the letter, you'll have your answer. And now,' she gave me a quick smile, 'I would like to hear some news from the far south-west. How is my sister?'

I admired her courage to ask me about my mother's circumstances. As the years had passed it had become clear to me that, because of the Reverend's meddling, contact between the two sisters had ceased completely. My aunt had lost her sister, Mother might just as well have been dead. I remembered the letters, which at first arrived faithfully every week, but were never answered. And I knew that even now a letter arrived every month. My mother never read them. Mainly because the Reverend would be quick to intercept them, and if he didn't, she would place the letter unopened on the mantelpiece for the Reverend to find and destroy.

I took a deep breath and, somewhat hoarse, began to tell her about our simple life. I told Auntie about the cutters that fished for mussels, the manse, the church with its modest interior. I expounded on the little garden at the manse, the grocer's, the baker and the swing at the school. Why I told her about the swing I don't know, but my aunt listened attentively, smiling and nodding, every now and then wiping away a little tear. I pretended not to notice and kept talking about home and Mother. I did not speak about the Reverend. Some memories were hard to talk about and every time I told Auntie about Mother I pressed the nails of my right hand hard into the palm of my left, without Auntie noticing. The physical pain helped me to keep Mother's betrayal from her.

As I spoke, more and more memories emerged and I talked and talked, until we turned onto a sandy path and Auntie pointed ahead.

'There it is, we're almost home.'

I grew silent and watched as we approached the farm. Only the horse's clip-clopping, and the creaking and rattling of the wagon disturbed the silence. My eyes traced the familiar bends toward the farm. To the left, beside a small ditch, I suddenly noticed a familiar landmark.

'Jopie is still there!' I exclaimed in amazement. Grandpa had named the old, crooked willow tree Jopie, after an old, bent man from church who looked just as worn out as the tree but who approached each new year with renewed vigor.

'Jopie is still there.' I repeated softly to myself and I suddenly realized that it was also possible that the old man was still alive. I looked sideways at Auntie who cheerfully nodded as she clucked her tongue.

We entered the yard and I leaned forward and stretched my neck so I could have a good look around. Auntie held my arm, but I impatiently shook it off.

'Be careful, Maria, or you'll fall.'

'I won't fall.' Just let me savor and feel for a moment, it has been so long.

I inhaled deeply and my lips tasted the familiar smell of days gone by. No sea air, no blowing sand dust. I smelled mud and greenery and animals. I smelled the earth after a good rainstorm. No seagulls here, but sparrows and larks, finches and chickadees. No screeching, but twittering. Here were flowers, bushes and trees, instead of sand and dune grass. Even now in the fall with winter fast approaching, the surrounding growth reminded me of fields full of poppies and wild chervil, daisies and chamomile. One more time I inhaled deeply and smelled the familiar smells of home. My home. For now.

We both grabbed a handful of straw and rubbed down the horse. It was odd how natural it was for me to join in this task after so many years of absence. When we were done I looked on while Auntie brought the horse to the stable. Ever since I met Auntie at the train station I had wanted to know what she thought of me, how her opinion of me was colored by the words in that letter. The letter was waiting for me in the house.

I looked forward to entering the house. It held so many fond memories for me. It may sound odd, but to me it seemed that the house breathed compassion, as if it had a human personality. But I could of course not go in by myself, I had to wait for Auntie Be. She smiled at me as she walked toward me.

'You'll be surprised!' she said, as if she had been reading my mind.

'Why? Have there been a lot of changes?' I couldn't bear the thought that there might have been. Together we went to the door, which led to the entrance hall. I couldn't wait to go in, into the open kitchen.

'You'll see for yourself. I hope you'll appreciate it.' Auntie opened the door to let me in. The delicious aroma of a stew that had been on the stove for hours welcomed me and I remembered that I was hungry. At the entrance to the open kitchen I stopped and I absorbed my surroundings with excitement. Everything was just as it had been: Grandpa's chair with its green seat covering, the kitchen table with seven chairs around it, two large cabinets against the wall, and the red tiled floor. I noticed that Auntie had acquired a new stove, it was beautiful and decorated with colorful painted flowers, but that was the only change I could discover at first glance. Relieved, I clapped my hands together and turned to Auntie.

'Nothing's changed at all!'

She stood behind me, smiling, but now she also entered the kitchen, walked past me to lead me to the front room. She went straight towards the box bed and opened up the doors. To my amazement I did not find a mattress and blankets, but tidy rows of shelves filled with empty canning jars. She opened the other box bed and there also I found a spacious storage cupboard, filled with linens and a few boxes as to which contents I could only guess, instead of the bed I had expected to find.

'But where do you sleep?' I asked after I had recovered from my amazement. For this had always been the adults' sleeping area.

'Follow me.' Auntie Be hurried ahead of me excitedly, and I followed her through the kitchen to the attached barn. It was chilly there and I wrapped my arms about me as I continued to follow Auntie Be. She headed straight for the stairs and climbed up.

At the top of the stairs was a small landing with three doors, two to the right and one to the left. Auntie led me toward the doors to the right and proudly opened the first door. Again she let me enter ahead of her and this time I found myself in a comfortable bedroom, which clearly was my aunt's. There was a beautiful bed in the center, but it was the large dressing table against the wall that drew all my attention. It was a table with attached to it a large mirror, consisting of three sections. It was pure extravagance. It would be unimaginable to find something like this in the manse. There we had all of one small mirror, and that was used by the Reverend while shaving. I saw my own reflection and looked at it for a moment. It was hardly noticeable. Nothing to worry about. Almost nothing.

Embarrassed, I placed my hand on my stomach, made a fist, then turned away from the mirror to have a good look at the rest of the room. I admired the wallpaper that decorated the walls with cheerful flowers. Pink and white colors were a recurring theme in the room, and the view from the window was breathtaking.

'What a lovely room!' It was so different from what I was used to at home. What we had was dark green curtains, brown furniture, small beds and bedspreads in muted colors. No flowers. Especially no flowers. When was the last time that Mother and I had danced through the meadows, both carrying a basket that we filled with all the wildflowers we could find? Daisies, dandelions, buttercups, wild chervil and the lovely scented chamomile. I closed my eyes and could see us skipping, hand in hand with big smiles. I shivered and quickly opened my eyes. Where did these memories come from?

'Come along, I'll show you your room.' Obediently I followed Auntie and she opened the second door for me. I hesitantly followed her into the room. I squealed with delight when I saw, on the bed, my old teddy bear. Auntie had made it for me when I was young. I had not been able to bring it with me when we moved, and I had been devastated over it for weeks. I searched her eyes and gave her a grateful nod. In silence I walked through the room, my hand tracing the washstand, which held a beautiful wash basin and a jug. I recognized it, Grandma had always been very proud of it. There was no dressing table, but above the washstand was a mirror, and on the small night table stood a vase of chrysanthemums. The curtains were of the same material as those in Auntie's room and the bedspread was a colorful quilt made of bits of left over material, probably sewn by Auntie herself.

'What a lovely room,' I whispered.

'So you like it?'

I nodded. 'It was a very good idea of you to use part of the attic and turn it into bedrooms. Absolutely beautiful, Auntie. What is behind the third door?'

Auntie Be went ahead of me and opened the door. I looked over her shoulder and saw the hayloft as I remembered it. There was plenty of room left I saw.

'Fairly soon after you and your mother left, Grandma decided to renovate. She always hoped that you would come and stay for a visit as a family and she wanted to have rooms prepared for that occasion.'

I silently nodded and thought of Grandma and Mother and Auntie. Poor Grandma, she never could have imagined that her granddaughter would end up staying in this room as a pregnant outcast.

'Of course we did not need the rooms for ourselves, but when Grandma passed away and Anna still had not come, I decided to alter the box beds. I prefer sleeping in a spacious room over sleeping in a cramped box bed.'

She closed the door again and we went back downstairs.

'I am very impressed, Auntie, Mother would absolutely love it.' The words left my mouth before I realized it and I quickly fell silent. Mother wasn't interested in the least. Didn't I know that? She would, most likely, never get to see these renovations to her old home.

'You know, we asked her for permission to do this,' Auntie said while she led the way downstairs. 'Unfortunately Anna never sent a reply, so in the end Grandma and I decided to wait no longer for a response.'

I thought of al the letters that arrived monthly and were destroyed unread, and it weighed on me, but what should I do? Should I tell Auntie Be that all these years she had been writing letters that went unread, or should I just watch every month as she posted a letter, which I knew was written in vain?

How had Auntie reacted the day that finally this one letter arrived, the letter that spoke of her niece, the letter she would let me read? Would she have smiled expectantly, or would she have opened the letter with trepidation, anticipating bad news?

'Would you like some tea, dear?'

Again we stood in the kitchen, and I nodded. The letter. What was in the letter?

'Go on and sit down, you must be tired,' Auntie said and she pointed to Grandpa's chair.

'I can't sit there! That's Grandpa's chair.'

'Grandpa is no longer here and you are exhausted. Go on, sit down. It's the best chair I have.'

Cautiously I lowered myself onto the green fabric of the chair. It stood close to the stove and the warmth radiating from it enveloped me like a warm blanket.

'Here is your tea.' I must have dozed off for a little while, for the words startled me.

'Would you like to read the letter right now?'

I nodded. My body was exhausted, but my mind would have no rest until I knew what I wanted to know. I was so grateful for Auntie's consideration. She seemed to know exactly what to say and what not.

Auntie Be found the letter and handed it to me without a word and then she left the kitchen. 'I'll be in the barn if you need me.

It took a few minutes before I had the courage to actually read the letter. Here I was, sitting in Grandpa's chair, staring at the envelope with on it in the Reverend's handwriting my aunt's address. My first question was answered. He had written the letter. Of course. How could I even have considered the idea that my mother would have been involved in this? Undoubtedly, she would have detached herself from the situation. Did she even know what was going on? Did she even realize that I was pregnant and that she would be a grandmother?

As was usually the case, it was the Reverend who organized, decided and commanded. If God would ever be in need of someone to organize his affairs in heaven, the Reverend would be first in line to offer his services. He would put everything in such order as he desired, he would lead the praise and preach the sermons. He would be lord and master in heaven. There would be no room left for God or the saints.

The paper in my shaking hand rustled.

It was time.

I was trembling when I opened the envelope and pulled out the letter. It contained merely one sheet of paper, filled with his sharp and angular handwriting.

My eyes skimmed over the letters as they shaped words, sentences, a story. All those letters lumped together and blended into one monstrous word. The accusation jumped off the paper. Whore.

The word he had used again and again, until even Mother had nodded in agreement, the word that had, in the end, destroyed what was left of my dignity. Every time he used that word, he shattered to pieces the small remains of my youth and dreams, and with his heel he pulverized them.

Whore.

The letter fell from my hand and fluttered to the ground, peacefully, like a feather, but it was as sharp as a knife.

I hid my face in my hands, and my body folded over. Behind my closed eyes it turned black, then white. The emptiness had it's own color, and it had plenty of room for the accusation his lips had uttered. Whore. Filthy whore. Nobody in his congregation was to know, but in the face of those who might love me, he was abundantly clear. First Mother, now Auntie. There would be no one left for me. Everyone would follow his judgement and judge me accordingly. No mercy for a whore.

I did not hear Auntie return. Much later she told me that I had heard nothing at all, for she had called my name several times, but I had not responded. It was only when she took my hands and stroked them softly, when she kissed my cheek and whispered kind words in my ear that I returned to my senses. Auntie said that I was as white as a sheet, and I knew it was true. My arms and legs had lost all feeling, I felt paralyzed and it would not have surprised me if all blood had flowed out of my body, simply leaving me in this hateful shell. This shell I despised for everything it carried.

'Would you like to tell me about it?' Auntie asked me, much later. She had given me some tea and another warm sweater to fight off the cold, which had taken hold of me and made me shiver.

I shook my head, but at the same time I opened my mouth to offer at least one piece of clarification. Barely a whisper left my mouth.

'I am not a whore.' I swallowed. 'There is no boy friend, no man, nobody.'

I wasn't sure if I had actually spoken those last words out loud, but it felt good to deny the existence of anything male in my life – including the Reverend. I repeated the words to myself, over and over. There is nobody. Nobody. He is nothing, a nobody. The words gave some relief, even if temporary.

Finally Auntie rose and began to set the table. I wanted to stand up and help her, but my legs were still too weak and I fell back in the chair.

'Don't get up, sweetheart.'

Auntie lifted the lid off the pan on the paraffin stove and again I smelled the stew. The aroma reminded me of meals I had had in this house in the past. I watched while Auntie stirred the contents of the pan and filled two bowls with a generous serving. Then she walked over to me and stretched out her hand.

'I look like an old woman.'

'You're just tired.' Auntie helped me up and walked with me to the kitchen table. I sat down and waited for Auntie to join me at the table. She sat down on the seat across from me and when she folded her hands I knew what she was going to do. Insincerely I bent my head, but in rebellion I did not fold my hands. I kept them hidden underneath the table. It remained silent and I looked up at Auntie in surprise.

'I won't make you do anything you don't want to, Maria, least of all this.'

I could feel my face turn red and I slowly shook my head in denial of what she had suggested, but I did not have the courage to speak.

'Listen, I pray at every meal and I also thank the Lord afterwards. I read from the Bible several times a day, but I will never force you to take part.'

Now I nodded, although I found it heard to understand what she meant and found it even harder to believe her. Then Auntie bowed her head and prayed in silence. I watched her dumbfounded. After her prayer Auntie picked up her spoon and started to eat. She nodded at me invitingly, so I also picked up my spoon. I started to eat for the first time without asking a blessing over the meal first.

When the meal was over I helped Auntie with the dishes. I pumped water into the large kettle and placed it on the fire. Auntie took a small zinc basin and placed it on the table. Next she took the pan of stew from the stove and placed it on a wooden cutting board on the kitchen counter to cool off.

The water boiled and I added the boiling water to a bit of soap in the basin. Then I quickly added a bit of cold water from the pump, took the bowls and washed them. Auntie joined me with a tea towel and she dried everything quickly and efficiently. She worked so fast that the bowls were put away before I had washed the utensils, and all that time she hummed a melody that somehow sounded familiar.

'What song is that?' I asked in the end.

'You don't remember?' she asked. 'Your Grandpa used to sing it. It's Luther's Psalm, A Mighty Fortress is Our God.' I nodded and tried to recall the rest of the words, but I could not draw them back out of the fog of my memory.

I felt so much better after my meal, but Auntie still insisted that I rest.

'You just take it easy indoors today. It's a cold day, you're tired and…' She didn't finish her sentence and in my mind I added the word that was clearly implied. Pregnant.

Would we continually feel awkward when my circumstances were mentioned? How would we cope when I started to show and could no longer hide what was growing inside me? It took me three large steps to walk to the door.

'Please excuse me, I need to visit the privy.' I yanked the door to the barn open. The privy was underneath the stairs, just where it used to be. I walked quickly and ignored the cold that soaked from the floor into my socks. I violently pulled the door open and I let it slam closed behind me. I just stood in the half dark narrow space, breathing furiously.

You're pregnant. You whore. Nobody can deny it. Nobody will deny it. His voice seemed fearfully close by, despite the distance between us. I closed my eyes, forced him out of my thoughts by slowly counting to ten. Then I slid the lid to the side and sat down.

I had to return to the kitchen of course, back to Auntie, but I refused to look at her and I pretended nothing had happened. Auntie didn't though.

'I can't bite my tongue every time, Maria. If you don't mind I'd rather call a spade, a spade. By not speaking of something it won't disappear, so we may as well face up to the awkwardness of the situation. Do you agree?

I nodded slowly.

'I'm glad. It will be a lot safer for my tongue.' She smiled and I smiled with her.

'Good. What I meant to say was, you are tired and pregnant, and you need to rest. So, today you'll stay here, close to the fire. You go and rest up, do some needlework or read a book, whatever you like, as long as you don't do any hard work.'

Dubiously I looked at her. Was she serious? Did I really have to be an idle spectator all afternoon?

She nodded. 'Tomorrow you may help me. That'll be soon enough.'

'Thank you.' I felt relieved, for I was more exhausted than I had expected and the idea of staying inside appealed to me. I was still shivering, despite the thick sweater, tea and the warm meal. To go outside now seemed to me the least desirable thing to do.

'Do you like to read?' Auntie did not wait for an answer, but brought me along to the hall.

'Here are my books. There's not many of them, but I enjoy reading them all.' She let her hand glide over the backs of the books, some of which already looked tattered, and she pulled two of the books partially off the shelf. 'You may like these two.'

'I'll have a look,' I said politely.

'If you would prefer to do needlework, everything you need is here,' said Auntie, and she drew open one of the drawers of the large cabinet. All sorts of colored yarn and material appeared.

'There are two things I love to do,' Auntie said, 'embroidery and cooking.' She rubbed her ample stomach. 'And eating of course,' she added with a smile.

We returned to the kitchen and Auntie stepped into her wooden shoes.

'If you need me, I'll be in the barn or at the stables, but I won't be long. I'll soon be coming in too.

I nodded and Auntie left. It was raining again and I saw her walking across the yard with her head down. The dog jumped around her feet, barking and she pushed him off with her hands. Auntie seemed to be a cheerful woman, full of life.

My feet were tingling and I sat down again in Grandpa's chair. I would do some needlework later, but first I needed a rest.

The remainder of the afternoon flew by and before I realized it Auntie had milked the cows and we sat down at the table to eat some bread. When we finished our meal I could feel what energy I had left drain from me and I sat drowsily in my seat. Auntie Be noticed it and brought me to the guestroom. She helped me with my clothes, found my nightgown in one of the suitcases and tucked me in snugly. I thanked her without words and we kissed goodnight. It was dark, my first night.

5

Those words on that sheet of paper. Each letter was full of venom. It torments my soul. May I please write to you? I won't expect a response from you, all I want is someone who'll listen to me. What can I expect of my stay here? I am afraid that I will have to live here for four months under the disapproval and contempt of an aunt I barely know. Is that better or worse than living in the manse?

I climbed down the stairs, uncertain. I had no idea what time it was, but it must have been later than Auntie's regular rising time. What I wanted to do most was quietly creep downstairs, crawl and hide in a corner unnoticed, but the stairs creaked with every step I made.

Finally I was downstairs. I stood for a moment and listened for noises that could tell me where Auntie was, but all was silent and I walked to the kitchen.

I knocked on the door and carefully pushed it open. It was nice and warm in the kitchen and my eyes were immediately drawn to the stove. The warmth radiating from it was so pleasant, and I realized that Auntie must have been up for a while already. I closed the door softly behind me and walked into the kitchen. The smell of freshly baked pancakes hung in the air. Pancakes! When was the last time I had eaten pancakes?

On the table was a note. I went to see what it said. *'I'm looking after the pigs. I'll be right back.'*

I looked out the window, half expecting to see Auntie, but the window was too small and the distance to the pig house too far. Besides, Auntie was most likely still in there. Should I go and see her?

Meekly I sat down on the edge of a chair. I kept my legs demurely together and lay my hands in my lap.

What would Auntie say when she returned? I could tell that she had been up for hours already while I had been in bed sleeping all that time. Of course she would ask questions. Again, I looked out the window, afraid I would see her coming already. I was afraid that she'd come straight at me with large, determined steps. I expected her to ask me after the father of the child and she naturally would want to know how far along I was. She would chastise me, discipline me and maybe even call me names. My hands began a life of their own and started to pull on the fringes of the tablecloth. With quick movements they made a little braid. When it was done my fingers took three more strands to make another braid.

'Have you got a touch of the flu, Maria?' Mrs. Kleut's remark sounded innocent enough, but she hung over the counter in a curiously interested manner and she took a good look at me. Her smile seemed insincere and I felt my cheeks burn.

'You're looking a bit under the weather lately.'

'Mother would like a pound of sugar.' I said.

'Anything else?'

'Flour.'

'How much would you like, Maria?'

'One pound, no, two.'

I pushed my hands into my coat pockets and stretched myself as long as I could while trying to suck in my stomach.

'Have you seen Helène lately, Maria?'

'What do you mean?'

'Oh well, you know. That woman from the west side.' Mrs Kleut shook her head toward the west side. She didn't wait for my response, but hissed at me: 'They say she's pregnant again.'

She looked at me with her eyebrows raised suggestively.

I did not know what to say, so I just put the money on the counter and took my groceries. Without saying goodbye I rushed out the store. I tripped at the entrance but managed to keep my balance. The sugar started to slip from my hands and almost fell. I managed to hold the package in place with my chin. After a little ways I stopped and knelt down to rearrange my groceries. My fingers were trembling and I held on tightly to each paper bag to make sure that nothing would fall. Mrs. Kleut's words echoed in my head. Helène is pregnant. Pregnant. *The horrible truth, which became more and more clear to me, made me shiver.*

There were twelve small braids hanging off the tablecloth when I suddenly heard the clip-clop of wooden shoes. A quick glance at the window told me that Auntie was on her way. I feverishly started to pick at the braids trying to untangle them. I was sure Auntie would be angry with me if she saw what I had been doing. I had to make sure she wouldn't see any of it.

'Good morning, Maria!'

'Good morning, Auntie Be.' I wasn't quite finished taking the braids apart, and, while fumbling clumsily, I tried to position myself in front of them.

'Did you sleep well?'

'Oh, yes, I did. Thank you.'

'What are you fumbling with your hands, do you always braid the fringes of tablecloths?'

'I… I'm sorry… I didn't mean to…'

'Don't worry about it. It's all right. Can I see?'

She came and had a closer look at one of the braids.

'Just like when you were young, I remember it well.' She had a beaming smile on her face. 'Do you like pancakes?'

I nodded and placed my hands in my lap again. Straight backed and with my stomach as flat as possible I stayed seated, quietly. What should I do? What did she expect me to do? Would this be when the accusations came? Maybe Auntie wanted to wait with that till after the meal? I closed my eyes and shuddered.

'Come and have a look, Maria.'

I quickly rose and walked to her.

'I'll just show you where everything is, so you'll be able to find your way in this kitchen.'

'Dishes, pots and pans are obvious of course,' Auntie said as she gestured towards the plate rack. The spoons hung there as well, and underneath them was a blue pan shelving unit. The pots and pans were on the top shelf and on the lower shelf were the lids. Just as I remembered from when I was young.

Auntie moved toward the large kitchen cabinet and opened up the doors.

'This is where I store my sugar, salt and flour. There are more things in this cabinet, so feel free to take your time one of these days and see what's all in here.' She closed the cabinet and walked toward the little steps that led to the 'opkamer', a room that was built at a slightly raised floor level to accommodate a cellar below. She swung the steps upward, which allowed her to open the door to the cellar.

'I'm sure you'll remember this.'

I followed her down into the cellar and saw in the semi-dark shelves along the walls, filled with canning jars and Cologne preserving pots. These canning jars were all filled.

'You have plenty of stock, Auntie.'

She turned and looked at me, smiling.

'Yes, and now we can enjoy eating it all together.' I turned back to the four steps that led us back up to the kitchen.

'We'll eat soon, would you mind setting the table?'

I nodded and took two dishes from the plate shelf, found utensils and two mugs for milk. Auntie disappeared again into the cellar and emerged with butter and a jar of jam. She pulled a pot of sugar from the cabinet as well and soon we sat down to eat. I watched how Auntie asked for a blessing over her meal. With eyes wide open I looked at her face, the round red cheeks, the slightly moving lips. She looked beautiful and kind, I thought.

6

untie has not yet condemned me and seems to be a kind woman. Sometimes I wonder if some of her traits may be found in my mother, very deeply hidden away. Sometimes it is obvious to me that they are sisters who are very much alike, yet other times they seem to me so totally different that you would think there was no family connection between them at all. I have told Auntie as much as I could about her sister. She seems happy to finally know more about what has been happening over the past ten years, there has been such distance for so long. I can't help but wonder if things are the same for me. Do I no longer exist to my mother, or to him who calls me his daughter? Have I been forever erased from their memories, and do they tell their friends that I have died, have disappeared? The idea of it frightens me, because, if they proclaim me dead, then what am I, who am I?

During the following days I noticed that I looked forward to good meals and I felt more and more energized. It was peculiar, but it seemed as if only here at the farm, my stomach started to grow, as if only now there was room for it, room for my shame. I also felt less exhausted, and when Auntie asked me if I would like to help her harvesting the apples and pears, I nodded. My mind went back to my younger days. I could almost smell the pan of stewed pears.

The next day we started picking fruit. When we had finished

looking after the animals, Auntie took the wheelbarrow. She handed me the picking tool and asked if I was ready to come along. Together we walked toward the small orchard, which held several kinds of apple and pear trees. Auntie had already picked part of the harvest before I had arrived, but we would together finish what was left.

Auntie put the wheelbarrow down beside one of the trees and stepped onto the small wooden plank she had placed on it. This way she could reach most of the branches. It was my job to shake the branches with the picking tool so the fruit that was higher up in the tree would fall down.

I held the hook up high, meaning to shake one of the branches, but suddenly I stopped, lowered the hook and closed my eyes. I used to help Grandma with this. I used to pick up the apples she had dropped, but...

'Auntie, shouldn't I first lay down the straw?'

Auntie turned her head to me and nodded.

'Shall I just get some from the barn?'

'I made a few straw mats, just have a look here in the wheelbarrow.'

'You brought them already? Why didn't you say?'

Auntie smiled, but she gave no answer. Instead she hummed a tune and continued picking fruit.

I went over to her and took the straw mats from the wheelbarrow, brought them to my tree and spread the mats over the ground. Once again I raised the picking hook and shook the branches. The apples easily let go of the branches and they fell onto the straw mats without too much bruising. A few apples rolled away. Those were the first ones I collected, and after that I emptied each straw mat, gathered up the mats and moved on to the next tree.

My thoughts wandered to Mother who always would explain to me in detail how I ought to perform each household task. She always seemed to be right on top of me while I worked, ready to give directions and she would be angry whenever I made a mistake.

Auntie had simply given me the picking tool and had not even mentioned the straw mats. I was so glad I had remembered about the straw myself.

The following days were spent taking care of the fruit harvest. We peeled for hours, and I soon ended up with several blisters, discolored fingers and the odd cut from when my knife had slipped. We cooked pots full of fruit into puree, jam and jelly. I could tell that Auntie enjoyed the work. She hummed while she cleaned out the canning pots, distilled them and filled them with our handiwork. Every day there was a new batch of jars. Painstakingly she would apply a label to each jar, with every detail written on it, from picking date to canning date.

'Why do you write all that information on there?'

She winked at me before she answered.

'Just because I like to.' She pointed at a label she just finished.

'You see that? I like to give a suitable name to everything I prepare, I like to think it tastes better that way.' *Picked Together* it said on the label.

I smiled, and peeled another apple for the applesauce we were cooking today.

'Shouldn't you write to your family and friends?' The question came out of nowhere and startled me. I quickly made up a nonsensical excuse.

'The postman would recognize my handwriting and start asking the Reverend questions.'

Auntie Be burst into laughter and without a word she shook her head. I was relieved she didn't pursue the issue. What could I have said? That I refused to entrust even the smallest detail about my new life, let alone a whole letter, to my mother or the Reverend? That besides the two of them there was no one whom I had left behind in the village even though I had lived there for so long? No girl friends to write to, or to miss, no happy memories to share.

I was in the middle as we skipped along, arm in arm with Elzemarie and Joanne. We sang a happy tune and tumbled into the kitchen, laughing, and Mother welcomed us cheerfully. She had just poured us some lemonade and placed a small dish with cookies on the table when the door flew open.

'What's the meaning of all this, Anna?' His head jerked towards my mother.

'Maria brought along two friends. Will you please introduce them, Maria.' I noticed how Mothers cheeks flushed red, how her voice shook, but I didn't understand why. I stood up and as I stood behind Elzemarie first, and next behind Joanne, I introduced them properly, as I had been taught to. They both remained seated, fascinated by the man who called himself my father, their new preacher.

'I cannot tolerate such a racket. Make sure they're quiet, Anna! How do you expect me to receive God's word when these *children*,' he spit the word out with vehemence, 'make such devilish commotion!'

He gave each one of us a piercing glare and left the kitchen, but not without slamming the door closed with a loud bang. I found it hard to swallow as I tip-toed back to my seat and sat down. The cookies looked a lot less appetizing and the lemonade didn't taste as sweet as it used to.

In silence we sat at the table. Then, way too quickly, Elzemarie had finished her cookie and lemonade. She rose from the table, walked to my mother and politely shook her hand.

'I need to hurry home, Ma'am.' She spoke the words softly, but clear enough for me to hear. Before Mother could reply, Joanne had also stood up and followed Elzemarie's example.

Mother accompanied the girls to the door and waved them goodbye. *I remained seated as I heard them leave. I didn't say goodbye and I didn't wave them off.*

'I think you should at least write to your father and mother. They will want to know how you're doing.'

I could barely contain my annoyance when Auntie brought the subject up again. She meant well and she could hardly be expected to understand my reluctance.

'We'll add your letter to mine each month, all right?'

I nodded, knowing full well that the letters would turn to ashes, without ever being read.

In silence we continued peeling apples until there was a big pile of apple pieces on the table. Auntie rose and took her largest pot from the shelf.

'Shall I put them on, or would you like to do it?'

'May I do it?' I eagerly stood up. At home Mother had never allowed me near the stove. She'd say, 'You'd just start a fire, Maria.'

'Of course you may. Go ahead. If you inherited your mother's skills it's going to be a delicious applesauce.'

I raised my eyebrows and looked at Auntie. Was she serious? My mother's skills? Mother, who worked in the kitchen only to prepare plain, sober meals?

'What do you mean?'

Auntie smiled again and went back to her seat.

'Just thinking of her applesauce makes my mouth water,' she said. 'And her stewed pears. Delicious! Does she still make it the same way?'

I shook my head. 'I can't recall ever eating applesauce or stewed pears at home.'

Auntie looked up, shocked, and started to speak, but I was quicker.

'We only eat what our bodies need. God has given us the food and we ought to be grateful for it.'

I thought back to the bland meals we had every afternoon. Usually everything was mashed together into one, colorless, shapeless, unappetizing paste. For the rest we would only eat whole wheat or rye bread, and on Sundays there was a little bit of butter and a slice of cheese. Naturally, the Reverend had filled sandwiches everyday, since he was the head of the house.

'We only have extra's to eat when we have visitors, and that hardly ever happens because Mother can't stand a mess.'

'What has happened to her?'

Auntie sounded shocked, but I didn't reply.

'The applesauce...' I said instead, 'How do I start?'

We were not only busy with canning fruit. The regular daily chores also had to be looked after. Auntie's days started very early and I was determined to adjust to her schedule. Ever since that first late morning, I got out of bed early enough to help her with the chores. There were six cows to be milked twice a day. I could recall how Grandpa used to let me taste the milk while it was still warm, and I still remembered how he would sit on the little stool between the cows legs and pull at the teats to let the milk squirt out.

I had never done it myself, and now I watched while Auntie showed me. She had pulled out an extra stool for me beside her so I could sit up close and see well.

'First you rub your hands warm,' she said, 'because cold hands aren't very comfortable for the cow.'

When she was ready she held the teats in her hand and started to pull with slow, regular movements.

'You have to pull your hand down and at the same time you squeeze, but not too hard. If you do she'll kick you.'

I watched and saw how two streams of milk squirted into the bucket. It looked easy enough, I thought, and the cow stood placidly and did not seem to mind at all.

'Would you like to give it a try, Maria?'

For a moment I hesitated. I was very conscious of the fact that so close by a cow was large and warm, but I agreed to try it. We switched stools and Auntie put her seat behind mine and put her arms around me. She wrapped her hands around mine and placed them around the teats, her body against my back.

This is different, I told myself and I remained seated on my stool, motionless. She was a woman, she was my aunt. But she was also tall and strong. The pressure of her fingers forced my hands into the right direction, but my breath came faster and faster, and I could feel the world start to whirl around me. I swayed on my low seat and almost fell over, but Auntie's arms caught me.

'Maria, are you all right?' She pulled me up and had me lean with my back against her chest. I could hear her heartbeat. The rhythm of her heartbeat mingled with his. *Too close.* He was way too close. I tried to push him away, but he was too strong and too heavy.

'Behave yourself, Maria.'

Too close. The thumping sound in my ears became one with his heavy breathing. With much effort I managed to suck in enough air. *Too close.*

'Do you need something to eat, or something else?'

Concerned, Auntie slowly released me, but I could sense that she kept a close eye on me and I turned around so I could face her.

'I'm fine,' I lied. I slowly counted to ten, breathing slowly and deeply.

'It was just a dizzy spell, nothing more. I guess it's all part of it.'
I smiled weakly.

'Let's do this some other day. Just watch me for now.' Auntie
rose from her stool, took my hand and pulled me up. She looked at
me intently to see how I was doing. My legs were shaking, but I
stood quietly and did not look away. She did not need to know my
weaknesses. Auntie Be nodded, reassured, and sat down between
the cow's legs. With calm movements she continued, and when she
finished she took the bucket and stool over to the next cow. I followed her meekly and watched how she worked, but my thoughts
were elsewhere, in a lonely and frightful place.

It was not until Auntie had finished milking the cows and emptied the buckets into the milk pail, that the memories disappeared
into the background and I calmed down as I helped her washing
the buckets. Together we brought the milk pails to the wheelbarrow in the barn. After milking this evening we would have to put
all the pails at the road for the milk driver to collect.

Next we walked to the pig house where Auntie kept two sows
and one pig for slaughter. As soon as the door opened I could smell
the so familiar smell of long ago. Pigs were filthy animals and I held
my breath as we walked in. Auntie did not seem to take notice.

'Next week the butcher will come,' she said. 'It's too bad you
won't be able to join us, Maria, are you sure you won't...'

'No, Auntie.' I interrupted her before she could finish her sentence. 'Nobody must know that I am here. I will go to my room
when the butcher comes and I'll be fine.'

'It's a shame, though.' Auntie Be rubbed her hands with regret,
but seemed to resign herself to the fact that I would not be present
at the pig's slaughter. Personally, I was relieved to have a good excuse.

When I was young I already had a strong dislike for the butcher
who would always come for just one day to do his job. The man always wore a big leather belt, weighed down with all sorts of grue-
some tools. Grandpa was the only one who seemed to notice my
fear and he always made sure that at lunch time the butcher would
sit as far away from me as possible. Sometimes, during the meal,
Grandpa would give me a conspiratory wink.

'What will you do in the evenings, when neighbors may drop by for a visit?'

'I'll stay in my room then too, I'll have to. The Reverend was very clear in his letter. Besides...'

I stopped, but my mind wandered back to Mrs. Kleut and her remarks. I looked down and saw how my stomach revealed a slight swelling. I shivered and felt goose bumps on my arms. Auntie could think what she liked, but under no circumstances was I willing to be seen by anyone in this state, least of all the butcher.

Auntie fed the sows and we were soon back outside.

'Just the chickens now, and then we'll have breakfast,' she said and led the way to the chicken coop which was located a little bit further from the farmhouse. She carried a basket with her. I recognized the basket from my youth. Feeding the chickens had been one of the chores I had been allowed to do as a six year old, and I remembered how I enjoyed throwing the grain around for the chickens.

Auntie opened the coop and the chickens came out before the first grain cornels had even touched the ground. While Auntie generously spread the grain around, I stepped into the coop and looked for eggs. I held up my apron and laid the eggs in it one by one. Auntie had some good laying hens and I thought to myself that, if there were always as many eggs as today, these hens must make her a good amount of money on the market.

When we were finished, the day had started to dawn and, as the sun started to brighten the day, we returned to the kitchen where a pile of pancakes awaited us.

7

I know that inside me life is growing, but how is this possible when I feel so lifeless myself? I feel withered like a dried up autumn leaf, but without the warm golden color that gives warmth and life to an otherwise dead leaf. I hate this creature that has taken over my body. I find it horrible that I no longer have control over my own body, that it grows, but not because I eat, that it hurts, but not because I injured myself.

And I hate him, who is to blame for it all. Hatred is something powerful, I can gain some strength from it. And since I no longer have a mother to encourage me and no God to depend on, strength is what I need.

'Isn't it a miracle?' Auntie nodded toward my stomach, which seemed to grow faster each day. We were working on two more new dresses because of it.

'Why a miracle?' I was genuinely surprised. In my opinion my stomach grew into monstrous proportions because of a being I had never wanted.

'It's new life that is growing in you. If all goes well, it will have everything it should have.' Auntie's head was bent over the material and while she spoke, her nimble hands pulled the fabric quickly through the sewing machine, her voice sounded melancholy.

'I don't believe in miracles,' I said gruffly. I didn't want to speak of the thing that was slowly but surely taking over my body.

'Maria.' Now Auntie did raise her head. I noticed a moistness in the corner of her eye, but within moments it was gone.

'Woman was created to bear children.'

She looked down again and her fingers seemed to pull the fabric through even faster. Up and down, up and down, the dark blue thread easily slipped through the fabric and sewed the pieces together. I took no notice of her words, they simply slipped off me and I didn't respond. What could I have said, after all?

Auntie believed in God and in miracles. But I had turned my back to that God of hers. I saw a different god, though, one who punished and tested, a god who made some people his servants and gave them all authority, a god who refused to care about simple folk who send up hopeful prayers to him.

'What have I done?'

'You disobeyed, you lied to me.'

He towered over me and his presence alone was enough to make me utterly helpless. My voice turned soundless, my legs could no longer run, my hands no longer fight. Again he was there. And he was the one in control.

I don't want to be punished, God. I really tried my hardest, truly. Please call him back. Please call him to serve you, so he'll forget about me, let him be too busy serving you to bother and torture me. I cautiously glanced at him, expecting him to be called away any moment, to leave for church or a sick church member. I was convinced that he would leave and once more I sent up a silent prayer. *But there was no one listening.*

'Maria, Maria!'

I blinked, confused, and the first thing I noticed was a big knot in my thread, on top of the seam I had been stitching.

'Are you all right?'

I nodded, pulled on the needle and saw the knot tighten. Despondently I put away the needle and took a pin so I could untangle the knot with it.

'Let's call it a day. How about I pour us some coffee?'

I looked at the knot and thought of the dress we were making. I nodded, it had been enough for today.

The first dress was done. Without me noticing Auntie had untangled the knot and finished sewing the hem. She had even added a four-inch hem which she had decorated with a brightly colored embroidery of flowers and fresh green shoots. The embroidery was stunningly beautiful, way too beautiful for me and much too beautiful for this hideous dress. I swallowed hard and shook my head. Why did she do this? Didn't she realize that I despised this dress and everything it signified? Auntie watched me expectantly, but I couldn't be happy about this gift.

'Don't you like it?' Her shoulders seemed to droop a bit, as if they were already weighed down by the burden of my dismissing headshake.

'Yes, I do,' I whispered. Again I looked at the embroidery and I thought of the many hours she must have spent working on it. My mother called embroidering a labor of love, because it was so time consuming and because you got nothing in return for it besides beauty. A labor of love indeed. The words floated through my mind for a moment, but then they disappeared amongst the many loveless memories I had.

'I'll try the dress on.'

I turned away, avoiding Auntie's eyes, and brought the dress upstairs. I didn't want to see the disappointment on her face and I didn't want to apologize and tell her how I truly admired her handiwork. The dress was worthlessly beautiful. In a few months time, as soon as I would have no use for it anymore, I would burn the dress. So why did she go through such trouble? Did she really think she'd be doing me a favor?

I peeled off my old dress, which was too tight, and I let the new one slip over my head. I didn't want to look at the hem, her handiwork, as it just hovered over my feet. Instead I thought of new reasons why she shouldn't have done this. Didn't Auntie realize that the hem is the one part of a dress that always gets dirty and grimy? What was she trying to tell me? It may look beautiful, but it would always be covered in a layer of dust and grime. Did she mean to say that I was like this embroidered hem, always dirty and soiled?

I straightened my shoulders and went downstairs. I was determined not to speak another word about this dress. It was too beautiful for me, too beautiful for what it concealed.

8

*S*omeone has seen me. It was unexpected. I was supposed to keep my condition hidden from everyone. The Reverend was very clear in his letter to Auntie, and if she were to follow his wishes to the letter, I would be indoors day and night.

Yet, I take care for my own sake too, that no one sees me. I never leave the farmyard and never go for a walk without the dog. He hears any passer-by approaching from a great distance and warns me with loud barks. When the postman arrives, I hide in the stable or the farm-house, and when Auntie has visitors I make sure I'm in my room. Some of the looks I would get from people in our church, and the remarks by Mrs. Kleut taught me that no one is to know about the shame I carry.

'It's not good for you,' Auntie said recently, but I knew it could not be helped, so I shrugged my shoulders. Yet, she found a way around it. She just doesn't realize how hard it is for me to face other people now that I am so clearly... you know what.

'We're having a guest for dinner tomorrow, Maria.' Auntie's words startled me and I called out in surprise.

'What!'

'I have invited a good friend of mine. He has been our preacher for a year now and I am very fond of him.'

No! Not a preacher. *'You're a whore, Maria. The child is a bastard and cannot exist before God and the community.'*

'You can't, don't do it.'

'Yes, I will.' Auntie sounded determined. I sat down, defeated, holding my head in my hands. *I am a servant of Allmighty God, do not talk back to me.*

'Why?' I asked in the end.

'Why not? He's my preacher and a friend, Maria. Besides, he's a young man and it's good for you to meet other people.

'But my...'

'He won't condemn you, Maria.'

Yes, he will. It's his job, his privilege and his duty.

The chair almost fell when I rose and left the kitchen. I stepped into the wooden shoes that Auntie had brought me from the market, and I walked out. I called the dog and he ran around my feet, barking, but I ignored him. With my arms wrapped around my body I tried to keep the cold at bay, and I walked through the garden. It looked withered and dead. I continued toward the small orchard. I stood still, leaning back against the wall that separated the garden from the orchard, and slowly the cool outside air calmed me down.

A preacher is coming to visit, a preacher of all things.

I turned around and thumped my head against the wall. Then I spread my hands and hit as hard as I could. Over and over I hit the wall, until the skin of my hands tingled. I kept hitting, until I could feel my skin scratch and tear, until I saw blood on the wall. Only then did I stop.

Bewildered I stared at my hands and what I had done to them. Blood mixed with dust and formed lines in my palms. I spit in my hands and rubbed them together. I tried to ignore the biting pain and spit once more. Then I rubbed my hands on my apron and called the dog back.

'It's time to get to work.'

We're having a preacher over.

He was tall and his blue eyes were surrounded by little wrinkles. His hair was covered by a cap, but he removed the cap as soon as he stepped in the door. He had blond hair that was oddly flattened by the cap. Before his eyes met mine I turned away to the stove. A pastor with a cap? Why didn't he wear a top hat, and where was his black suit? He looked more like a farmer.

'It's vital that no one in church will be able to find fault with me, Maria. So I expect you to dress appropriately, and your behavior must be irreproachable.'

'I do my best.'

'Remember, you are the pastor's daughter, don't you ever forget that. People in church will watch you and will judge you.'

Condemn, is what he meant, he just didn't say it.

'Maria, isn't it?' His voice hesitated for just a second after he said my name.

I lifted up a bowl before I turned around to face him.

'Yes.'

I quickly circled around him and placed the bowl on the table, my hands moist with sweat. I could also feel a droplet of sweat at my nose. I quickly wiped it away and stood for a moment at the table, wondering what I should do. Should I sit down, or turn around to welcome the intruder? When he said my name again, I decided to turn around.

'Reverend Bosch.' He held out his hand in greeting. I stared at it, not knowing what to do. How could I shake the hand of this man, a servant of God? I kept staring, still not knowing what to do, until he lowered his hand and smiled at me.

At that moment Auntie broke the silence.

'Shall we sit down to eat?'

I was grateful for her rescue and I quickly took the chair nearest to me and sat down. I straightened my back, drew my chair close up to the table, so my stomach was hidden by the tablecloth. The way Reverend Bosch sat down told me that he was used to coming here and sit at the head of the table, on Grandpa's seat. What was he doing here?

Auntie allowed the Reverend to cut the meat and divide the pieces. I held out my plate and let him serve me. I was being served by this preacher, but I couldn't utter any words to thank him. All I could think of was how he would judge me.

Why did Auntie invite him? Did she want to humiliate me?

While the two of them said grace I could observe him without reserve. I searched his face for the hardness that was so familiar to me on the face of the other preacher, the condemnation that was so obvious in every line of his face, but I found nothing. Before he opened his eyes, I looked away and stared at my hands, which had become clenched fists in my lap.

Auntie and her guest picked up their utensils, so I did the same. With my head bent over my plate I started to eat slowly. I imagined that with every bite I took my stomach would expand so that in a few moments I would have to push back the chair and reveal my shame. The food was quite distasteful to me.

In silence I listened to the conversation between Auntie and her preacher. Every now and then a bit of laughter from one or the other would interrupt the dialogue. I squinted as I thought back to that other preacher. Did I ever hear him laugh or tell a joke? Had he been like that when he was courting Mother?

When Reverend Bosch started to talk about Dirk Jacobsen I suddenly paid attention to what was said. I remembered that name from when I was young. Dirk had been a big boy, always a ring-leader at school and he could never sit still in church.

'Last Summer I paid him a visit. He had been bedridden by then for weeks already and he complained about the lack of view.'

Auntie nodded, she clearly knew exactly what Reverend Bosch was talking about.

'After that visit I found two men and two ladders, and the three of us chopped a large hole at the spot where the linden trees met.'

'Ah.' Auntie nodded and clucked with her tongue, her eyes sparkled.

'At my next visit Dirk's mood had improved already. The gap between the trees allowed him a good view onto the street, so he could see folk passing by and he'd often wave to friends. But there was still one thing troubling him.'

Auntie leaned forward and I noticed that even I was curious to hear. I quickly straightened my back again and took another bite. No need for them to think that I was listening to their conversation.

'He hadn't seen his girl for a while and he was worried that she didn't want him anymore, on account of his crippled leg. How to solve that problem, he asked me.'

Reverend Bosch paused and took a bite.

'I nodded at Dirk and wrapped up my visit with him, but that very same evening I climbed the ladder again and changed the gap in the trees into the shape of a heart.' Reverend Bosch paused again. 'This was all half a year ago and yesterday I received word that Dirk and his girl are getting married as soon as his leg is fully healed.'

Auntie nodded, smiled and looked at me for a moment.

'I always wondered who it was that did that,' she said and winked at me, as if to say, 'Isn't he a nice preacher?' I ignored her cheerfulness. Who is to say that he really is what he seems to be? The Reverend also seems to be an exceptionally educated man, kind and courteous, until he steps into my room and closes the door behind him. I can't trust him, Auntie. I can't trust anyone.

'Dirk must be a contented man,' I said. My voice sounded just as suspicious as I felt.

'He sure is,' Reverend Bosch answered. 'Do you know him?'

I shook my head, even though I did know him, and by doing that I ended the conversation. Auntie seemed to realize that I wasn't about to go out of my way and try for the sake of her guest, so she changed the topic. She did not seem to be put out by my reluctance. She remained cheerful and obviously enjoyed her preacher's company.

I started to feel uncomfortable because of my own poor manners, but I knew it was too late to take any of it back. In an attempt to at least justify my behavior, I searched the preacher's face and eyes every time he looked Auntie's way, for signs of disapproval, disgust, and condemnation. But again, I found nothing.

I emptied my plate as quickly as possible, no longer listening to their conversation and ignoring him as much as I could. In my mind I counted the seconds until they made minutes, and I kept track of the minutes by quickly making little braids. Twenty six little braids later they finally finished their meal, and Auntie asked the Reverend to read from the Bible and give a thanksgiving prayer.

Obligingly he agreed and I was amazed to find that his voice didn't get carried away by a threatening tone of doom and gloom. Instead he performed his duties in a conversational tone. I refused to close my eyes during the prayer, until all of a sudden I noticed that he had opened his eyes too. Just at that moment he winked at me, closed his eyes and continued thanking God for the meal.

I was so startled I immediately closed my eyes, and kept them closed until I heard the 'amen'. I quickly moved my chair back and started to gather the dishes.

'Let me give you a hand with that.' Reverend Bosch rose as well and he gathered up the dishes as if it was the most normal thing for him to do.

'How about you just sit down here, then we'll look after these dishes,' he said to Auntie.

I almost dropped the plates, and I had to swallow a few times with difficulty before I recovered my voice.

'No, no, you're our guest. We can't have guests helping out with the dishes, right Auntie?'

'I think it's an excellent idea, actually.'

No Auntie, don't do this to me.

I wanted to protest, but then I saw that the preacher was heading for the pump with the water kettle in his hand.

'Just give that to me, I'll boil the water, please take a seat.' Maybe I could deal with it that way. I would have him sit with Auntie and they could nicely talk together. I was more than happy to do the dishes on my own. I'd prefer it in fact. But again my hopes were dashed.

'Please, let me help you.' He firmly held on to the kettle and was clearly determined. So I moved aside so he could pass. I held my breath and sucked in my stomach as he walked by.

While I pumped the water, he held the kettle. Every now and then he glanced at me. Did he see what I was? Unmarried, pregnant, unclean? The words he didn't speak were clearly audible in my head. *Don't you know that a fallen woman is an abomination in the eyes of God? I should punish you. God has given me that authority. You are a disgrace to your family and the child will be a disgrace. A bastard child.*

With relief I saw that there was enough water in the kettle, so I stopped pumping. The Reverend placed the kettle onto the stove and I put the wash basin on the table. Next, I excused myself. I didn't know what else to do while we were waiting for the water to boil. Better to spend a few minutes in the privy than in his company. I stayed away for as long as I dared to without being rude, and when I returned to the kitchen I saw that the Reverend had just started to pour the water into the basin.

I went to the pump and got some cold water to add to the boiling hot dishwater. I burnt my hands in the water because it was actually still too hot, but I wanted to have this over and done with as quickly as possible, so I washed the dishes regardless. We stood side by side at the table and I could tell by the way he breathed that he wanted to say something. When the words finally came he sounded unsure.

'It must be lonely here on the farm, especially now that winter has arrived.'

My hands fell still in the dishwater as I contemplated these words. Lonely. Didn't he understand that I had come here for exactly that purpose, to be lonely?

'Yes, it is.'

I lowered a pan into the dishwater and scrubbed it hard.

'I can understand that it's difficult...'

He stopped. I waited.

'I'm sorry, I didn't mean to... judge.'

Not? My eyebrows jumped up and I even looked at him for a moment.

'I'm not really sure how to put it into words.' He stammered and stumbled over his words. There was nothing left of the smooth talker who had entertained Auntie with his tales at the table. I took another pan and scrubbed even harder. Water splashed over the edge of the bowl onto the table. What could I say? More water splattered onto the table. If only the water could cleanse me, remove all the filth, so I could start over and wouldn't have to carry this shame.

'What Reijer means to say is that he would like to drop by every now and then, to keep you company,' Auntie's suddenly spoke from the corner where she was quietly knitting. 'That's very kind, don't you think?'

Reijer? Auntie called this man by his first name? Her own preacher? For the other preacher that would be unthinkable, not even Mother addressed him by his first name. Nobody did, or it just might diminish his authority.

I forgot to respond, so Auntie repeated her comment.

'Yes,' I finally mumbled in a shocked daze.

'Good,' Auntie said. 'It'll be good for you to see a younger person on and off.'

I was dumbfounded and looked at Auntie. Then I looked at the man beside me and saw a friendly face. Still shaken, I grabbed a few spoons and washed them.

The Reverend took them from me and dried them off. I looked for more dishes to wash, but there were no more, so I tidied up. While I was doing this, Auntie sat in her chair, singing psalms and knitting away at the little white socks that kept no secrets for him.

9

*Can hate turn into love? I always used to think it was impossible.
But maybe, just maybe there is a small chance...*

The creature in my stomach kept growing and struggled. Auntie
asked me a few times if I had any idea what it would be, a boy or a
girl, but I just shook my head. Sometimes she'd ask if I had thought
of names yet, and other times she'd be sitting across from me cro-
cheting or knitting and suddenly her hands would be still. Then
she'd look at my stomach with melancholy, her hands would
abruptly let go of her work and feel her own stomach.

I ignored her questions and glances, just like I ignored the
knowledge that she was childless and always would be. It wasn't
likely she would ever be pregnant, as she grew older and was still
unmarried. She would never feel life within her. I ignored her pain
and yearning. How could I possibly be hopeful for her, while I despised the creature living inside me?

'Maria,' her voice was soft as a whisper and I looked up from the
book I was reading. Auntie's eyes were friendly, but also sad. Her
voice sounded hoarse and the smile that forever hovered around
her mouth seemed to have disappeared. 'Surely, it's not right to
hate the child...'

Hate? Oh, yes, it sure is. I had to hate it. From this hatred I drew
strength, enough strength to endure all this. If I didn't hate the

child I wouldn't be able to cope.

Auntie rose from her seat and knelt down beside my chair. She took my hand and placed it gently on my stomach.

'You have to feel it, this life growing within you. Cherish it.'

I tried to pull my hand away, but she kept it firmly in place. To my great relief there was nothing, no movement, no stirring, no sign of life. Auntie's eyes held mine, and I stared back, expecting her to look away soon enough and let go of my hand, but her grip remained firm.

Then suddenly, I felt a stir.

I started and with a sudden movement jerked my hand free, and in doing so my nails grazed aunties cheek.

'Don't! Stop it, stop it!' I hid my face in my hands. I didn't mean to hurt or offend Auntie, but she shouldn't be forcing me to feel!

My whole body trembled and I wanted to run away and stay all at the same time. Would she be able to understand at all? I remained motionless, listening hard, expecting to hear her footsteps retreating with indignation. Maybe even a slap in the face because I had hurt her with my nails. Or harsh words…

It was quiet for a long time. Then I heard the sound of rustling skirts and suddenly felt warm arms around me. Her hands stroked my hair and in a soft whisper she sang me a lullaby as if I was a baby who needed comforting.

I wanted to escape, I wanted to get away from those hands, and I tensed my shoulders in silent protest. I made myself as small as I could, but remained seated and I could feel her tender touch while my face started to burn. Slowly my shoulders relaxed, but I didn't dare look up. I had hit her and she was comforting me.

'My dear, dear child. Is it that bad?'

She held my chin gently and forced me to look at her. I let my eyes wander. I could not bear the shame, the confrontation, but in the end I did look at her and saw a softness in her eyes.

Then she did something amazing. Again she took my hand and placed it back on my stomach. She pulled her own hand away and I was no longer forced to feel but was free to choose.

It was at that moment that I really felt life for the very first time. I really felt it.

That evening I went to bed early. I lay on my back and had both my hands on my swollen belly. Maybe Auntie thought I was still upset and that I had gone up early because of that, but that was not the case. Something inside me had become alive when I felt the stirring, and now I wanted more. My hands were patiently waiting and I smiled when I felt the movement again. I closed my eyes and thought of the little baby that was safely hidden within me. A baby only knew a mother's love, how strange. I felt another flutter and I whispered softly; 'Well done, little one.'

How could I have felt such hate? And where had it gone to? Just like when a canal lock is opened up and water streams away, my hate had flushed away in those few minutes.

In the quiet of my room I thought about the past weeks and everything I had done and felt. How could an innocent child have deserved such hatred? I sat up, slowly pulled back the blankets and firmly placed my feet on the floor. I quickly put on a dressing gown and warm socks. Then I quietly returned to the kitchen.

'Auntie?'

She looked up from her bible and smiled.

'I've made some porridge, will you join me?'

'Yes, I would love some.'

'It'll do you good.'

For Auntie food was the solution to every problem, and sometimes I believed her.

10

In all fairness, this young preacher is quite different than I had ex-
pected. Yet, I find it difficult, because the Reverend was different
too at first, wasn't he? He managed, after all, to win my mother's
heart. And Auntie still has no idea of the evil that is in him. Is this
what power and authority does to a man? Is this what power and au-
thority will do to this preacher as well?

It was one of those beautiful days in December, blue skies and a
weak shimmer of sunlight. Despite the cold I decided to hang the
laundry outside to dry. I tried to whistle a tune while working, and
I remembered Grandpa's incredible patience as he showed me how
to whistle. The very first time I managed to produce a sound, he
slapped his knees with amazement and started to laugh. The sound
I brought forth today sounded just as feeble as the sound I made
then. Yet, I enjoyed it and in an odd way I felt free.

'Ah, there you are.' I suddenly heard a man's voice behind me
and I felt my cheeks turn red, so I didn't turn around. How was it
possible that he got so close without me noticing? I was always so
alert about visitors! I never allowed anyone to come this close and
always managed to hide myself in time. My hands trembled and
the sheet I was trying to peg on the line slipped out of my fingers
twice. Both times I just managed to catch it in time and prevented
it from falling on the muddy ground. So Reverend Bosch had kept

his word and came to see me again. What could he possibly gain by doing this? Why didn't he just visit Auntie? She was part of his congregation, not me. I was the fallen woman. What he actually should be doing was steer clear of me, just like the Reverend would always make sure to avoid Helène.

Finally I turned around to face him, hoping my red face was no longer showing.

'Good afternoon, Reverend,' I mumbled. 'You startled me.'

'I'm sorry, I didn't mean to.'

I ignored his words. 'I really need to finish this.' I bent down to take the next piece of laundry from the basket and hang it on the line, expecting him to leave and join Auntie.

'Would you mind if I stay here for a little while?'

'No.' What else could I have said? But what was I supposed to do with this man behind me, watching me work? Again I took a piece of laundry from the basket and started to feel more and more nervous. Why was the man here?

Unwanted memories returned. Memories of a heavy male figure approaching me from behind, forcing me to stand still while big hands moved over my body and touched me in ways I didn't want...

'NO!' I screamed and then, startled, my hand flew over my mouth. I inhaled deeply and could smell the scent of the laundry detergent on my hand. I tried to calm down by breathing in this simple fragrance, but the memories were stronger than me. My feet started to move and I ran off, away from the horror. I heard footsteps behind me, overtaking me, and my terror increased.

'NO! NO!' gasping for air I kept running until I tripped and fell.

'Mother,' I whispered. 'Mother, where are you now?' I shivered and made myself as small as I could, while I waited for him to catch up. I couldn't escape from him. I never could. The opening lines would soon come, I could dream the words by now.

'Maria, you've been disobedient. As your father I will have to discipline you.'

'Don't do it,' I said with difficulty.

'Don't do what?'

'Touch me like… that.'

'Why not? Are you enjoying it?' he asked sternly.

'No, no. Not at all. I don't want this. *Don't. Stop it!'*

'Maria, are you all right? Maria?' The voice sounded concerned, a pair of rough hands calmly smoothed the hair out of my face. Then I was lifted up. I wanted to fight, but I knew I couldn't win so I kept myself as small as possible, my muscles tense but defenseless.

'What's wrong, Maria, did you hurt yourself?'

Finally the words got through to me. This was no sermon on obedience! This was not the Reverend! I opened up my eyes and saw that I was being carried by a different preacher. No, I had to get away from here. I had to get away.

He didn't look at me. His eyes were focused on the farm he approached slowly but surely. I tried to break free by flinging my arms and legs about. He tripped but recovered his balance and calmly kept going, holding me firmly. I didn't resist any longer. He was boss. He always was.

Finally he put me down on the bench beneath the roof's overhang at the farmhouse.

He said nothing, but stroked my hair briefly and went inside. Shaking uncontrollably I sat on the bench in the shelter of the farmhouse and looked back at my past with eyes that saw nothing but the Reverend and ears that could hear nothing but the words from his mouth.

'You've been disobedient, Maria. You know I have to punish you.'

'Mother, do you have a moment?' It annoyed me how my voice quivered unsteadily and I knew Mother heard it too as she looked at me in surprise. Yet she didn't seem concerned. Her hands never stopped their work, her fingers deftly pulled the needle through, and stitch after stitch the button was sewn back on. Fasten off, cut the thread and pick up another button. Nobody could sew as fast as Mother.

The things she used to sew had always been beautiful too, but nowadays she only sewed what was functional, a skirt, a blouse, a coat. She always sewed for those less fortunate in our church, always in black, without any variety.

'I need to tell you something. Can I talk to you?' I had rehearsed my words beforehand, but now they sounded stiff and insincere.

Mother said nothing and remained where she was, keeping her hands busy with needle and thread. I went to her and took her hand. I gently took her needlework from her hands and sat down close beside her. Mother kept her eyes on her needlework, but I held on to her hands and squeezed them softly. She looked at me again and I searched her eyes for something familiar from days gone by, the love, the light, and her warm understanding.

It could have been my imagination, but I thought I saw her eyes relax and look at me lovingly. This was enough to give me hope and I took a deep breath as I was finally going to tell her the truth. For four long years I had said nothing, but now that I had missed my first monthly period, and after that a second, I had tried daily to build up the courage to tell her. Although there was nothing visible yet, I knew it would not be long before everything would be out in the open. My hands began to shake while I took a deep breath to speak. I closed my eyes and opened my mouth.

Before I could even utter a word the door was thrown open with a bang and the Reverend came in. With his arrival, both my hope and the little bit of courage I had scraped together, disappeared into nothing.

'What do you think you're doing?' He stopped beside my chair and gave me a menacing glare.

'You're coming with me, right now.' He grabbed my hand and crushed it painfully hard. With a jerk he pulled me along. At the door he briefly let go and sneered at Mother that she had to stay put, but I noticed that she hadn't even made an effort to move.

Then he was behind me again and he pushed me up the stairs. A confusion of thoughts raced through my head. I didn't have the slightest idea what could have roused his anger.

He reached ahead of me and roughly threw open my bedroom door. With a bang the door slammed back and almost hit me in the face. I just managed to catch it with my hand. He didn't seem to notice, but impatiently pushed me into the room, onto the bed.

'What were you doing there, with your mother?'

I looked at him in silence, what should I say?

'Tell me!'

'I... we... I wanted to tell her...'

'What? What is of such importance that you need to tell your mother?'

I closed my eyes so tight that in the darkness little shapes started to dance before my eyes. If I had had the courage, I would have covered my ears with my hands to shut the sound of him out. But I didn't dare to and I thought about a possible answer. What could I tell him, the truth? No, that was impossible.

But he beat me to it. He no longer waited for my answer and started to speak about the fifth commandment and about his rights and duties as a father. All the usual words and I almost managed to let them slide off my back, until he caught my attention with a long silence. The words that followed shocked me all the more.

'You're pregnant, aren't you?'

I gasped for air and could feel the blood drain from my body. A roaring sound that seemed to start from somewhere behind me entered my ears and filled my head. There was nothing else but this roaring sound.

Then suddenly a harsh slap hit my cheek and cut through the roaring in my head. I opened my eyes and looked at the Reverend.

'Your silence speaks volumes. Whore. Did you really think you could keep this secret from me? Did you really think I haven't noticed how you pick at your food at breakfast? Did you really think I wouldn't notice the changes in your body?'

His hand slipped down from my shoulder for a moment, and I shuddered as he touched my breast. His hand lingered for just a quick second, yet too long, always too long.

I pulled back and saw his face twist in anger.

'You filthy whore.' He screamed the words in my face and spittle flew about. Disgusted to be sullied yet again by his body, I wiped it away with my sleeve. He had just turned around and didn't notice. I heard him thunder down the stairs. Then I heard shouting, shocked wails, and my mother's crying.

These sounds only slowly penetrated through the fog in my head. They floated up the stairs in slow motion and lingered at my door. But in the end they reached me. I stared up at the bare ceiling of my room, looking at nothing. Up there was nothing for me. No loving God. Not even a God to curse. What good had God brought me so far? Nothing but misery.

I heard footsteps on the staircase. It was the Reverend, followed by my mother.

With quivering finger he pointed at me and exclaimed loudly: 'Your daughter,' he spit at me again, 'Your daughter is a filthy whore.'

His dramatic act made the desired impact, for my mother's eyes opened wide in shock, her hand flew to her mouth and a shriek passed her lips.

I watched in silence while the Reverend screamed, beside himself, 'She's pregnant! No doubt she doesn't' even know who the father is.' He glared at me ominously and I said nothing. What could I say? It was obvious that I was the guilty one here. Me. Me. Me. Mea culpa. Mea maxima culpa. These were his favorite opening words for a sermon. Or final words. Or both if he really got into it.

I averted my eyes from him and tried to find my mother's eyes while she stood unsteady and touched the wall for support.

When the Reverend finally fell silent, Mother asked with a soft voice: 'Is it true?'

These words hit home with deathly precision on what hope I still had and they destroyed everything. When I nodded I saw how my mother's head sagged down to her chest and her shoulders fell. She turned around and staggered out of the room. I heard her stifled weeping and wanted to stand up, shout that it wasn't true, that it wasn't my fault.

'Whore,' he hissed at me before I could get up. 'You don't say a word. Not to anyone.'

His eyes gleamed menacingly in his face. I shuddered. Not the words he spoke, but the way he said them terrified me. *I nodded and knew I wouldn't say a word, to no one, ever.*

'Maria!' My Auntie's soft arms joined her exclamation and took hold of me with a warmth that chased away the cold.

'Maria, child. What happened, dear?'

All of a sudden my eyes came back to life and I could see the present. I could see her sweet face, her round blushing cheeks, her gray hair and sparkling eyes. She meant so well, but I had never yet told her everything, and I wouldn't do so now.

'I'm not sure what happened, Auntie,' I lied. 'Something startled me and...'

This was too complicated to explain in a few sentences. Besides, there was nothing on this earth that could possibly make me tell her and explain it all.

'I'm much better now,' I said and straightened up. 'I don't know what came over me, but I'm better now.'

Auntie looked at me with concern, but said nothing.

'I have to finish hanging up the laundry.' I got up awkwardly and walked back across the grass to the washing line and the laundry basket. My hands were shaking and I tripped twice before I reached the basket, but I had to do something. It seemed best to me to simply go on with my chore. I took extra care that no one was sneaking up on me, and often looked over my shoulder. I saw that Reverend Bosch was now sitting on the bench beside Auntie, and they were calmly talking together. It looked like he wasn't going to head my way anymore. Slowly the tension in my body disappeared and I stopped shaking. When I checked over my shoulder again I noticed that Reverend Bosch had stood up and was saying goodbye to Auntie. When he noticed that I was looking his way, he waved his hand at me in parting, but he didn't come. I couldn't blame him, I had offended him several times now after all, but I still felt an odd pain inside me when he simply left.

Stubbornly, I turned my attention back to the laundry.

All was well.

II

Pregnancy is usually not a topic of conversation. Swollen bellies are kept hidden away with wide flowing dresses, and sore backs are only stretched in relief when no one is around to see it. The idea that something is growing inside me is becoming more real by the day, especially now that I've felt the life stir. I had become so used to hate it, that moving creature inside me that is the offspring of adultery and fornication, of weakness and hatred. But a new feeling has awoken and is slowly pushing out the hatred. Is it love? Can this love exist or will it be blown away by the very first gust of wind that will come? Will it be taken away by a fresh spring breeze, or blown away by a strong fall storm?

Auntie however talks about the pregnancy as if she has no concept of shame about these kinds of matters. Maybe it's the farmers stock in her, or maybe it's because it's just us two women in this house. Maybe it's in her character or maybe it's simply because of the whole awkwardness of the situation.

I have fended her off, excluded her, hurt her. But how long will she be patient? When I see how she cares for the animals, I think her patience is unending and she has actually proven that already. She has been so very patient with me. Yet, I am not able to count on her love. I must not forget that there was, after all, once a time when I was a child who knew her father and mother's love and who trusted in a loving God. But in the name of that same God, all the love I knew was taken from me.

And Auntie worships that same God.

I noticed that increasingly often my hands would linger on the swelling of my stomach. Every day there was some moment where I was newly struck by the sensation of life moving deep within me. Was it a hand, a foot, or a knee?

Auntie kept a close eye on me and smiled with a nod when she caught me mesmerizing. When that happened I would quickly return to the present and make my hands continue their task.

My hands had changed in the last while. The soft, preacher's daughter's hands had turned into the rough hands of a farmer's daughter. The cuts I had suffered at the beginning had all healed and were replaced by tough calluses, my nails were cut short, and the palms of my hands were rougher than they used to be. It made me proud, they resembled Auntie's hands more and more. They were hands that could love and care. Would my hands be able to do that?

It was solely for Auntie's sake, because of her constant care and patient love that I had spent the last hour struggling to come up with words to put on the sheet of writing paper in front of me. Words that would explain nothing and at the same time say everything. I would add my sheet to Auntie's letter. Right from the start she had insisted I would write to them. She never checked my letters, so she wasn't aware that all I did was fill a sheet with lines, circles and scribbles, knowing full well that no one was ever going to notice. But now something had changed and I no longer wanted to deceive her.

The last thirty minutes I had been thinking of how to start the letter. *Father and Mother* was no good, since he wasn't my father and never would be. *Dear Sir, Mother* also didn't work, because I couldn't call him 'dear'. *Dear Mother* was a wish I didn't dare write down, so in the end I decided to write no salutation at all. I wasted three sheets of Auntie's expensive stationary before coming to this decision.

In the end I managed to come up with three full sentences that seemed sincere to me, but that didn't reveal anything about my true thoughts and feelings. I didn't dare to commit to paper my wish that Mother would reply and would tell me how she was. I knew very well that this wish wouldn't come true.

Auntie had also finished her letter. She stood up from her seat and opened the door to the barn.

'I want to show you something, come along.'

I followed Auntie obediently up the stairs, not knowing what she was up to. To my surprise she opened the third door, the one leading to the hayloft, a place where I hardly ever came. Her hand held an oil lantern and she quickly lit it. The little flame lit up the dark room with whimsical shadows and Auntie's long shadow followed her as she walked to one side of the hayloft. I stayed as close to her as I could and tried not to touch anything. Everything was dusty and I knew there would be big spiders here. Probably mice too, and who knows what else.

'Ah, that's where it'll be.' Auntie moved a few steps to the left and gave me the lantern. 'Would you hold the light for me, please?'

I stooped over and the light fell over a large sheet that covered some lumpy objects. With one jerk Auntie removed the sheet and I sneezed because of the sudden dust cloud that reached my nose. I sneezed again and only then did I see what Auntie had uncovered.

'A cradle,' I whispered in surprise.

I came closer and put my fingers on the beautifully entwined wicker.

'I didn't know you had one.'

'This was your own cradle once.'

'Oh.'

'Your father was simply overjoyed with your mother's pregnancy. He worked on this cradle for weeks without Anna knowing about it. It was such a surprise for her.'

I felt a lump in my throat. My father. He had made this for me and together with my mother he had placed me in it. My father. Even if I closed my eyes, I couldn't remember him, only his curly hair and the warmth of his voice. But were these really memories or wishful thinking?

'Come, let's bring it down.'

Auntie gave a tug and with a creaking sound the cradle slid across the floor.

'I'll help you.'

When we were in the kitchen I could have a good look at the cradle. Father had twined the dark and light wicker alternately and it had created a beautiful pattern.

'We'll have to give it a good scrub,' said Auntie, 'and we'll make a new little canopy and some new bedding.'

I looked again and I saw her beaming.

'That's why I wanted you to see it. Tomorrow, at the market, I'm going to buy fabric for it, what do you think?'

'But there is still bedding in it.'

'It's old and discolored. Or do you like it?'

No, it wasn't beautiful at all, but that was no reason for Auntie to go and spend money for the sake of me and my...

My thoughts halted before I dared to think the word. But then I allowed the thought. Child. My child.

A cradle for my child.

'I have some money left from the journey,' I suddenly remembered.

It looked like Auntie first meant to protest, but then she nodded. 'That's good. You can give it to me, and I'll find something nice.'

She took two mugs and poured us our some coffee. Then she took her loaf tin and walked to the table.

'Come, sit down for a bite.'

We sat down beside each other, so we could both look at the cradle.

'What color would you like?'

'I haven't thought about it. What color would go with a baby?'

'Any color is good, as long as it isn't black.'

I nodded. 'As long as it isn't black.'

I went to bed and fell asleep with one hand on my stomach as it changed shape with the child's movements inside. I could almost imagine that the child was calling to me and wanted to know me.

I had picked flowers for Mother, pretty yellow and red ones. I held the little bunch tightly in my hands. The stems were already starting to wilt, so I had to walk home quickly and cheer Mother up with these flowers. I would find a pretty vase and place the flowers on the kitchen table. It would be a nice surprise. Mother loved flowers. Mother loved me, and I loved Mother. The sun was shining and the birds sang their songs and I started to whistle along. I couldn't whistle all that well yet, but I practiced a lot and was getting better and better at it.

Father had been able to whistle really well and he had shown me how to do it. Father himself had learned from Grandpa, who could whistle with his fingers as well, really hard. Sometimes I tried to do that, but then you heard nothing, and all I ended up with was wet fingers. But now I could sing along with the birds. I looked up at the blue sky and felt just as cheerful as the birds I could hear. I saw a butterfly and chased it, into the sky. It was a tiny black speck against the blue sky, and I followed it, higher and higher, closer and closer to the sun. I could feel the sun's warmth on my face and I basked in the glow of it with my eyes closed. The sunlight shone just as brightly behind my closed eyelids. Even though my eyes were closed it wasn't really dark at all. It was a cheerful darkness. Yes, that's what it was, a cheerful darkness.

But all of a sudden the cheerful darkness disappeared and turned into a frightening darkness. It was real dark now, black, like the night with its scary sounds. A cloud had blocked the sun's light. It was now dark as the night and a watery moon shimmered in between the clouds, and then it vanished again. I could feel how it suddenly turned cold. My arms, back and legs were covered in goose bumps.

My hand let go of the flowers. Yellow and red fluttered to the ground, withered and forgotten.

'No, no!' I stammered the words, but beyond my lips there was no sound, just silence, a silence that embraced me in the darkness.

'No.' A tear found its way from my eye down my cheek. My knees gave way, legs that had carried me up into the air moments earlier, had lost their strength and I collapsed. I crushed the flowers in my fall.

'No.'

Suddenly he was there, standing over me.

'Maria, get up.' His arms stretched out to me as he stooped down and lifted me up. High over his head I flew. The black night could hold me even better now and choked me as I floated. I couldn't breath as the darkness oppressed me. His strong hands had a crushing hold on my stomach, I saw his black eyes and felt his black breath, hot breath that cut like a knife through my body.

'Don't!' The words resonated in my head, loud and clear, but in the night they were stifled and they were lost before he heard them. He didn't hear and continued to hold me with the big hands that pulled away clothes and that scorched my exposed skin.

Why, why? Where is Mother, I want Mother.

But she wasn't there, she never was.

12

Sometimes it seems to me as if the present and the past merge to-gether in this place, though I know that nothing will ever be quite the way it used to be. The hatred I feel for the Reverend is still there and I don't think this will ever change. I'm not even sure if I want it to. My hatred for him gives me the strength to go on. I no longer wish to loose the child I carry, but I often feel the weight of shame pressing down on me. It's impossible for me to face people. It would make my misery unbearable. But it's also impossible for me to live the rest of my life in isolation. With the new year drawing near I start to have many new questions. But I'm not yet ready to face up to the answers.

As I woke up on the morning of New Year's Eve I smelled a fragrance that brought me back to the past. I got out of bed and slowly came down the stairs, one hand pressed on my ever-growing stomach. I no longer was troubled by nausea, so whenever I smelled delicious aromas that reminded me of my younger days coming from Auntie's kitchen, I was always tempted to eat a lot.

I opened the door and saw Auntie standing in the kitchen with a cloud of steam around her head, and I saw how she just poured out a large ladle full of batter onto the waffle iron on the stove.

'Waffles!' I exclaimed.

She turned and smiled broadly.

'Of course. We can't have New Year's Eve without waffles.'

I returned her smile and thought of how Grandma used to bake waffles at this time of year. She had told me once that the waffle iron used to be her mother's. She had baked her first waffle when she was seven years old, and Grandma had promised me that she would teach me too when I would be that age. That never happened, of course. At seven I no longer lived on the farm.

But this memory was a new one. The years had come and gone without me ever thinking of it, but now that I saw Auntie standing there in that cloud of steam and I could smell the waffles, it all flooded back to me. I remembered just how it used to be.

Grandma used to stand in the kitchen all day baking, and Grandpa would, after his daily chores, come in and set up the long tables in the barn. He would attach three long tables and arrange long benches to go along them.

The whole neighborhood used to be invited, and the tradition was that at around nine o'clock in the evening everyone would show up. Many of the guests would bring delicious treats such as battered apple rings, chicken soup, or oliebollen, the traditional New Year's doughnut balls. But the only one who made waffles was Grandma. Nobody else was allowed to bake them, and nobody else was allowed to bring them.

'The butter, Jochem!' Grandma would call to Grandpa when he was finished setting up the tables and benches. I had so often watched him when Grandpa would pick up a milk can and pour the milk into the butter churn. Next he would get to work with the big churn dash. He often let me help him. With his big hands folded over mine we would hold the dash together and move it up and down in a regular motion. After a while little clumps of butter would appear floating on the milk and I would look up at Grandpa and smile. Again with his big hand over my small hands he would help me scoop up the butter grains and place them in the butter bowl. One time I had forgotten to place the cheesecloth in the bowl so we had to return the butter grains to the churn. Grandpa never got angry with me, but he patiently explained to me that the cheesecloth was important because it allowed the liquid to flow away. He showed me how to do it, and after that I never again forgot to place the cheesecloth in the butter bowl.

After kneading the butter we had to salt and rinse it, and then it was ready.

'You go and ask Grandma for a spoiled waffle.' Grandpa would tell me. I would skip to the kitchen and beg Grandma for a waffle that hadn't turned out well, just so that we could taste and see if the butter was good. Of course the butter always was just right.

Grandpa would spread a thick layer of butter on, and sprinkle it liberally with icing sugar. When he had done all that he would take a knife and very carefully cut out five heart shapes. I would always get three of them and he would always have the other two.

The very first waffle was always the best. That very first waffle...

'I haven't had waffles in years, Auntie.'

Auntie turned around and placed her hands on her hips. 'Well, this year you'll have them again, you just wait and see. There may not be any guests this year, but I intend to enjoy these waffles with you. I'm using Grandma's recipe and you'll see that I make them as delicious as Grandma used to.'

'That sounds wonderful, Auntie.'

'Will you help me?'

'I've never done this, though.'

'It isn't difficult. I prepared the batter this morning already, so the only thing left to do is bake them. You take a big ladle full of batter and pour it onto the iron, then you close it and slowly count to one hundred and twenty. Then you press this here,' and Auntie pressed on the handle and I saw how the iron turned over and now lay on the stove the other way around, 'and again you count to one hundred and twenty.'

Auntie counted quietly and then opened up the iron.

There was a beautiful, golden brown waffle all ready for us, and she skillfully popped it out of the iron with a flat spatula. She added it to the mound of waffles she had baked already that morning.

'Would you like to try?' She held out the soup ladle. I nodded and took her place at the stove.

I took a ladle full of batter and poured it onto the waffle iron. The hissing steam cloud startled me, but Auntie was right beside me and she gently helped me close the iron. Then I started to count. At one hundred and twenty I quickly glanced at Auntie and when she nodded I pressed the handle and the iron turned over.

Again I counted the seconds and then opened up the waffle iron.

The waffle had turned out marvelously and I looked at Auntie with excitement.

'Why don't you sit down and can eat this one,' she said.

I hesitated for a moment, but then I shook my head. 'You sit down instead and have it. My first waffle is for you.'

She smiled at me and took the waffle from me, and while Auntie ate her waffle at the kitchen table, I made another, and another.

That afternoon I made butter myself.

Evening fell and we sat together in the front room, a room I hardly ever entered, since most of our daily chores centered round the kitchen. In the front room was a flat top stove that radiated a pleasant, warm glow, but it was unusual for me to be sitting here and I felt uncomfortable. The clock ticked away the seconds and the year would soon be over. Only a little longer and it would be all behind us. If only it was this easy to put other things behind you as well.

I thought about the year ahead of me and I shivered as I considered all that was yet to come.

Auntie suddenly interrupted my thoughts. 'Do you also feel uncomfortable sitting here?'

'It is a little strange,' I admitted.

'Then come, let's welcome the new year in the kitchen.' Auntie already got up and lifted the bowl of waffles from the table. I got up too and took the icing sugar and butter. I followed Auntie to the kitchen. Immediately I felt more at ease and I smiled at Auntie as I sat down.

We both had just grabbed another waffle when, all of a sudden, we heard footsteps outside. Startled by the noise I quickly pushed my seat back and stood up. My sudden movement made the chair fall back onto the floor, so I quickly picked it up. Auntie motioned me to calm down and waited at the door until I had left the kitchen by another door. Quickly I climbed up the stairs and tiptoed into my room. I lay down on the bed. It seemed I would be entering the new year in solitude. I thought of the waffle lying on the table downstairs and I rubbed my stomach in regret. As long as there were visitors I wouldn't be able to have any more waffles.

I sat up when I heard a creaking on the stairs.

'Maria?' Auntie knocked on the door.

'Reverend Bosch has dropped by, will you come down again?'

Reverend Bosch? In that case I most definitely would stay up here.

'I...'

'He came especially for your sake. He thought our New Year's Eve would be a bit lonely.'

'But I want...'

'It's up to you, Maria.'

Auntie looked at me for a moment and waited for me to make up my mind. When I didn't respond she closed the door and I could hear her footsteps go down the stairs. Quickly I climbed off the bed and followed her without really thinking my decision through.

'Auntie, wait, I'm coming.' I followed her down the stairs and was relieved to see her waiting for me. Together we returned to the kitchen and I nodded in greeting to the preacher. He rose and waited for me to take my seat before he sat down again himself.

Then followed an awkward silence that Auntie broke by offering the Reverend some waffles.

'That sounds delicious,' he said.

Relieved to be able to do something I pulled my plate toward me and cut my waffle into five pretty heart shapes. I started to eat in silence while I wondered to myself how I could have been so stupid as to come down with Auntie. I took a quick glance at the clock and saw that we still had an hour and a half to go. I sighed so deeply that the icing sugar went flying like a cloud of dust and made me sneeze.

Reverend Bosch burst into laughter, at first hesitantly, but then wholeheartedly. Auntie also laughed and wiped her hand over my face. Then she showed me the white on her finger.

I remained gruff and silent, but when the two of them didn't look at me any more, I smiled and took another bite from one of the heart shapes.

13

*I*t won't be long now and I'll be a woman with a child. Will I be like my mother? That idea frightens me. Should I blame her for not protecting me, or should I be grateful to her for the happy years we shared?

Now that I haven't seen or spoken to her for so long, I find it harder and harder to understand why she never protected me. Was he really that powerful? Was she unable to stand up to him and protect me?

My hatred for him is as strong as ever, and every thought that turns to him I smother in the flames of my anger, and the fear I once felt for him now seems to be unjustified. I am stronger now, my hatred gives me strength.

For several days I had tortured myself over the knowledge that there was nothing for it but to involve Auntie in the necessary preparations.

In the end Auntie Be brought the topic up herself.

'How much longer now, Maria?'

Her question took me by surprise and I suddenly realized that I wasn't really sure! From the moment that I had discovered what was going on with me, I had tried to ignore the fact that I was pregnant, that I had a child growing inside me, with such determination, that I never paid any attention to the date and least of all looked ahead anticipating the moment that this child would leave my body. My mouth fell open, and for a while I stared into my auntie's eyes, speechless.

'I don't know.'

'We'll need to make some preparations, you know, like the doctor…' Auntie Be rose up from her seat and started to pace through the kitchen, waving her hands about wildly. I had never seen her like that before.

'I had thought you would at least know when the child is due!' She kept pacing and waving her hands about, mumbling words I couldn't hear.

'The doctor. First the doctor.' Finally she stood still and spoke clearly again, but her words scared me.

'No doctor, please, no.' I knew I was begging, but how could I possibly allow her to invite a strange man into the house who would examine my body and who would determine how far my pregnancy had progressed? It was unthinkable.

'Auntie, don't do it! I just need to think things over first, I'll figure it out.'

Auntie's eyebrows jumped up in surprise. 'Think things over first? What is there to think about? You're pregnant, child, whether you like it or not. What we need is a doctor who can examine you and determine how far along you are.'

I shot up and stood close beside her. I placed my hands on her shoulders and said very clearly: 'No doctor. Please. I'll count back and figure it out, really Auntie.'

She shook her head and I felt fear and disappointment.

'The exact date is important, but it is just as important for someone to have a good look at you. We have to call in the doctor.'

I shook my head. I was being stubborn and disrespectful. I was afraid.

She sighed deeply and I could smell her breath. It had a hint of the laurier licorice she liked to nibble on every now and then. I knew I had won.

'I'll call Mien instead.'

Mien!

'Is Mien still alive?' Mien used to be a midwife and to my mind she must be as old as the large oak tree in the yard. She had helped deliver me, my mother, my aunt, and I suspected she had also been around at my Grandma's birth but I wasn't sure of that.

'She's still alive and as bright as ever. You won't mind if I ask her to come?'

I shook my head reluctantly. I would have preferred to spend my days in seclusion within the safe walls of the farmhouse. But my confinement would come to an end and maybe sooner than I had expected.

Five days later Mien arrived. Auntie had sent her a message by post and she had, also by post, informed us of her arrival time. She had caught a ride with the postman and nimbly walked onto the yard. She walked just as quickly as she used to, and her short little legs moved with a speed that amazed me. Auntie Be had to laugh and assured me that Mien probably wasn't quite as old as I thought. I had my doubts but wasn't about to argue the point.

'Maria, Maria. It's been so long since I saw you last. You're so grown-up!' Mien was just as I remembered her, down to the flow-ered apron. The only difference was that I was now taller than the tiny midwife.

I let her embrace me, and a few of her escaped hairs tickled my nose and almost made me sneeze. I wasn't sure what to say. After all, my belly spoke for itself.

At first Mien didn't comment on it. She moved her basket to her other hand and followed Auntie inside. She had a seat in the kitchen with something to drink. Auntie Be and Mien caught up with each other about all the news from the area, and I sat with them, quietly listening and feeling my stomach protest. It felt like the nausea from the first few months had returned and I felt more and more miserable. My hands held on to the tablecloth and felt for the fringes. My restless fingers started to braid and knot and braid yet some more.

Auntie Be didn't comment on my busy hands, but suggested that Mien have a chat with me first. She had a few more chores to take care of, she said, so she disappeared outside and left the two of us together.

Mien looked me deep in the eye, silently, and then nodded slowly.

'You don't have to tell me anything, and I won't ask you any-thing. Does that sound all right?' she said finally.

Immediately my stomach settled down, and I inhaled deeply and exhaled even deeper as I nodded. My fingers relentlessly con-tinued their restless braiding, but Mien didn't seem to mind and for me it was a most welcome distraction to keep my hands busy.

'I would guess you're about seven months now,' Mien said sud-denly. She gestured for me to stand up and she placed her hands on my stomach, pressing her fingers in the skin here and there. She grumbled a little and nodded, next she fumbled around in her bas-ket.

I was about to tell her that it was a bit more than seven months, but she was too quick for me. She grabbed a measuring tape and measured the girth of my waist. Again her hands moved over my stomach, but I felt no fear the way I used to when he touched me. I knew she was doing something different. She was looking for the child. In the end she nodded with approval.

'Eight months is closer to it, isn't it?' She asked finally.

I nodded and sat down again. In my mind I had traced back time and figured she was right, eight and a bit I thought. Maybe a week or so more, but eight months sounded about right to me.

'The child is positioned very well. Can you feel it move?'

I nodded again.

'If it is moving, all is well. If it stops moving for a few days… then something is wrong. Pay attention to it.' The words sounded curt and abrupt. For a moment I considered how I would feel if the child would stop moving. Wasn't that just what I had been wishing for all these months?

'Your aunt will have to send someone for me when the time comes, but it's very possible that I won't be here in time. In that case, she will know what to do. Do you know what to expect?'

I nodded, then shook my head and shrugged my shoulders. I didn't dare to look her way and I allowed my fingers to go back to their game with the tablecloth's fringe.

She started to tell me, and didn't mince any words about it. She talked about the blood and the fluids, about the pains and of how long giving birth could take. I listened to the words without really understanding them. I wanted to crawl into a corner, ignore everything and know nothing. Why would I care about pains and blood, umbilical cords and afterbirths?

She concluded by saying that many women died in labor, but that I was young and healthy and that I would be all right. If I had any questions, I should ask them now.

Finally I lifted my eyes to meet hers, and I saw her sitting there across from me at the table, old - though not as wrinkled as Sister Olivia had been – and so confident. She had witnessed so many deliveries.

I hesitated. Of course I had questions, lots of them, but I didn't know how to ask them. What could I say about the images she was conjuring up in my mind? That I thought it would be horrible, unnatural, deathly? I saw how Mien rubbed her hands and I considered how these same hands would take my child out of my body. I shuddered. But no word came out of my mouth and no question came over my lips. Instead I stood up and went out to call Auntie.

14

I t's still the middle of winter. We've had frost already and snow a few
times. I sometimes can't help but think that it's a good thing I was
sent to Auntie's at this time of the year. How would it have worked
if it had been springtime? There would have been a lot more work to be
done on the farm, the days would have been so much longer and visitors so much more frequent. Now, as it is, there's only one person who
knows about me and occasionally visits me.

'I don't want you to do any heavy work anymore, Maria.'

'But I feel fine. Please just let me muck out the stable.'

'No, from now on I want you to take it easier. You can collect
the eggs, cook dinner and…'

We were still discussing this when there were footsteps in the
yard and the dog started to bark. I wanted to escape upstairs, but
Auntie stopped me.

'You can stay, it's Reverend Bosch.'

'I'd prefer to go up.'

But I was already too late, the door opened and a gust of fresh air
blew in with the Reverend who greeted us with a smile. Since I had
not been able to escape in time, I decided to ignore him instead.
Despite his visit on New Year's Eve and his pleasant company that
night, I still found it difficult to face him. I turned my back to him,
ignored his greeting and continued the conversation as if his arrival

had not interrupted us.

'I want to do something. You can't expect me to sit still and just sit around for thirty days or maybe even more.'

'Then stay in and do some needlework,' Auntie suggested.

I shook my head.

'The weather is so beautiful, please let me help with the work outside.'

'I don't think it's a good idea…'

'You can help me.' Reverend Bosch interrupted, and I send him an look filled with annoyance. Only after several seconds it dawned on me what he had said.

This was not at all what I had meant.

'What could she help you with?' Auntie asked in my stead.

'I'm going to chop some firewood. Maria can help me stack them up.'

Auntie nodded thoughtfully, I wanted to change my mind and thank him kindly for the honor, but Auntie was now smiling in agreement.

'That's a very good idea, excellent.' She nodded toward Reverend Bosch and he put his cap on with an exaggerated gesture.

'Are you coming, Maria?'

No, I'd rather not.

But slowly I walked to the door and slipped into my wooden shoes. Auntie had taken my coat and helped me in it. I looked at the ground, and then at my hands as I buttoned up my coat. The coat was tight around my stomach, even when I stood straight up and held my breath.

Reluctantly I shuffled after Reverend Bosch towards the stables where Auntie had a pile of wood that needed to be chopped. The blocks of wood were large and Auntie had commented once how difficult it was for her to split them. It dawned on me that normally Auntie would call in a neighbor or a hired hand for the heavier tasks, something she couldn't do now because I stayed with her. Apparently Reverend Bosch had offered his assistance.

The stables were just about as cold as the outside, and our breath created little clouds in the air.

'If you'll stack the wood, I'll chop.'

I nodded and watched how the Reverend placed a block of wood on the chopping block and hit it with his ax. It didn't take long for the wood to split, and the Reverend grabbed a new block. I crouched down and picked up the two smaller blocks. With some effort I raised myself and brought the two pieces over to the wall where a small supply of wood was still piled up. I neatly stacked the two new pieces with the rest and returned to the chopping block. There were by now four more pieces of wood on the floor and the Reverend was already on the next one.

The ax struck with a crack.

And again.

Another two pieces of wood were on the floor.

I couldn't work as fast as that. I couldn't bend down, so I had to kneel down, and when I stood up my knees creaked and it took me a moment to find my balance. Nonetheless I picked up as many pieces as I could each time and I didn't complain. It clearly didn't go fast enough, for after a few minutes the Reverend struck the ax onto the chopping block and he bent down with me to gather blocks of wood in his arms. Within seconds he had cleared them and then he continued chopping.

'Thank you.'

He drew a sharp breath and struck his ax hard.

He split a new block in two.

He probably hadn't heard me at all.

The rest of the morning we worked in silence. The only sounds were the falling pieces of wood and the striking of the ax. I soon felt the sweat on my forehead and I felt the extra weight I carried with each step I took.

'That was the last one,' the Reverend said while he wiped the sweat off his face with his sleeve. As quick as my feet could carry me I returned from the neat stack along the wall to the chopping block where a whole pile of wood still awaited me. I carefully picked up as many pieces as I could hold and stood up. For a moment I stood unsteadily, but then I continued and returned to the stack at wall.

'I didn't realize it was this heavy for you.' Reverend Bosch all of a sudden stood behind me and obligingly stretched out his arms to take the bunch of wood from me. 'Please, let me do this.'

With a shriek I suddenly dropped all the wood pieces. Gasping for air I looked from the chaos at my feet to the Reverend and back again. But it wasn't him.

I have to punish you, Maria.

No, it wasn't him, not here. This was someone else.

I hid my face in my hands and closed my eyes.

'Are you all right, Maria?'

I had difficulty breathing.

Yes. I was all right.

'Yes, Reverend. I'm all right. I'm just fine. I'm only tired.'

And scared. Go away and leave me alone.

'Come and sit down for a moment, right here.' He placed his hand on my shoulder and I winced, jerked to the left, and the hand fell away. When I looked up I saw a bewildered look on his face.

'I'm sorry.'

I walked toward the chopping block and sat down without giving him another look. My breathing was still unsteady and I slowly counted to ten to calm myself down. In the meantime the Reverend stacked all the wood that I had dropped on the floor. Then he walked toward me.

I wrapped my arms about me and waited.

He sat down on his haunches in front of me and looked at me.

'I didn't mean to startle you, Maria.'

I shook my head, but didn't speak a word. He didn't say anything else though, so in the end I broke the silence.

'You don't need to apologize, Reverend. I was tired, I got startled and dropped the wood. That's not your fault.'

'Yet, I feel responsible.'

'You shouldn't.' Not for a woman like me.

Reverend Bosch quietly looked down and traced a line with his finger in the thin layer of dust and sand on the floor. Then he made another line. It looked like he randomly made lines, until I noticed that they were letters. I tried to read what they said, but he erased them with his hand and stood up.

He walked to the door and I thought he was going to leave without looking back. But he didn't. He turned around and walked back to me.

'I would like it if you would call me by my first name.'

With a shock I jerked up my head.

'Really. Every time you call me 'Reverend' I feel…'

I shook my head. 'I can't do that.'

'I'm not that old. And you're not…'

'I'm not what?'

'You're not a member of my congregation.' He turned red and lowered his eyes.

I smiled briefly. Would he want that, though? An unmarried, pregnant woman in his church?

'I don't think it's a good idea.'

I stood and beat the wood shavings off me. As we walked back to the farmhouse I thought about his suggestion, and I realized that I couldn't even remember his name. He walked behind me and when we got to the door he caught up with me.

'Your aunt also calls me Reijer.'

I shrugged my shoulder and shook my head. That's what it was, Reijer.

'I would like to be a friend to you, and that is impossible if you call me Reverend. Please think about it.'

'I will.' Reverend. Reijer.

15

ebruary. It's a week earlier than I had expected, but I know the time has come, though I haven't told Auntie yet. The pains come and go and I'm wondering how much more excruciating it can possibly get. I try to stay calm and do my chores, and it works well in between the contractions. I refuse to let fear take over my thoughts and I also refuse to think about what's ahead. My concern is not so much the delivery itself, but the child that's coming. It is unavoidable now, even though I tried to deny it all these months.

It's important to me that I think about other things, so I tidied my room, straightened out the bed linen, laid out clean linen. And all this time I didn't say a word to Auntie.

I didn't want to tell Auntie too soon and I just told her I was tired and would lie down for a little while. She looked at me with concern for a moment, but then she nodded and I disappeared to my room. I pulled off the dress that we had made together and put on my nightgown. Then I crawled into the large bed. The pains came and went in waves, and I searched for a comfortable position.

It was as if the rest of the world ceased to exist, it was like a fog, so distant. I closed my eyes and looked inward, all that existed was pain and rest, pain and rest. My breath became hurried, until I focused more and I inhaled and exhaled slowly and deeply. Mien had told me something about this, but at the moment I couldn't remember what it was. The only thing that mattered was that I kept my teeth clenched tight together so no one would notice what was happening to me. My shame must not become known beyond this household, and for as long as no one knew, there was still the possibility it wasn't actually true. I couldn't event tell Mother, he had forbidden it.

'Mother.'

There was no answer so I walked in. Mother was probably pouring the tea, that's why she hadn't opened the door.

I stepped over the threshold, but the kitchen was awfully quiet.

'Mother?'

I hesitated and contemplated where she could be. Then the idea came to me that she probably was in the outhouse, that was very likely. I simply had to wait for a few minutes. I pulled out a chair and sat down, and I let my legs swing cheerfully back and forth in a rhythm all of my own design. The ribbons in my stockings fluttered in the breeze I created and I laughed.

The time passed and again I started to feel concerned.

'Mother?'

I rose up from the chair and walked about the kitchen. Where could I look? There were many places in the house where I wasn't allowed to go. In fact, I was only permitted to enter the kitchen and the room at the top of the stairs. I listened in the hallway, but heard no sound. Warily I looked at the door of the study. That's where he would be sitting, busy with his work. I shook my head. No, don't go there. I trembled at the thought of his words, the scathing words he would speak. *Be quiet Maria, I'm busy!*

His voice seemed to hound me and made me feel both desperate and angry. Time and time again I heard his voice, accusing me of disobedience, fornication, wanton behavior, adultery. It seemed as if he was physically present here in the room where I had felt so at ease from the day arrived. Why did he have to be here now, at this moment? Had Auntie informed him? Did he want to witness the birth of the child he had fathered? Why was he here? I wished he'd leave and that Mother would appear in his stead. Mother was the only one who had the right to be here, to hold my hand and talk soothing words to me, but when I opened my eyes she wasn't there.

Little droplets of sweat ran down my face. I could feel his large hand, how it moved slowly and with such familiarity over my face. He smiled at me and then hurt me. The smell of his skin and the touch of his soft, limp fingers revolted me.

I felt nauseous and moved my back against the headboard while pressing a pillow against my stomach. The contractions seemed to come quicker and quicker. I wanted to call Auntie but couldn't find the strength to walk across the room, open the door and call out for her. How would I manage that?

While I moaned in pain, the teddy bear looked on patiently. He had been sitting on the night table, on guard since the day I arrived. His brown eyes were warm and seemed to smile. In a brief moment of peace I stretched out my hand and picked up the lifeless bear so I could hold it close against me when the next contraction would come. The warmth of it's fur comforted me a little, I put my teeth into the fur and bit down with all my strength to avoid any sound coming over my lips. The bear didn't protest.

New pains came and went, came and went, and I finally screamed out in agony while I slid down so I could lie down on the bed.

There was a sound of stumbling on the stairs. I heard her concerned voice and felt a cool hand on my forehead.

'Mother?'

On and on came the pains. I groaned, arched my back, reached out to feel her presence. Finally she had come, she was here. Mother had found me, she had finally managed to free herself from his dark hold on her and she had come to find me. Would I also be able to escape from his darkness? If she helped me I could summon up the strength. I grabbed her hand to pull myself up, away from the darkness, far away to a place of safety, a place where he wouldn't be able to come. We would go together, hand in hand, helping each other to keep going. We would make it. Together we could find ourselves a new home, live there together and find pleasure in small things.

'Come on, Maria.'

The voice sounded kind and familiar, but something wasn't right.

'Mother?'

The voice was silent, but before I could ask again the pain was there. Why did I have to endure this torment? Was there no other way, some way to make everything that had happened unhappen? I cried out again and clenched my hands around the bear, hid my face in its fur. Mother was here, but she was no longer a comforting and encouraging presence. The Reverend was in his study and needed peace and quiet.

'*Behave yourself, Maria!* Not a peep, you know that.' Mother whispered and threw a glance over her shoulder, then squeezed my shoulder and grabbed my coat.

'Go and play outside, not here on the square, but elsewhere. You mustn't disturb him. *Remember, no shrieking.*'

The sound of my own voice suddenly reached my ears and I abruptly slammed my jaws together. He mustn't hear me, if he did it would just mean another punishment. I had to keep quiet, ignore the pain. If I screamed he would have another reason to punish me. My silent tears were liquid nourishment for his ego, and my anguished screams were like honey to his soul and only spurred him on to more pleasure, more pain.

'Don't. Don't. It hurts, really, it really hurts.'

'Shut your mouth, Maria.'

I shut my mouth, but another fearful cry escaped my lips in further humiliation.

'Maria, wait, don't push yet.'

Was that Mother's voice? Was she here to help me through this lonely hour of torment? Again I stretched out my hand and this time I found her hand, warm, patiently holding mine. Her warmth spread over me and comforted me. For a brief moment I knew all was well, Mother was kind and would always help me.

'Wait a little longer. You can almost push.' She was silent again and I knew why. This pain was different and seemed to be even more destructive. Whether I wanted to or not, I had to deliver this child, there was no way back. My body seemed to know instinctively what to do, but the pain was excruciating and all of a sudden I could feel his hands pulling the clothes off my body and touch my skin.

'*No, don't. Don't!*' But it was no use, my words brought no relief, and neither were my prayers answered. Power and strength were unto him forever and ever. *Desperately I tried to cover my body with the ripped clothes, to cover my nakedness, but he wouldn't allow it, he put his hands in between and touched me.*

'Go ahead, Maria.' Voices mingled and confused me.

The blood on the bed sheet. What was I to do about it? Mother mustn't see it. I had to hide it, wash it without her knowing about it. I ignored the pain and rose from the bed. There wasn't much blood, but it was clearly noticeable. The bed spread had slipped and was partially on the floor, the blanket and bed sheet were in a jumble. I quickly pulled everything off and piled it on the chair in my room. Now the bottom sheet. I pulled it off the mattress and folded it up, hiding the stain. Maybe Mother wouldn't notice. Of course she would notice. I had to clean it myself. I secretly had to boil some water, and somehow get a hold of some soap. I had to find soap without her noticing. How would I ever be able to get rid of those stains?

I shuddered and felt the intense pain where he had humiliated me. Pain became my life and filled my mind. Behind my own eyes I saw flashes of his piercing eyes glaring at me, his mouth calling me whore, his hands resting on my mother's shoulders while at the same time touching me. Her eyes filled with sadness looking at me, speaking to me apprehensively.

'Is it true, Maria?'

The pain deep inside when she turned away, to him.

'*No!*'

But she was gone already. She had never really been there for me.

Darkness surrounded me and I groped around in the emptiness. The silence was intense and sounded more piercing than all the sounds I knew. Where was I, what had happened? The pain seemed to be gone, my body felt weightless and oddly absent. I wanted to look down, see my legs, but everything was black, there was nothing. The emptiness around me filled me with fear, it stretched out its tentacles toward me and smothered me. I tried to breath and wanted to call out, but no sound came over my lips. Once again I tried to use my eyes to see, my hands to feel, but fear was all I found.

I wanted to run, shriek, flee, or fight, but my body no longer was obedient to my will and I could do nothing. With my eyes closed I waited for what would come, his hands, his breath, his voice, his body, his punishment. My body arched forward and I tensed all my muscles in desperate resistance.

Then there was a loud shriek.

Suddenly a bright light appeared.

'Maria, you have a beautiful daughter!'

More shrill screams reached my ears and all of a sudden I was able to move and open my eyes.

Light.

I saw real light.

Only now did I realize what the words I had heard actually meant. Was it really true? Had I given birth to a child, a little girl?

'Here she is, she's a beautiful child.'

Blurred outlines turned into clear images and I saw Auntie with in her arms an incredibly small bundle that she tenderly handed to me. A pink little body, wrapped in blankets. I looked at Auntie and saw tears in her eyes. Had she noticed it too, the darkness, the emptiness?

I opened my mouth to ask her, but she handed me the bundle and smiled.

'Look, your daughter.' Here voice faltered when she spoke, but I ignored it.

The small weight in my arms squirmed about and I saw my child's blue eyes. I smiled and brought her tiny body towards me so I could stroke her cheek with mine. She was so soft, I had never felt anything like it.

For a minute I glanced up at Auntie to share my joy with her, but to my amazement I saw pain and sadness in her eyes. When she noticed me she quickly smiled and said, 'It's a miracle, so amazingly beautiful.'

I nodded but said nothing. For a moment I considered her pain, Auntie would never be able to experience motherhood. But then I was quickly distracted by those tiny eyes squinted so tightly, that tiny, O-shaped yawning mouth, and I smiled softly. A miracle? Maybe.

'Just hand the little girl to me for a moment, Maria, then I'll wash her.' I had no idea for how long I had been admiring my daughter, but it was difficult for me to let go of her. I was reassured when I saw how tenderly Auntie cared for her. I leaned back against the pillow and looked on while Auntie gently washed away the stains with a wet cloth.

After that Auntie gave her a diaper and next she dressed my child in the white garments she had laid out. I observed everything she did. So here she was, finally. And despite the fact that her origin and conception had been evil, this child was good.

Auntie was finished and laid my little girl in the old cradle we had cleaned together and re-upholstered. I had no idea when Auntie had brought the cradle into my room, probably during the contractions when she was walking about getting everything ready. A wail of protest came from the cradle as Auntie nestled my little girl in it, but she took no notice.

'Just let her cry for a little while,' she said when I sat up and already stretched out my arms to hold her. 'Now we first need to look after you. When you're done it's her turn again.'

'But she's crying.'

'Of course she's crying. It's a strange world she's entered.' Auntie smiled as she spoke, but I couldn't smile. A strange world, indeed. A cruel world.

'I'm going to wash you first, and then you can hold her again.'

'No.' I shook my head. 'I'll wash myself.'

I couldn't bear the idea of her hands moving across my naked body. No matter what, I would no longer accept anyone except myself to touch my body in such an intimate manner. I had had enough.

'You're exhausted now, let me help you.'

'No. I'll do it myself.'

'Absolutely not.' Suddenly she was a stern farmwoman and, just like Grandma, she stood with her hands firmly placed on her hips.

'I've seen it all already, girl, there's no point in worrying yourself about that anymore. I'll wash you.

I wanted to protest, beat her hands away, get up and run off, but I lacked the strength.

She came back again with a bowl of warm water and fresh cloths and she pulled back the sheets.

'You just sit straight now.' Her voice was kind and soft and I obediently did as she said. Then I closed my eyes shut and with my fists I scrunched up the stiff sheet beneath my body. For a moment I could feel cold air on my skin, and then there were the soft, warm cloth and slow, gentle movements. Light and darkness battled, but her gentle voice seemed to attract the light and push away the darkness more and more.

I listened to her voice as it mingled with the wails of my daughter and I allowed myself to be distracted by their presence.

'I'm calling her Mara.'

I hadn't thought about it beforehand. Despite the fact that I had been feeling closer to the child inside me, I had never been able to accept reality to the point that I had come up with a name. The thought had not occurred to me. Now that I had seen her though, it was impossible not to name her.

I looked expectantly at Auntie, curious to see her reaction. She disappointed me enormously when she simply turned away and left the room without a word. Had she not heard me, or did she disagree with my choice?

I thought about it for a while, but I soon forgot about my annoyance. It was much more important that the little girl would get to know her name. So I whispered in her ear, over and over, how beautiful she was and that her name was Mara.

After I fed her and she almost fell asleep in my arms, I called

Auntie, so she could put her in her cradle.

When she came in I was shocked to notice that her eyes were red.

'Did you cry?'

I thought that she shook her head slightly in a quiet denial, but I wasn't sure. When she had picked up Mara and turned towards the cradle, she spoke.

'It has been a long night. I'm tired.'

Her voice sounded listless, sad and unsteady, but I ascribed that to her tiredness. After she had gently tucked Mara in under a woolen blanket she left the room without another glance at me.

Soon enough I had forgotten about her strange behavior and I fell asleep, comforted by Mara's soft mumbling baby noises.

Only a short while later I was woken up by Mien's loud voice. She had arrived and made a big fuss about the fact that everything was over already.

'You little rapscallion.' She stood by the cradle, sternly waving her finger at tiny little Mara. 'You did it all way too quickly. That poor mother of yours.'

I silently watched and smiled when I heard what Mien was telling my daughter.

'You're a beautiful child.' Mien bent over the cradle and I thought she kissed Mara. Then she walked up to me. Her wrinkled hand took mine and squeezed it gently. I couldn't help myself squeezing back, though I wasn't sure what she expected of me.

'So you do have some strength left,' Mien spoke. 'It's a beautiful girl in that cradle.'

I nodded and smiled, but before I could speak Mien continued to talk.

'Let me have a look at you.' With a jerk she pulled the blanket away. 'Just go and lie down now.'

Though I didn't want to, her voice and hands forced me to obey. As I lay down she washed her hands in the basin beside the bed. She gently examined me and after a few minutes looked up and pulled the blankets back.

'You did very well for a first one, a bit fast, but very well. You're young and healthy though, you'll heal quickly.'

Again she washed her hands and kept on talking.

'I'll give your aunt instructions. I know Be, she'll look after you very well. I'll come and see you regularly to make sure you're healing properly. You mustn't get out of your bed too soon, you hear?'

I shook my head, then nodded. No, I wouldn't leave the bed too soon. Yes, I heard her. 'You'll also need to know that you'll soon have sore and heavy breasts. You're producing milk now and you'll feel the pressure of it. In your case it'll be more difficult than usual, but I'll give your aunt instructions for this too. It usually lasts only for a few days. Do take care not to catch a fever during that time. You can easily catch something. You'll be very susceptible to the slightest cold. In a week or so your body will have forgotten everything, and...'

Her words poured over me and immediately slipped off me. My thoughts remained with the little miracle in the cradle. My daughter. A few of Mien's words suddenly caught my attention.

'It's the best thing for you and the child. Don't you agree, Maria?'

Of course I wanted the best thing for me and my child. I closed my eyes and tried to think back to what Mien had just said, but the words had floated off like leaves in the wind and I couldn't recall.

'Do we agree, Maria?'

Mien spoke with more emphasis and I looked at her, then nodded my head. Yes, sure, we agreed, I wouldn't exhaust myself too much, I would obediently do as Auntie bade me, and I would love the child I had given birth to.

'Good. I'll be back tomorrow.'

She turned to leave, then stopped for a moment at the cradle to murmur something to my child. Then she looked over her shoulder, gave me an encouraging nod and left.

Before the door was even closed I had already lowered myself into my bed and closed my eyes. I was tired and wanted to dream of my joy.

The remainder of that first day and night passed in a daze of sleeping, feeding, enjoying my daughter and sleeping yet more. I couldn't understand how Auntie managed to be there every time to lift Mara out of her cradle and hand her to me. After all, she had so many other chores to look after, but she was there each time, just so I wouldn't have to get out of bed.

'You must call me immediately, Maria, when you're done with her,' she said every time she laid Mara in my arms.

I nodded, but when Mara was finished feeding I didn't call her. I held my daughter close to me and smelled her neck and cheeks. I admired the shape of her tiny ears, I put my index finger in the palm of her hand, and she would hold it tightly.

In the end Auntie would return on her own accord. Mara had by then already fallen asleep in my arms.

'Why didn't you call me?'

'She's so beautiful.'

'You should have called me immediately. You must only feed…'

'Auntie, she's beautiful, my Mara.'

'Just give her to me now, I'll change her diaper.'

So I gave her my daughter and watched how Auntie expertly changed the soiled diaper for a clean one.

'Reijer has popped in to see how you're doing and I told him you have a daughter.' Auntie said while she was busy changing the diaper. 'He'll be back tomorrow.'

I nodded, but didn't respond. I hoped my body would heal quickly so I could learn how to look after my child myself. When I watched Auntie, it didn't look hard at all. I wanted to ask her to show me next time, but I was too tired and closed my eyes before the words could cross my lips.

16

It took me a while to notice. The silence in my room, the blankets draped over the side of the cradle, Auntie Be quietly sitting on the chair beside my bed. No child in her arms. A heat rose through my body and I threw the blankets aside.

'Where is Mara?' My voice shook, sounded shrill, shocked and broken. What started as a whisper grew into a shriek at Auntie, who turned ashen as she looked at me. My question was answered by what I saw in her face. With great effort I hoisted myself up, despite the pain, and I grabbed a hold of her shoulders as I stood in front of her.

'Where is she!'

'Mien took her. It's the best thing for everyone. You never said you wanted it otherwise, Maria.'

That simple answer silenced me, my mouth closed shut, my ears began to hum, my knees wobbled and I fell on the floor. You never said. The accusation hit me like a hammer hits hot metal, and it shaped me. It turned me back to that miserable state I was in for so many years. I never said.

No, I had never said anything. I had been the one who hadn't wanted my little girl. For many months I had denied her existence, denied her growing within me, wished her dead. For a long time I even refused to think of her as a child. The words I used were thing and creature. To me the child had been unknown, unnamed and unwanted. Mien and Auntie had only done what had seemed best to them.

Auntie Be kneeled down beside me.

'Did you hurt yourself?'

The absurdness of her question made me laugh out loud, of course I had hurt myself. Life had been ripped out of my body and had been taken away, my heart had been left outside in the freezing cold and had frozen into an icy still life.

She pulled me up, helped me back into bed and carefully pulled the blankets over my cold, shivering body. Then she placed a warm cloth on my forehead and asked if she could do anything for me.

'Get her back.'

She shook her head in silence.

'You need to get your strength back. I'll bring you some food, it is better…' She stopped, then turned and left the room, leaving me alone, alone with an empty cradle.

I lay in bed and cursed my weakened body, I *had* to get out, I had to get my child back. She was mine. I had held her in my arms, fed her at my breast, given her my love. She could not leave me now, the only good thing in my life could not be taken away from me now. She had entrusted herself to me and I had promised to protect her. Never would I let her down. But already I had broken that promise.

I tried to get up several times, but each time I slung my legs over the side of the bed the world turned black and I had to lower myself onto the bed again. In the end I decided to try it anyway, and I stood up. I fell down and everything turned black. When I saw light again I stubbornly headed for the door, crawling. I must have made quite a lot of noise, for Auntie had heard me and she entered the room just as I had reached my first goal, the door.

'Let me go, I have to find her,' I gasped, sweat dripping down my back.

'Back to bed with you.' Her voice was full of authority and I dared not disobey. I turned to crawl the whole distance back. Seeing this, Auntie scolded me and helped me up.

'Were you planning on crawling down the stairs, breaking your neck and then go look for your daughter? Back to bed now, and stay there.'

She tucked me in again, not quite as gently as usual, yet still patiently. She wiped strands of hair out of my face, moist with sweat, and she gave me a drink of water. Then she placed a small pile of linen cloths on the bed.

'You need to wind these tightly around your chest, to help you dry up your milk supply.' She unrolled the cloths and wanted to help me. I shook my head angrily.

'Please turn around.' My words sounded curt, but she did as I asked without a fuss.

I sat up straight, pulled my nightgown and undershirt up under my chin and wound the first cloth awkwardly over my breasts. I carefully fastened the cloth with the pin Auntie had given me. I took another cloth and wound that one also around my body. When I was done I lowered my nightgown again. I remained seated straight up in my bed and I looked down my body. It seemed oddly shapeless. I had to dry up my milk supply, I had to put everything behind me and forget everything.

I suddenly remembered Mien's words, about how my body would soon forget, and I was afraid of the other things she may have said, the words that I simply hadn't paid any attention to. Was it possible that Mien had told me about all this? That I had been told and never said a word? I shivered, sagged down in my bed and pulled the blanket up.

Auntie noticed my movement and turned around. She tucked me in again and kissed my forehead but she couldn't take away my pain.

'Stay in bed, Maria. I'll see what I can do.'

I nodded listlessly. I was exhausted and closed my eyes, in the darkness I tried to conjure up visions of my child found and returned into my arms. A beautiful dream.

Before Auntie left the room she turned around.

'I'm sorry, my child,' she spoke softly. 'I really thought that this was for the best, that it was what you wanted too. I hope that one day you'll be able to forgive me. Maybe in the future, when you're married and will have children within wedlock…'

'No!' I opened my eyes and the beautiful vision I had a moment ago disappeared. I screamed at her and beat the mattress. I didn't want any other children, I didn't want to get married, never again would I touch a man or would I allow a man to take possession of my body. The only thing I wanted was my own child, my child, who was the result of an intimacy I hated, but whom I had come to love despite everything.

'Auntie, please help me!'

'I'll do my best, Maria, but I can't give you much hope.' Auntie shook her head and left, closing the door behind her.

I watched her leave as I lay in bed.

Mara. Mara. In my head I sang a lament for the little girl that I had been allowed to hold in my arms for only a short while. The child that I had carried with me for nine months. I remembered the hatred I had felt from the very first moment, the denial, the revulsion, and I felt the guilt weighing down on me. Had I not deserved this? Every moment of her life I had cursed her. Only much later, at that time when Auntie had made me *really* feel, had I realized that a child was growing within me, my child, my own flesh and blood.

Out of habit I placed my hand on my stomach and I remembered the light kicking that had been annoying at first and later on became reassuringly familiar. Now my stomach was flat and empty, life was no longer in it, the contact we used to have had been severed as abruptly as the umbilical chord that used to bind us together.

I thought of all the times that I had sat with my hand on my stomach, simply savoring in quiet amazement this connection with my baby. Finally I had realized that a light shines brighter in the darkness than during the daytime. I had learned that something beautiful can come from something evil, and I had slowly started to accept the fact that I was going to have a child. Suddenly I saw her eyes before me, focusing solely on me, declaring me a mother.

And now I was childless. A childless mother.

A wail passed my lips and pierced through the silence. I screamed until I had no breath left. A sharp stabbing pain in my breasts warned me of what was going to happen and I wrapped my arms tightly around me. The wrappings around me were meant to slow down the milk flow, suppress its supply. How precious were those few moments that she lay in my arms and eagerly filled her tummy. And now it was all flowing away for nothing.

Then, with sudden fury, I threw back the blankets, pulled up my nightgown and yanked off the cloths. I would let the milk flow freely over my body. I would in no way willingly remove my daughter from my life. I would allow my milk the freedom to flow. And who knows, maybe Auntie would find my child before my milk dried up. Maybe I would be able to hold her at my breast again today, or this week.

I left the blanket where it had fallen, even though I got colder and colder as a draft blew over my damp clothes. What did it matter anyway. I turned my head to the window and could just see the top of the oak tree in the yard as its branches moved gently in the breeze. I thought of its young leaves. It made me think of nests built in trees, of birth. And of loss.

I heard a stumbling on the stairs and I knew Auntie Be was coming up. She was probably coming to bring me a cup of sweet tea, or a bowl of broth, or a small bowl of dried apple pieces sprinkled with sugar. I stubbornly refused to turn my head in her direction. Why would I? What would I see in her face?

'Maria.' Her voice was muted behind the door. Auntie knocked again, but I had no strength left to answer her and continued to gaze out the window. Finally I heard a soft creaking sound and imagined how she'd be peeking around the corner carefully, afraid to wake me up.

'Maria, are you awake?'

I ignored her in silence and I banned her presence from my mind. I looked at the sky, the oak tree, the branches and the wind. Where had they taken my child? Had the wind swept her off to a faraway place, or was she still close by and could I run into her in the streets?

'Maria, you'll catch a cold that way.' She moved quickly, closed the door, and hurried over. I smelled the aroma of chicken soup, and I heard the sound of a bowl being put on down, and then I felt her soft hands.

'You'll catch a cold, please my child, look after yourself.'

What good is it to me to be healthy?

She pulled the blanket back over my body and I realized suddenly how cold I had become. My damp undershirt and my nightgown were icy cold and my skin was covered in goosebumps. Auntie was busy fussing already and pulled a clean nightgown from the closet.

'You put this on now, and I'll give you some clean sheets, my dear.'

She handed me a clean undershirt and nightgown and hurried toward the door to leave. 'Will you manage with that on your own?' she asked quickly before she opened the door.

I nodded morosely, and she was gone.

Listlessly I opened up the buttons of my wet nightgown and laboriously struggled out of it. After that came the undershirt. My nipples were stiff with cold and I knew that no milk would flow now. I felt a pain in my breasts however, that was just about unbearable. All this food for my baby girl, so much, and all of it wasted. I wasn't there for her to offer it.

I was just working on the last few buttons when Auntie returned.

'I brought you an extra blanket. You mustn't catch a cold or end up with pneumonia.'

I nodded, although I really couldn't care less. Auntie helped me out of the bed and onto the chair beside the closet. She quickly stripped the wet bedding off the mattress and briskly made the bed again.

'Now, back in bed with you, quickly.'

I realized I was shivering and was grateful that I could lean on her as she helped me back to the bed. My feet were numb and my fingers were stiff with cold.

Auntie fluffed up the pillows behind my back and had me sit down in the bed. Then she pulled the blankets up to my chin.

'And now you're going to enjoy a bit of soup, it'll perk you up, you'll see.'

Auntie fed me chicken soup and I ate obediently while I listlessly sat in bed. Only my face showed above the blankets and I slowly felt the soup warming me from the inside. The thick blankets did the rest.

'Reijer came again today to ask how you are doing.'

I swallowed a spoonful of soup and waited for the next spoonful. 'Why didn't he come sooner, and why didn't he stop them from taken her? Or did he know about it too?'

'I think he knew about it.'

Another spoonful. I burnt my tongue, but suppressed the pain.

'So he just came to gloat over me?'

'Maria.' Auntie spoke no further, but patiently fed me the remainder of the soup. I was left to my own reflections and they swung back and forth between the present and the past, between love and hate, between holding in my arms and yearning for.

Mien came again and she examined me. I meekly let her. I no longer cared that she touched my body with her hands. It wasn't important. The only important thing was for me to find my child back, so I hung onto Mien's arm and begged her for information.

'You're sixteen, Maria. You can't expect anyone to allow you to raise the child yourself. No one would ask that of you, and besides, you don't have a husband to support you. The shame of it. Think of the child!'

'What about the child? She belongs with me. I am her mother, I'm all she needs.'

'What would a child do without a father? Be glad that she now is part of a family where she'll have a mother and a father. She won't grow up with the shame of a fatherless family. Think of your child.'

I was silent. What could I say in response to this? I tried to follow Mien's reasoning and understand why she was being so harsh, but I couldn't. Didn't she realize that every father was a possible monster to a child that wasn't his? Didn't she know that it was better to be the child of a fallen mother than of a stepfather?

'I want her back. I can offer her a safe and loving home.'

'No, you can't.' Mien's voice was determined and she had placed her hands firmly on her hips.

'Believe me when I tell you that she's found a good home. Your own father has been involved and don't you think he'd know? She's now with a family in one of his former congregations.'

Her words provoked a thundering roar in my ears. At first all I could hear was a thumping noise on the inside of my head and it seemed to roar upwards and became louder and louder. I wanted to slap my ears to banish the noise, but I knew it would make no difference. Mien's movements seemed to slow down and blurred out of focus and I closed my eyes in an attempt to banish her words, but they only hit home harder. The Reverend. The Reverend. First he had planted her life in me against my will, and now he had taken her from me, against my will.

Slowly my hearing returned and I stared at Mien with shocked, wide open eyes.

'Who better to ask than your father, after all?' Mien smiled, her rosy cheeks round as apples beneath her eyes.

'I wrote him immediately and of course he was willing to find a family. I have no doubt whatsoever that your little girl has found a good home. Doesn't that make you feel better?'

NO!

Mien gave me an encouraging nod, took my hand and squeezed it softly. Then she rose and placed her things back in her basket.

'You'll get over it, you'll see. She won't be a bastard, Maria, and you won't be a disgraced woman.' I closed my eyes and licked my lips.

'Helène is a fallen woman, Maria.' The words were always spoken in a whisper and Mother would look nervously over her shoulder, afraid someone may have overheard.

'Did you ever see her little boy?' She waited a moment and continued when I nodded.

'He is a bastard.'

I didn't know what a bastard was, but judging the tone of Mother's voice, I could hear that it must be something horrible. I didn't understand why though, for the little boy holding Helène's hand looked very cute, with his round cheeks and blonde hair.

'Never become like her, child. Women like her...' Mother spat on the ground, something she never did. Slowly we continued down the road. Helène was on the same road, headed our way and Mother steered us to the middle of the road, so we could take a wide birth around the woman and her boy. I didn't know where to look. My eyes darted round until they rested on Helène. I looked at her intently and decided she looked cheerful. She was always dressed in colorful clothes and her cheeks were rosy. Today was no different. With a shock I noticed that she smiled and winked at me. She smiled at me! *I quickly looked away, afraid I'd be contaminated and would turn into a bastard.*

'The people who came to pick her up seemed really friendly. Your father wrote to me that they were unable to have children of their own and that they were overjoyed with this arrangement. It is the best for everyone concerned, Maria.'

'Not for me.' I hadn't realized that I spoke the words out loud, but Mien responded immediately.

'For you too. You'll find a husband, you'll marry and have more children. This wasn't your one and only chance, Maria.'

Didn't she understand that I didn't want that at all? That my body belonged to no man, that I didn't wish for marriage and more children, but only for my child? The child I had delivered after so much pain?

I let Mien leave without saying goodbye to her. My thoughts kept coming back to those few words she had spoken. Your father. Your father. Your father. My child was gone, given away to a family only the Reverend knew and I was under no illusion that he would ever tell me who they were and where they lived.

I faced the window and looked at the oak branch that moved slowly in the wind. My last hope just burnt to ashes and was carried away on the wind of truth. Unreachable.

'Did you know about it, Auntie, did you give her the address?'

'Your parents' address? Yes, of course.'

'So you knew?'

'I thought that it was what you wanted, Maria.'

'Then why did I have to love her?' My voice cracked when I remembered the moment I could feel her, my hand on my stomach, a short moment of contact.

'It isn't good to hate.'

'Now I hate all the more.'

Auntie was silent, we both were. She patiently offered me a bowl of soup, a spoon, and a napkin. In silence I started to eat.

'Maria.' Auntie began, then stopped, and began again. 'Maria, if I had known…'

She stopped and I didn't ask further. What use was regret to me?

I finished my soup and Auntie took the dishes from me. She kissed me on my forehead, bade me good-day and left my room. I refused to answer her and I turned my head away from her kiss. When the door closed behind her I lay down again to look out the window.

I saw clouds, thick gray clouds and I knew it wouldn't be long for the rain to come. I closed my eyes and I dreamed that I was blown away with the ashes of an incinerated body. I flew tumbling through the air. I grasped around me, trying to catch as much of the ashes as I could, trying to make something new of it. I was looking for new hope. My eyes swept over the fields I flew by, but because the wind blew me so fast I wasn't able to see anything clearly. All I saw were vague black dots where cows stood, gleaming mirrors where there was water, but no baby anywhere. The distance was too great. And she was too small.

I shouted and stretched out my arms. I kept searching until I was blinded by a thick cloud of dust. I stopped tumbling in the air and fell straight down. The earth rapidly came closer. The wind whistled in my ears and pulled at my clothes that were flapping about me. I closed my eyes and resignedly waited for death.

When I woke up, the first thing I noticed was the empty space where the cradle had been. I knew that there was nothing left now that could remind me of the existence of my child. Everything was gone, thoroughly removed. Pulled out like a weed.

My body was young and strong, and after a few days already I felt strong enough to come out of bed.

Auntie Be took me by the arm and carefully guided me to the kitchen, while keeping a close eye on me with every step I took.

'Here, sit down now, girl.' She gently pushed me in Grandpa's chair and I carefully lowered myself.

'How are you feeling?'

'Fine.' My breath came in short bursts and my voice was hoarse. 'In a few more days I'll feel like my old self again.'

Auntie nodded. She turned and walked to the teapot simmering on the stove.

'Would you like some tea?'

'I'd love some, Auntie.'

I didn't know what else to say, words between us had become pointless. Just the sound of my voice was an accusation, no matter what words came out. She placed the tea beside me and sat down in silence at the table. I looked about me and it was as if I saw everything for the very first time. The pots on the shelf, the little bundles of dried herbs hanging of the beams, one of Grandma's embroideries. The embroidery was of some wise words I never understood as a child, but I knew the meaning of them only too well now. *Do unto others, as you would have them do unto you.* But was there anyone in my surroundings who had taken these words to heart? Maybe I should also stop conforming to other peoples' wishes, but simply do what I wanted and no longer obey those who considered themselves to have authority over me.

We sat together in silence and I looked round me, drank my tea and thought things over. Every now and then I would glance Auntie's way and to me it seemed as if she had shrunk, shriveled up. She sat quietly and lonely at the table with the six chairs. But not lonely enough.

How was it possible that this woman had collaborated in this betrayal? I had grown to love her, she had slowly started to fill the hole left behind by my mother as she had withdrawn herself more and more over the years. So, again I felt emptiness, such bitter emptiness.

'The tea was nice, Auntie.' I reached for the newspaper that was on the table and pulled it toward me. I started to read, ignoring Auntie, but the words on the paper didn't interest me much. I read about a tramp who had been taken into custody, I read about the growing unemployment and about people in financial trouble, but how important could money be compared to the love I had for my child?

As I read, Auntie pottered about in the kitchen. I suspected she'd probably like to talk to me if I would give her the chance, but I kept reading, ignoring her presence. In the end she left the kitchen and I could hear her wooden shoes clip-clop through the attached barn. She would find comfort with her cows and she would have no shortage of other things to keep her occupied after that.

Now that Auntie had left I could close the paper, and I stared out the kitchen window without seeing anything. My breasts hurt and I could feel moisture escaping. Reluctantly I rose, slowly. I had to get back to bed. Just then Auntie returned to the kitchen.

'I'll walk with you.'

Auntie came toward me and hooked her arm solidly into mine. She smiled at me. I looked at her in silence and clenched my teeth hard together, because inside my head echoed all the words and accusations I wanted to shout at her. But not a word crossed my lips, and her eyes told me this may have been the harshest accusation of all.

17

Seven days passed in a whirl of thoughts and dreams. I slept many hours of the day, and when I was awake, all I could think of was Mara. Each day my body ached less, my breasts were less full and the pressure became less as my milk dried up. But every now and then I still felt the, by now so familiar tingling sensation and I still regularly had to change my undershirt because the milk had started to flow again. I cherished every stain and wished the milk could keep coming, so I could feed her when I would have her back.

Auntie looked after me very well. She was kind as always and baked something special for me almost daily. The meals were nourishing and substantial, but I often pushed my plate away as soon as she had left the room. We didn't speak.

Auntie tried, but I couldn't find any words to say to her. Every word I thought of got tangled up in hatred and I couldn't get it out of my mouth. She had let me down so very much and there was nothing left of the easy bond we used to have. I also couldn't think of Reijer without feeling betrayed by him, and every time Auntie told me that he had asked about me, I would turn my head away, close my eyes to lock them both out.

After the seventh day I decided I was strong enough to get up and stay out of bed for the day. I didn't talk to Auntie about it, but simply picked up my clothes in the morning and got dressed. Auntie was in the kitchen baking pancakes. My arrival didn't seem to surprise her. She greeted me kindly and soon enough we sat down at breakfast together as if nothing had happened in the last week.

The only difference was our silence.

In the end, after reminding me three times not to tire myself out, Auntie left to do her work. I didn't respond and just stared at her, waiting for her to leave. She left soon, but quickly returned with a book that she put on the table in front of me. Then she left for the barn and I warily picked up the book and opened it. The words just danced in front of me and wouldn't form sentences. Where would Mara be? How could I be sitting here reading a book while I should be looking for her? I tried to figure out a way that I could find her back, as I had been trying so often these days, but every time I ended up with the same problem. Without help I wouldn't be able to find her, and there was no one willing to help me.

Then I heard her crying.

With a jerk I was pulled out of my contemplations and I sat rigid in my chair. Incredulously I lowered my book slowly and stood up. I held my breath as I listened closely, wondering if I would hear the sound again.

Yes, there it was again!

She was near by! With relieve I started to laugh out loud, a noise that sounded very strange to my own ears. I turned around on the spot and tried to locate the origin of the crying I had heard. On my socked feet I started to walk through the kitchen. A hot burst of anger at Auntie, who had been responsible for all this, flashed through me, but it was quickly chased away by the joy I felt when I heard the crying again. It came from upstairs, I had to go up.

With two steps at a time I ran up the stairs and I threw open my bedroom door and stood still at the threshold. No, of course, not here. Not here. I had to look in Auntie's room. I returned to the little hall and pushed down the door handle as carefully as I could. The door creaked open and I looked inside. At once I saw that there was no cradle, no child.

But the crying...

I closed my eyes and concentrated again. The sound was still there, but now it seemed to be further away than before. I closed the door of Auntie's room and slowly climbed down the stairs. Had I really been mistaken?

Maybe she was in the front room, or in the 'opkamer', the little room above the cellar, or in the cellar?

I entered the kitchen, determined to search the whole house, but Auntie was in the kitchen and looked at me with an odd look in her eyes.

She had lied to me!

'Is something the matter, Maria?'

'No, nothing at all.' My voice quivered, but I looked her straight in the eye and forced her to think that nothing had changed.

'I made some tea. Come sit down.'

Obediently I sat down. In silence we drank our tea. My anger grew and grew. Did Auntie really think she could keep this secret from me? I could hear my own child crying and she sat here beside me, drank her tea and acted as if Mara was no longer here. How could she do this to me?

I poured my tea from the cup into the saucer so it would cool faster and I drank it as quickly as I could. Then I pulled at the little fringes of the tablecloth and quickly made little braids. Three strands entwined, four, five, six. I tried all sorts of combinations and impatiently pulled at the strings that wouldn't stay put. Finally Auntie had finished her tea and left the kitchen. I waited a short while until I heard her wooden shoes clip-clop in the barn and then I got up to.

The crying had stopped, but I knew what I had heard. I knew she had to be here somewhere. I first checked the front room. Nothing.
Then I searched the 'opkamer'. Nothing.
The cellar next. Nothing.

Again I went upstairs and this time I also checked underneath Auntie's bed and also underneath my own. I pulled open the closets to look for her. Then I remembered the third door and I went to the hayloft. She could be anywhere!

I returned to my room to get a lamp. I lit it and returned to the hayloft. I started on the left, the side where we had found the cradle, and I searched the loft yard by yard.

But there was no child.

Defeated, I slowly climbed down the stairs. I returned to the kitchen. Then I remembered that I hadn't searched the attached barn. As I searched I held my breath and kept my ears alert. I had heard her, maybe I would hear her again.

But there was nothing.

Without hesitating any longer, I stepped into my wooden shoes and went out to look for Auntie. I found her in the garden and when I called her she looked at me with hope in her eyes and a smile at her mouth.

'Where is she, Auntie?'

Her face turned pale, and her smile disappeared.

'What do you mean, Maria?'

'I heard her.'

'Who did you hear? What are you talking about?'

'Mara is here, isn't she? Bring me to her.'

I went up to Auntie with large steps, my hands on my hips and ready to take her on. She couldn't take my child from me.

'Mara? My child, she isn't...'

'I heard her crying. I could hear her crying, Auntie, don't deny it.' I swallowed my despair and remained strong for my daughter's sake.

'You must have imagined it, there is no child here. Mien took her away.'

'Don't lie to me!'

She shook her head, and I stamped my foot on the ground. Then I turned around. I would look for her myself, as long as it would take for me to find her. I stomped over the yard and kicked at the chickens and the dog. I threw the doors open and pulled everything out of everywhere. I searched every corner of the farm, all day.

I found nothing.

And at night, in bed, after a silent meal with Auntie Be, I still thought I heard her crying. From somewhere deep. I listened intently. The sound remained constant, even when I covered my ears with my hands and hid under the blanket. Then I realized that the

sound was in my head. The sound was only inside my head, se-
curely lodged inside.

It was all I had left of her. She was gone.

Forever gone.

18

Why is it that the woman I have grown to love and trust, has turned out to be a traitor? Sometimes she looks at me and her large eyes speak to me. I see regret in her eyes, but I don't know if it is regret for what she has done, or regret for what has come of it. Our relationship has turned cold. I only speak to her when I need to. In the end she has turned out to be just like the rest of them.

How much can a person bear? How much am I able to bear?

After my desperate search of the farm I no longer allowed myself to be kept confined to a chair in the house, despite the pain to my body. I had decided to go back to work, and my hands worked at high speed as I scrubbed the floor of the 'opkamer'. The soapy water turned my fingers raw and I felt a burning, piercing pain, but I ignored it. I just got myself more hot water, inflicted new pain, and I scrubbed.

I felt a hand on my shoulder and I shook it off impatiently. I didn't want to be touched. I wanted no contact. Leave me alone. I don't want to talk. I don't want to live.

Again there was a hand on my shoulder, then two. Auntie held on to me and no matter what I did, she wouldn't let go. The only way to free myself would be by force and I couldn't possibly do that. Instead I scrubbed even harder and put my full weight on the brush so I could get all the grime out of even the deepest grooves.

The result was quite the opposite. The bristles of the brush bent uselessly sideways with the pressure I put on them.

'Get up, Maria.'

I considered her words and wanted to ignore her again, but her hands remained on my shoulders and seemed to leave a burning impression. Finally I got up. Her hands still remained on my shoulders.

She guided me down the steps and brought me to one of the kitchen chairs. She placed a cup of coffee on the table in front of me and sat down, facing me.

Instead of looking at Auntie, I looked out of the window. It had some dust on it and a few flies. I would have to wash that. I made a mental note to boil some water in a minute, lots of hot water, so the windows would gleam. Weren't windows like the soul of a house? With clean windows, people who walked by could enjoy the welcoming warmth of the home, and people inside could look out and have contact with the people outside. Windows ought to be clean. I already moved my feet in preparation to push back my chair. The coffee stood on the table, untouched.

But Auntie's voice held me back.

'Don't you dare get up now, Maria!'

She spoke the words with such authority as I had heard from her only a few times before. I relaxed my feet, and the chair stayed where it was.

I glanced at my hands and looked closely at the red cracks, the white swollen edges of my nails, the cuts between my thumb and index finger where the skin had split and now was swollen as well. Now that I was no longer scrubbing away at the floor, little droplets of blood had a chance to dry. It was like life emerging, but congealing before it had a chance to really make a difference.

'We can't go on like this, Maria.'

I heard a soft movement and saw in the corner of my eye how she stretched out her hand to me across the table. Another meaningless gesture. I had admired this hand before, because of its strength and patience, but this same hand had betrayed me, had taken my child and carried it off.

I looked at the coffee that was steaming hot and patiently waiting for me on the table and I toyed with the notion of throwing it over. Would the hot liquid reach the traitorous hand and scar it? Would she keep her hand outstretched despite the pain, or would she pull her hand back?

'I want you to look at me.'

More words. Another command. Was there nothing left for me? No room, no freedom at all to make my own choices? Was I doomed to live my life tied to bonds that others controlled and tightened around me? The only difference between the Reverend and Auntie was the way they went about it. He tortured me with his power to condemn me, and she tortured me with her love that also condemned me. What good had love brought me so far?

Only betrayal.

'Look…at…me.'

My eyes glided from the coffee cup with the flower pattern to her hand, still lying there with the palm facing upward, vulnerable. From her hand I slowly looked up her arm, her neck, her chin. I took care not to meet her eyes.

'Look at me, Maria.'

She still wasn't satisfied. It was never enough.

Again my legs moved underneath my chair, I pushed off and stood up. I moved so sudden that the coffee spilled over the cup into the saucer.

My soapy water was cold by now, but I would prepare new water. I had to scrub the floor and after that wash the windows. I didn't have time to chat. I didn't have the strength.

As I threw water from the rain barrel against the windows with a wooden spoon, I heard the dog barking behind me. For a moment I felt the familiar urge to run away and hide from visitors, whoever they may be, but when I looked down at my flat belly, I realized that this was no longer necessary.   I heard steps approach me and I glanced over my shoulder to see who it was.

Reverend Bosch. Reijer.

He stopped a few steps behind me and I positioned myself in such a way that I could still throw the last bit of rain water at the windows, yet keep a good eye on him.

'Good afternoon, Maria.'

I nodded in response, but said nothing. This was the first time I saw him since… Mara. With the disappearance of my big belly, it seemed as if a barrier had fallen away between us. I felt no shame as I saw him now, only the same impatience and anger I felt toward Auntie. It was very easy now to call him Reijer instead of Reverend Bosch.

'Afternoon, Reijer.' I was angry, and he was allowed to know it.

'Your aunt told me you're all better now?'

He spoke as if I had caught a cold, had been in bed for a few days, and was fully recuperated now. Did no one understand then that it was more than a small illness, that the white stretch marks on my stomach would always remain? That a piece of my heart was missing because I could no longer hold my daughter in my arms? Auntie, Mien and now also Reijer, everyone acted like it was just a passing ailment.

I threw the wooden spoon with force into my bucket and took a firm hold of the bucket while I considered filling the bucket and throwing the contents over Reijer's head. I didn't do it.

'Oh yes, all better.'

'I'm glad to hear that.'

I nodded. Angrily.

'Is your aunt inside?'

'Yes, she'll probably be in the barn,' I said, though I didn't have a clue as to where Auntie was or what she was doing at that moment, and it didn't interest me in the slightest. As long as he would leave me alone.

Reijer hesitated for a moment. He fumbled with his cap and then went inside. I watched him go in silence. Then I grabbed my things and moved on to the next window. It suited me just fine if the two of them were going to sit and chat together in the kitchen. They didn't need my help with that. They could manage just fine without me, just like I would manage just fine without them. I had other concerns. I wasn't finished yet with the windows.

'Maria!'

I didn't respond. She'd stop calling me soon enough.

'Maria!'

I remained silent and kept cleaning.

'Maria!'

I heard footsteps in the yard and they came my way.

'Oh, here you are. Come on in, child, I've made you some tea.'

'I don't want any.'

'Reijer is here too, come along and join us.'

'I know he's here.'

'Maria, child...'

Reluctantly I turned to face her. I saw a tear on her cheek, but I ignored it and side stepped her. I just missed bumping into her and I felt a sense of satisfaction.

She had brought this upon herself.

I walked along the attached barn and used the barn doors at the back to enter. Instead of walking straight into the kitchen, I washed my hands at the pump in the barn and as I stared at the flowing water I wondered to myself if I was treating Auntie too harshly.

And was I treating the world too harshly too?

Had my own behavior not been much, much worse than Auntie's when I had hated my child and had even wished it to be dead?

But that was before I had seen Mara and had held her in my arms!

I dried my hands, turned round, crossed the barn and headed for the kitchen. Tea was on the table already and Reijer and Auntie sat together talking in muted voices. When I entered, their voices became silent.

'Come and join us, Maria,' Auntie spoke after a brief silence. Reluctantly I took a chair and gazed at the steam rising up from the tea. Auntie offered us a cookie and I refused gruffly. I drank my tea as quickly as I possibly could. Despite the heat of the liquid that burnt my mouth and throat I didn't want to pour the tea in the saucer to cool it off first. With a slam I put the cup back on the saucer. I got up and wanted to leave the kitchen again.

'Maria, it's you I came for actually.'

'I can't talk, I've got too much work to do.'

'Give me a chance, Maria.'

I stood still, unsure, and Auntie got up and left the kitchen.

'I'll leave you two alone.'

Why won't anyone listen to me? I don't want to talk. I am invisible, indistinct and insignificant. I'm sorry Reijer, forget it. I'm out of here. If it's a conversation you want you'll have to find Auntie back. Don't expect anything from me anymore.

I started to move, ready to walk out.

'Why do you punish us all?'

I don't punish anyone, what are you talking about? The only one being punished is me. Over and over again. That was the reason I got pregnant to begin with. You didn't know that, did you? You didn't know it was a punishment. The Reverend knew though, every mistake I made was an excuse for him to come to me and rape me. And in the end that was how he left inside me the seed that brought forth Mara. Oh yeah, by now I know all about it. Did you know all this? All that what a man and woman do together? Sure you do. You're a man and a servant of God besides. Any idea yet which woman you're going to select for your filthy games?

Mara. Mara has been punished too. She was taken away from her mother, even before we could get to know each other. What do you think, has she been punished enough for my sins?

My mind raged, but my mouth remained silent.

'Maria, I want to help.'

He stretched out his hand across the table and looked at me, pleadingly. I closed my eyes and turned away. Very deliberately I walked out of the kitchen.

My feet felt heavy as I lifted them into my wooden shoes. Why did I behave like this to people who were trying to be good to me? Did I really mean to be this harsh, hurt the people close to me, and go through life sad and alone?

I opened the barn door by leaning against it. I tripped over the threshold and let the door slam closed behind me with a loud bang. Another mistake. You'd think I was angry.

I wasn't though. I was just so...

Sad?

Without seeing or hearing anything I crossed the yard, walked past the pig house and the chicken coop and looked for an opening in the bushes where I could climb through. My skirt got caught on the thorns of a wild black berry bush, but I tore myself free, not caring that I ripped in my clothes. I trampled on some young shoots that had just started to grow. At the same time I held on to the branches and I tore off all the young green leaves that were growing on them.

My hands quickly were filled with red stripes, and they ended up soiled by the green juices. It stung. I sat down on a fallen tree and put my face in my hands. I smelled the juices of the crushed leaves on my sticky hands. Now I was really alone, I had managed to distance myself from everyone.

It wasn't until Reijer sat down beside me on the tree trunk, that I noticed I had been followed, and he carefully put a warm arm around my shoulder. I jerked up, startled, and moved away from him.

My sudden move made him pull back his arm and he said nothing, but continued to sit silently beside me. It was strange to sit on a tree trunk beside a man, and it was as if I could still feel the pressure of his arm on my shoulder. I wiggled about uncomfortably. The fabric of my dress rubbed over the rough bark of the tree and it pulled every now and then. My thoughts darted from staying on the tree trunk to running away, from remaining silent to screaming out all my misery, from fighting to suffering.

I swung my feet back and forth until I realized I was doing it. Then I started to fidget with my hands, traced a red stripe on my palm with my index finger. The pain was irrelevant, I simply studied the structure of the damaged skin. Why had I done that? I quickly closed my fist in an attempt to hide the scars.

What would happen if I hit him and shouted at him? Would he leave me alone then for good? It seemed like a good idea.

But it was a lonely one.

So I stayed seated and didn't hit him, but stared at a spider climbing over my wooden shoe. I could shake it off, or crush it. Or leave it be. Was this how God regarded people? Did he choose to cruelly crush some, to repel and merely wound others, and to leave others in peace? I thought about it for a long while but couldn't come to a satisfactory answer, and when I glanced at the wooden shoe again, the spider was gone.

My shoulders had slowly relaxed and the sleeves of my dress lightly touched the fabric of Reijer's jacket. I imagined how an invisible thin piece of thread united us and I shuddered. I quickly moved aside, but not too far.

I listened to the sparrows chirping. In the distance I could hear the dog bark and close by I heard an insect buzzing. Finally I made my decision.

'Thank you, Reijer.' *That you came after me, that you took the trouble to see me, that you're still friendly to me.*

Reijer didn't respond for a few seconds. I looked aside and saw him smile.

'I'm glad you said that, Maria. You mustn't run away. Not for me and not for your aunt.'

'It's all harder than you think.'

'She has told me a few things. I am trying to understand the two of you. And I'm trying to help too, but there are no easy solutions.'

'So am I simply supposed to resign myself to how things are?' I dug my heels into the sand.

'I'm not sure about that. I don't have a clear picture of the situation.'

From the corner of my eye I saw how he shook his head, but his answer was of no help to me.

'But it is so simple, I am her mother.' I twisted my heels fiercely and dug deeper into the dirt.

'Yes, that you are. What is her name?' he asked suddenly, as if the question just struck him.

'Mara.'

'Your child is now in a family that is very happy to have her.'

I took a deep breath and wanted to interrupt, but he raised his hand.

'You have to believe that. Mien has done this kind of thing before.'

But she has never asked the Reverend for advice before, and what did she know of him?

'Mara will have a father and a mother, she can grow up without shame.'

'And without me.'

He ignored my remark.

'You're sixteen. How would you raise a child and hold a job at the same time to support yourself, find a place to live for you and your child, and also, how would you live with the shame when people look on you with contempt?'

His words were true, they were all true, but so harsh and cruel. I wrapped my arms around myself and slowly rocked myself.

'Of course you would have been able to find a temporary solution, but you have to look further, Maria. How would it be in five years' time, or ten? What about when you're older and you would like a family, a husband, more children?'

I stopped short and suddenly sat very still. Then I slowly started to rock myself again.

'Your aunt wanted to do what's best for you, Maria.'

I kept rocking back and forth and considered his words, everything he had said. Maybe it was true.

But she was still my child.

I pulled my wooden shoes out of the sticky dirt and softly put my feet down again. Again I rocked back and forth and again my wooden shoes sucked themselves into the dirt.

Auntie meant to do what was best for me. Maybe it was true. But Mara was still my child.

I don't know for how long we sat there, but finally he helped me up and we walked back to the house together. At the door he tapped his cap and left.

19

I feel so much doubt after my conversation with Reijer. Can it really be true that Mara is better off with other people than with me? Auntie Be, Mien, Reijer, they all seem to agree.

Why am I still here? I don't know what else I can do to find her, and if I can't find her, then why would I keep hoping? What has life brought me except for fragments of happiness that were all too quickly snatched away from me? Happiness is nothing but the counter balance of misery, the more happiness, the deeper the misery when that happiness is taken away.

I am very diligent in doing my chores, so Auntie won't have any reason to complain, and I think about what I can possibly do. There are so few options.

In truthfulness, there are none.

No, if I'm really honest, there's only one.

Farewell, my dear friend.

The hayloft, a place where I never used to come, now became a place of refuge for me, a place where I could feel at ease just sitting or lying down on the hay while I thought about everything that had happened. I heard footsteps on the stairs and silently waited to hear if Auntie was going to call me. I hadn't told her that I spend many hours here. I didn't know if she knew where to find me if she was worried, but I didn't want to share this secret with her.

The door opened up and a ray of light fell across the loft. Without a noise I lowered myself behind a few of the hay bales and I held my breath. I almost had to sneeze because of the smell and dust all around me, but I managed to hold it in and silently waited.

'Maria.'

It wasn't Auntie who was looking for me, it was Reijer. I hesitated, not sure whether to answer him or not. I could hear his footsteps crossing the loft and I could feel the floor tremble under the weight of his steps.

'Maria, your aunt told me your were here.' He stood still and seemed to hesitate. Like me, he hadn't brought a lantern and it must have been hard for him to see anything while his eyes were still adjusting to the darkness.

He made another careful step and bumped his foot against a bale. I saw him bend down and touch it, then he sat down.

'I would like to talk to you.'

I remained quietly crouched down. I was sure he would leave soon enough. He had to understand that I didn't want his company. This was the only place for me where I could think in peace. Did that have to be taken from me as well?

'Have you thought about our last conversation?' he asked, as if I was sitting beside him and we were having a normal conversation.

I said nothing, but inside my head I answered him. *I haven't been able to think of anything else. Clearly, the decision wasn't mine to make, but others. And everyone has decided that I am unsuitable. Unsuitable and useless.*

'Have things improved between you and your aunt?' he continued.

No, things haven't improved between us and it isn't going to change either, but don't worry, she won't be burdened by my useless presence much longer. Everything will change. Everything will become peaceful.

I made up my mind and suddenly took off my wooden shoes and stood up, walked four, five large paces towards the door that Reijer had left ajar, and said: 'I don't want to talk, Reijer, please leave me alone.'

A few more steps and I had reached the door and then the stairs. I quickly went down and in the barn I put my wooden shoes back on. It had been enough. More than enough.

The barn door was still ajar and I opened it further. I glanced over my shoulder, but Reijer didn't follow me. Good, what a relief.

I started to run, quite determined now. I had to get away, away from myself.

I ran without looking, I blindly pushed my way through shrubs and jumped over obstacles. The dog's barks reached me from afar and accompanied the noisy thumping of my footsteps.

In my head voices echoed telling me what I had to do. Everyone knew so well, and they all said the same thing. *Maria, whore. Be glad that you're rid of the child. Be happy with this solution, grow up, find a husband, have a family. Submit yourself to the leadership of a godly man and you'll be blessed. Of course he has authority over you. Yes, over your body and soul. But that is the order of creation, that is how it's supposed to be. Why do you fight it? Because you're a whore, and always will be. No one can wash you clean from the sins you've committed. It's no use. You won't find your daughter back. She's in a place you'll never find. Everyone wants to do what's best for you, really, everyone.*

My breath came faster and faster, my throat felt dry and raspy. I felt a stabbing side ache and it angered me, and hurried me on till the pain became unbearable and I slowed down. For a moment I stopped and leaned with my hands against the white bark of a birch, my body bent over. Then I heard Reijer calling my name. He was following me after all and again I ran.

No, Reijer, you will not take this from me. I will not let myself be found again, I don't want to anymore.

I ran slower now, held back by the pain in my side and my bruised feet inside the wooden shoes. I tripped and almost fell, recovered and kept running. I had only one goal, one solution.

I had to go on, to the end of the earth and then off it, that was the only option left to me. It was no longer a question of where I should go, but whether I would make it in time. I followed a wide bend and turned right, ran straight through a thicket and I felt the branches of some large berry bushes hit my face. One painful lash must have left a red welt on my cheek, but I ignored it. I had set my goal and was determined to reach it. Goaded on by a voice I knew and at the same time didn't know. A voice that silenced every other voice in my head. Gone were all the good intentions. All that was left was the voice with the one remaining solution that would make all things well. For Mara, for Auntie, for Mother, for the Reverend, for everyone. Also for me.

I reached another path and knew it wasn't much further. Now that I had reached a proper path I was no longer hindered by branches and bushes. I made quicker headway and knew I had almost reached my destination.

In the distance I could see the blackness glistening and with renewed vigor I ran faster and faster. My feet ached and I kicked off my wooden shoes without slowing down. It didn't matter anymore.

On my socked feet I could feel every little stone, and a surface root hurt the bottom of my feet, but it mattered no longer. I had reached the end of the path and ran the rest of the way across the grass, next a short stretch of sand and then I walked into the shimmering blackness. Immediately the water slowed me down as it soaked my skirts, but I doggedly moved on.

The cold seemed like a friend to me, it numbed my painful scratches and bruises. It became more difficult to continue as my skirts became heavier and heavier. I could feel the water pulling on me and I knew all was well. I turned round and looked up at the sky one more time, then I let myself fall back and let the water close over me. There was nothing left to fight for anymore, no chance to turn back, the water had taken a hold of my clothes and I slowly drifted away. All was well.

Water plants entangled and embraced me, as if they wanted to gently rock me in their arms, cradle me like a baby.

The cold numbed all my pain. The pain I felt inside me also seemed to disappear as the watery depths welcomed me. I blew some bubbles and sank a little deeper. My eyes followed the bubbles as they rose to the surface and there they popped like sweet dreams.

The water plants' arms cradled me into the depths of the water. Back into Mother's arms, safe as a little baby. Finally all was well.

I felt firm slaps on my cheeks and my head swung from left to right. I was so cold. Strong arms lifted me up and carried me. There were bumps and jerks, and voices calling. The cold, I felt so cold. Fingers were touching me, pulling the clothes from my body.

No. Not again, no! Don't do it, don't do it! It's quiet in my room, I'm in bed with my blanket pulled tightly over me. I don't dare to crawl under the blanket any further. Mother is gone, and I don't want to miss any noises by putting my head under the blanket. My heart is thumping with fear, my hands hold on tight to the blanket. I can't avoid it, I can't do anything about it. Why do I listen so intently? Why do I want to know when he comes?

The third step on the staircase creaks.

Now I pull the blanket over my head.

When I can't see him, he can't see me, right?

The door opens with a creak. I smell my own breath as it is trapped under the blanket. It smells of fear. Three steps, two steps. He stops. He waits. All he does is wait and I know that it is enough. My hands tremble, and I blow on them, again I smell the sour smell of fear. He waits. Every minute he waits, his impatience grows. He won't drag me away from under the blanket, but he'll win anyway. Mother, where are you? Mother.

My feet start a life of their own and suddenly they push against the end of the bed. My body slides up and my hair feels the cool air in my room. The blanket moves and fresh air enters, and a soft light enters my room from the hall. A shadow hangs over my bed. His shadow.

'Maria.'

His voice is enough and I know that he has won again. My eyes are closed, but the image on my retina won't disappear. I know him too well, I know how he is, how he feels, how he punishes. I have to open the buttons of my nightgown myself. He doesn't need words anymore. My hands are his servants and do their duty. My body stiffens with cold, and offers him warmth pleasure. *And my misery.*

The hands are gone now. They are replaced by a warm blanket, but even the blanket can't chase away the cold. Why didn't the water keep its hold on me, keep me in its powerful embrace?

'What happened?'

I could hear Auntie's voice, shrill and full of distress. Where did Auntie's voice come from? And where is the water? I start to thrash about me and I open my mouth in an attempt to swallow water and sink deeper, but all I swallow is air.

'She needs to be kept warm. She's chilled to the bone.'

I want to nod my head, but I can't. Yes, it's cold. It's terribly cold. I shut myself off to my surroundings and refuse to listen anymore, again I allow myself to drift off with the cold. There is no water now, but maybe the cold is enough. Simply the cold will do. I drift with my eyes closed, my arms spread out. I look up at the blue sky. A single branch from an old oak tree is hanging over the water and I follow the direction it points to. For a moment there is a small robin sitting on the branch, then it flies off. I try to fly along with it, higher and higher, but instead I sink further and further. For a moment I feel the need to breathe. I flail my arms about, momentarily gasping for air, and I feel the sun on my hand as it reached up above the water. But then I realize that there is nothing up there except misery and heartache. I close my eyes and escape into darkness.

'What else can we do?'

'Just pray.'

Familiar voices call me. Their words are like stars in a dark night. They shed a bit of light, enough to see by. I rise and feel the odd sensation of my body shivering. Uncontrollable shivering. The cold that's nestled inside of me seems to try and find itself a way out. My hands, arms, legs, yes, even my stomach, they all seem to shiver uncontrollably. My breath comes haltingly, but I know that I am breathing air, not water.

A strong cocoa smell enters my nostrils and it almost chases away the cold. My eyelids flutter, and suddenly I want nothing more than to open them and look around me. I need to know where I am, with whom and why.

I hear mumbling voices and I focus my eyes in the direction of their sound and I see them, Reijer and Auntie. They are both sitting beside my bed, each with a bible on their lap. Their hands are folded, their eyes are closed and their lips are moving. They each have their own rhythm, either one incomprehensible to me. I continue to watch them as they pray. I notice how Auntie reaches out for the hand of her pastor and how he suddenly leads her in a clearly audible prayer, as if they had planned it that way. When he stops, she continues and her amen is for him the start of a new dialogue with his God. There seems to be no end to their pleading, until Reijer opens his eyes, seemingly without focus, but he looks straight into mine. His voice falls silent and he smiles.

'There you are,' he whispers softly as if to a sick child that just woke up from a feverish dream.

'Maria!' Auntie rose and puts her arms around me, which warms me more than all the hot water bottles she heaped around my body.

'Auntie.' My voice is no more than a hoarse croaking and I shut my mouth, startled. Has the water damaged my voice?

'You've swallowed a lot of water and vomited a lot as well. Your throat must be sore.'

Only now I notice that she's right and I nod slowly.

'Do you think you can you sit up?'

I have to think about this question, and I focus my attention on my limbs. They are still trembling, but it's less severe. I even feel some warmth that seems to emanate from inside me and not from the bottles that Auntie has put all around my body.

I nod my head but don't speak. It is as if my body is no longer capable of doing more than one thing at a time. I know that after nodding my head I now need to do something. I turn onto my back so I can push myself up.

Then, as I push myself up with my feet against the end of the bed, it all comes back to me, the hands that touched me! My clothes being pulled off my body. The warmth I felt on my skin.

'No.' It is no more than a whisper and they both couldn't hear it. No!

'Go away, go away!'

My voice is louder now and they both look up, startled. Again I feel a trembling deep inside me, but it isn't the cold this time, but a cold fear. I won't look at Reijer again, but I wait to hear the sound of his leaving footsteps.

But instead I feel Auntie Be's comforting arms around me again, and she lifts me up as she presses me against herself, and she sits me up against a pillow.

'Maria, it's all right, just calm down.' She hushes me, and softly speaks kind words into my ear and strokes my hair. Somewhere there's a vague realization that I hear indeed the retreating footsteps I had been waiting for and I now dare to open my eyes. Her face is close to me, and she smiles lovingly. Little wrinkles appear around the corners of her mouth and I can't stop myself from speaking.

'Those hands, my clothes.' I can't think of anything else to say, but she seems to understand.

'You were wet and cold, Maria, deathly cold. Reijer helped me, but only with your gown and socks.'

'Those hands,' I say again.

'I was the one who touched you, darling, with my hands and with a towel. I had to rub you dry, rub you warm, don't be upset.'

The sound of clattering cups tells me that Reijer has in fact not left, but is pouring the cocoa I had smelled earlier. I feel new shame when I realize that he has heard everything and must have understood my suspicion.

I look at him warily as he hands me a mug. His smile is friendly, not threatening. His eyes are blue, not black. His hands are soft, not forceful.

'Thank you,' I whisper.

During the following night I had fits of frightening dreams. My struggle with the water and those hands, the cold and the warmth, everything played a part but none of it made sense. When I woke up, Auntie was sitting beside my bed and looked at me with concern. She dabbed my forehead with a cold wet cloth, and every now and then she felt my pulse.

'You've got a fever, Maria.'

I shook my head and told her that I didn't feel anything, that I was fine. There wasn't anything wrong with me, but before I could speak, my eyes fell shut and I was enveloped again by a new dream. He came to me and brought God's wrath down on me with his accusations. I had brought this upon myself. Didn't I know that

Judas was burning in hell for his unbelief and betrayal, and worse, for the suicide he had committed? Was I planning on following his example? I should be grateful that someone had rescued me. He laughed shrilly and his cheeks glowed red when he told me what I had to do. My refusal infuriated him and I wasn't able to resist anymore, so my hands did his bidding. My soul cried out and begged for deliverance, but there was no one who listened and the Reverend always did as he pleased.

I shut him out and again floated away on the water. Why had I not been allowed to stay there, to be carried away by the peaceful currents that could bring me to utter nothingness? A place where I didn't need to be afraid anymore, a place where the Reverend couldn't reach me?

Again I woke up and opened my eyes. I saw a vague figure sitting beside my bed, but couldn't remember who she was. Was it Mother? My lips seemed to crack when I tried to ask her a question, and my tongue was like dried leather and I closed my mouth without uttering a sound. The heat that soared through my body took turns with a shattering cold. On those moments I had no idea where I was and why I wasn't drifting. Wasn't the cold supposed to make me numb and carry me away?

I shook my head from side to side and called out, but there was no one who listened. There never was anyone.

Later, Auntie told me that I had been hallucinating and thrashing about for three long days. She had sat at my bedside for those three days almost uninterrupted. Whenever she could, she fed me small amounts of broth, and she would often squeeze a few drops of water on my lips with a wet cloth. She had called for the doctor, but he couldn't do much more than tell her that the fever simply had to break on its own accord.

Reijer had been the only one who assisted her. Every day he came by and took care of her chores so she could sleep for a few hours. He helped her run the farm, and it was because of him that she could stay at my bedside almost all the time. I frowned when she told me about this and wanted to ask her why a pastor would bother to do a thing like that.

But I said nothing, although the question kept circling round in my head. What kind of a pastor had the time to sit at the bedside of a church member – no, not a church member, but an unwilling, unrepentant, fallen woman? Why did he do that?

On the evening of the third day I opened my eyes and asked with a clear voice for something to eat. Auntie, who sat beside the bed, jumped up for joy and immediately left the room to prepare something for me. At that moment I had no idea of what Auntie had gone through, how much she had worried about me.

I turned my head to the side so I could look out the window. There wasn't much to see, it was twilight and the oak tree's outline was blurred. In a short while I would be able to look at the stars. Maybe I'd be able to see the moon too.

I heard Auntie's footsteps on the stairs and I looked at the door. When she came in I smiled.

'Why am I in bed?'

'You've been ill, Maria. Very ill.'

I nodded and thought about what she'd said. I had a vague notion that the illness had been caused by cold. Slowly I remembered that I had walked into the water, that I had caused this illness myself, and that someone had saved me from drowning.

'Why?'

It was no more than a whisper that passed my lips, but I trembled as I spoke and wanted nothing more than call Reijer to account for what he had done. Why had he come after me and pulled me out of the water? Why go through all this trouble for someone who has given up on life?

Reijer was at my bedside and auntie Be was downstairs. She had decided that I needed more rest, although I considered myself quite capable of going down to the kitchen to eat.

'How are you now?'

Auntie had asked me the same question several times, yet it somehow felt different this time. Was it an accusation? I suddenly realized that Reijer must also have ended up soaked right through to the last thread of his suit, but he had not ended up sick.

'I'm fine. Thank you.' My voice was soft but clear. I had been eating and drinking more lately and my voice had become stronger because of it.

'I'm very glad to hear that, very glad.' He was silent and seemed to be lost for words. He held his cap crumpled up in his hands, his elbows were leaning on his knees, and he let his head hang despondently. He was silent.

'Why?' I asked him. 'Why did you take me out of the water?'

His head rose up and I saw the pain in his eyes as he looked at me. His face seemed to age as I looked at it.

'So it's true,' I thought I heard him say. He brushed a hand through his hair and made a mess of it. Then he answered me.

'I saw you struggling in the water, of course I rescued you.'

'You should have left me there.' It was peaceful there.

'You were struggling. I could see you were in distress.'

Struggling? I had no recollection of wanting to escape the water. In my mind and in my dreams I had always been peacefully embraced by the water and I had let it carry me to new worlds, to safe places.

'I followed you and saw your hands splash above the surface. Then everything fell silent and there was nothing left but some ripples in the water. I ran towards you and pulled you out.'

Reijer continued, but it was more like a summarized account than an answer. It was as if he was trying to memorize for his own benefit how everything had happened. He sounded remote.

I closed my eyes and now I recalled the frightening sensation I had felt when I knew I couldn't breath anymore. I had opened my mouth in an attempt to breath, but had tasted water instead. I had stretched out my arms to the heavens, and for a moment I had felt the dry air with my fingertips. Then I had let myself slip away into the cold water.

'I think I ought to thank you,' I said after a few minutes of silence.

'You did already.'

Again Reijer fidgeted with his cap. He straightened it out, then crumpled it up again.

'You'll ruin your cap that way,' I couldn't resist telling him.

He looked at me in surprise, then looked at his hands and saw the crumpled wad he held.

'Yeah.'

He straightened the cap out again and placed it on his knee. Then he looked up at me.

'Why Maria? Do I have any right to know why you did it? Was it me, did I drive you to it?'

I closed my eyes and turned my head away. Of course he would ask that question, I should have known. Wasn't it a pastor's duty to address every sin committed by his flock?

What should I say in response?

I struggled with the possible answers I could give him, but Reijer didn't wait and continued.

'I don't think you're ready to confide in me yet, and maybe you'll never be.' He was quiet and held his hand out and took my hand in his.

'Look at me, Maria.'

I shivered at his touch. I saw the large, rough, hairy fingers, and I thought of those other large fingers, smooth and soft. I closed my eyes, then opened them again. The sweat on my hand formed a thin, slippery film between the palms of our hands. I squeezed his hand with all my strength while I tried so hard not to run away again, even if just in my mind. I couldn't do it though and I pulled my hand away with a jerk. I hid my face behind my hair and didn't dare to look at Reijer.

'You may not be able to trust me, but your aunt is a good woman. Tell her what's troubling you. I'm convinced she'll be able to help you.'

He waited until I met his eyes again and he nodded at me before he stood up, his cap in his hand again.

'Goodbye, Maria.'

I closed my eyes, didn't answer, and let him go.

20

It is strange how irrelevant and meaningless my former anger at Auntie now seems. There is nothing left of my hard feelings. Everything has been washed away by the water that carried me. I don't think I am capable of feeling anger toward Auntie any longer. I understand some things better now. What I don't know yet is what to do with my knowledge.

Instead of my child, a letter from the Reverend arrived. It was addressed to Auntie, but after she had read it, she quietly handed the letter to me. My eyes swept over the words, which were as unpleasant as his voice, but I felt nothing. No anger, no fear, no love, no longing. In silence I read the words that summoned me back home now that everything was resolved. In all of two sentences Auntie was thanked for her time and effort – there was no mention of repayment of her expenses – and if she could please drop me off at the station for my train journey home. I was expected to leave in a week, exactly six months after I had been sent off. Just like a parcel, return to sender.

The letter made me think about my future. So far, I had not had the courage to look beyond the next chore, but now I had to face the fact that I was expected home in a week. No, not home. That was not my home and it never would be. I was expected to return to my personal hell, under the watchful eye of god's servant.

I picked up the letter again and crumpled it in a furious gesture. The crumpled ball of paper in my hand brought me no satisfaction and I straightened out the paper. Then I continued by tearing strips off it, tearing up the letter sentence by sentence. I ripped the sentences into words, the words into letters and the letters I threw into the stove. Ashes you are and ashes you'll remain.

I would not return to that place. Not even for Mother, for she would continue to fail in her task of protecting me from evil, just like I had failed to be a good mother to Mara, despite my intentions.

I preferred to stay here on the farm, it was the only place where I had felt safe, the only place where I had been happy. But it was also the place where I lived in anger, although the anger was now starting to crumble away. My anger seemed to be no longer justified. It now felt more like an easy solution for an impossible problem. For, as long as I felt contempt for Auntie and blamed her, I was free to consider myself blameless.

'Maria.' Instantly I was aware of the pain that came through in that one word. As if I had been deaf and now suddenly could hear properly, it was her tone that spoke to me, not the word itself.

I looked up and met her eyes without really seeing her. If I were to stay, I would be living with this woman. I couldn't throw up barriers and ignore her for the rest of my life. I could no longer turn away from her hopeful, loving heart. Right now was the time to make a new choice. Right now I had to face the question: which of the two will I be able to bear, his judgment or her love?

My hands slid over the fringes of the tablecloth and I slowly picked apart one of the braids I had twisted earlier. The envelope that the letter had arrived in lay on the center of the table, like a dividing line between us, between our two worlds. Finally Auntie was the first to move as she stretched out her hand to pick up her cup of coffee to have another sip. I followed her example and in silence we drank our coffee. The coffee was cold by now. When our cups were empty, I heard the scraping of her chair as she pushed it back across the tiles. I looked up and stopped her with my words.

'I'm staying here.'

Again I met her eyes, this time to really see her. And in her eyes

I saw more than just the here and now. I also saw how she had put me at ease on that day when she came to collect me at the station. I relived the fear I felt when she handed me the letter that day and allowed me time to read it on my own, undisturbed. I remembered her warm bosom comforting me that day.

She stretched her hand out to me and I, unsure still, let mine fall into hers. All of a sudden I remembered that there had been another time when she had held my hand, even though it had not been her name that I had called out. She had been the one who had stayed by my side through all my pain, she had sat by my bedside and cared for me. Auntie was the one who had never spoken a reproachful word. Again and again I had experienced her patience, seen her smile and every now and then heard her words of wisdom.

I stood up and made a small step in her direction. Could I dare hope that she would hold me again? Was there a small chance that I had not alienated myself from her forever with my hateful behavior?

Another step. She pushed back her chair. She stood up, and I made one last step.

'I would like to stay, if that's all right with you.'

'I would love that, Maria.'

'Even now?'

'Yes.'

Her simple and short reply convinced me and I crossed the last few inches, flung my arms around her waist and pressed my face into her shoulder. We stood like that, free from time's restrictions, like a mother and daughter.

'You bring me such happiness, Maria.'

'I'll write them,' I promised her.

'They won't allow you to stay.'

'Yes, they will.' My calm assurance seemed to convince her at least of the fact that I could try. But I was quite sure that there wouldn't be any problems. My letter would be absolutely clear. The Reverend would have no choice but to accept when I laid out the choices to him. How he was going to inform my mother of my decision was his problem. I couldn't care less. The only thing I knew for sure and without a doubt, was that I wanted to stay here with

Auntie. Here on the farm, with her, I was at home. Home, as much as I could ever be at home anywhere.

21

Which way should I go? Is there a way, an option? They wrote that they will come here soon. But when will that be? Do I have a month to prepare myself for their arrival, or a week, or a day? Not knowing is making wearing me out and each new day begins with worries and ends in sleeplessness. I am trying to be strong, and ready for the confrontation.

Auntie is looking forward to seeing her sister again, but she doesn't know that the woman she knows as Anna no longer exists. Whenever she speaks about her sister, it's as if she is talking about a stranger, someone I may have known a long time ago but have long lost touch with. Is it really one and the same person with that name, one mother, one sister, or are they two different persons?

I don't dare to speak about the Reverend to her. I'm afraid I'll say more than I should, that I'll throw the whole filthy truth on the table. I'm not sure anymore of what I should do.

We both have our own expectations as we await the imminent reunion. Dare I hope for a happy ending?

'Is it someone's birthday?' As I spoke the words my voice trailed softly into a quiet, fearful whisper. I knew it wasn't anyone's birthday. What I saw could only have one meaning.

'No, no. There's no birthday. We'll be having visitors, Maria, you know that!'

Auntie measured a bit of flour on the scale and emptied it into a large bowl. She cracked an egg above the flour, she added sugar and began to stir. A pinch of salt. Some butter.

I saw what she was doing, I understood, but didn't want to believe it.

'Who are you making that cake for then?' I spoke the words slowly, and articulated each word carefully.

'For your father and mother, of course.' Auntie hummed a tune and put both her hands in the bowl to knead the dough.

'Not my father,' I managed to say after a moment.

'And your mother,' she added, smiling cheerfully.

I stomped my foot on the floor in impotent fury, but without my wooden shoes the effect was unimpressive, Auntie didn't even look up. I stomped again, hard, just so I could feel the pain, but Auntie noticed nothing. She had no idea, this woman. She had been cheerful ever since the moment she had received the letter notifying us of her sister's visit.

And now she was baking a cake for them, as if the ten years that had passed without any interest from their side, had never happened. The only use the Reverend had had for Auntie was to let her deal with the shameful situation of my pregnancy. And she had taken on this task without complaint.

What would happen now? Didn't she understand that they meant to separate us, that they meant to put an end to our peaceful togetherness?

'They're not coming for a friendly visit, Auntie.'

The words that crossed my lips sounded as harsh as I meant them, but it didn't seem to faze Auntie. Still humming she shaped the dough into a ball. The dough looked smooth and perfect, as it always did when she baked something.

'At least they're coming.'

'Yes, they are.' I turned away and walked out of the kitchen. She didn't understand, and wouldn't understand. She would have a shock, the moment she would see my mother, but by then it would be too late.

Carrying a basket, I plodded along to the garden behind the farmhouse. Auntie once told me that Mother had planted that garden, and she had even tried to tell me that Mother was unequaled in talent in the kitchen, but I had gradually come to the conclusion that she and I were talking about two different women.

Regardless, I had discovered that I enjoyed working in the garden. The whole winter we had enjoyed turnip, black salsify, parsnip and curly kale. Now, throughout the summer season, strawberry plants and several kinds of berry bushes would supply us with their fruit.

A few weeks ago we had planted the first seeds for the summer vegetables in small containers filled with dirt. They stood in a row in the kitchen. We made sure we kept the dirt moist and soon I could see the first signs of green shoots pushing their way through the dirt towards the light. Auntie had shown me which of the plants could be transplanted into the garden first and yesterday I had planted and watered them.

There was a tall fence, grown over with blackberry bushes, that separated the vegetable patch from the little orchard with its plum tree and several varieties of apple and pear trees. The blossoms had flowered abundantly a month earlier and the first buds of new fruit promised a good harvest.

The only question was, would I be around to enjoy it all? Mother and the Reverend were coming to take me away from here, away from this garden, I knew that full well.

I crouched down, dejected, on one of the steppingstones that were spread around the garden, and I started to pull away the weeds that had come up. The frost was now completely gone from the ground, and it had been sunny for several days after last week's rain. The soil was still moist. My hands stirred up the moist dirt and I pulled the weeds out with precision, shook the dirt off and threw the weeds in the basket.

I had to take care that the herbs weren't choked by weeds. My gaze swept over the lady's mantle which had withered during the winter, but new leaves had been lying in wait for more sun and new hope. Despite the cold, the little plant had survived underground.

If only there was an underground reserve for people to draw strength from when troubles arose. The only one who could help me was Auntie, but she was completely blinded by the anticipation of being reunited with her sister. Could I warn her and at the same time gain her support?

My hands hurried on while my thoughts busied themselves with the problems I had to deal with. My thoughts circled around the same problem continually. I needed Auntie's support, she was able to stand up to the Reverend and convince him that I should stay here.

But Auntie wasn't gearing up for a confrontation, the only thing she was looking forward to was a reunion with the sister she hadn't seen for so long. She was expecting a happy homecoming. How could I prepare her for the shock and at the same time convince her to help me?

I didn't pay attention as my hand grabbed a small nettle and it stung me viciously. In anger I yanked the plant out of the ground and threw it in the basket, but in doing so it stung me yet more. My hand throbbed and burned and I looked around me for something to alleviate the pain with. In desperation I dug my hand into the cool, damp soil and I let the cold numb the pain to some extend. I looked up and shouted my frustration at the heavens.

The pain persisted, but I pulled my hand out of the dirt and continued with my work. Wilder now, I roughly pulled young shoots out of the ground and ripped them. I knew that I was leaving the roots behind and the weeds would return, but I didn't care. Finally I sank down on my knees and hid my face in my hands. I curled myself up, tried to brace myself and ignore the thing I feared, but the images kept coming back to haunt me.

'*Mother, why are you so quiet?*'

'What do you mean?'

'You used to be different, we would play together, we would drink our tea and have some cookies. We would pick wildflowers and brighten up the house with them.' I could have given her more examples, but Mother sat quietly shaking her head, her knitting needles moving faster yet. I said no more.

'It's all vanity. Nothing but vanity.'

'Is it wrong to do those things, things we enjoy?'

'You listen to the Reverend's preaching when you're in church, then you'll know the answer to your question.'

But Mother, I miss how it used to be. Is it really better like this?

I didn't say the words out loud, how could I have? But inside my head I told her everything, and she would listen to me and pull me to her bosom and comfort me. Then she would speak her mind to the Reverend and shake her fist at him in my defense. Then the light would switch on in the darkness and expose his sins in her presence.

Then we would walk out of the manse together and leave him behind, alone.

'Don't you miss those days?' I tried one more time. Maybe, if she said yes, maybe I would find the courage.

'No.'

I fell silent and we sat together without speaking further. That night the Reverend came to my room and I knew she wouldn't hear me, wouldn't rescue me. She didn't miss those earlier days. *I did.*

My knees were wet and sore from kneeling on the ground. The Reverend would come, despise me and humiliate me. And then, when we would return to the manse, everything would go on as before. How could I face him when he'd arrive? I knew I would tremble and stutter, I would obey his every wish. Hadn't I always done that? Never had I stood up to him or ignored his wishes. Would I be able to now?

Again I concluded that I needed Auntie's help and I decided to ask her. First I would tell her about the situation at home, that would convince her, and then I would ask her for help. If necessary I would beg her. I couldn't return to that place, I just couldn't.

I stood up and stretched my sore limbs. My dress was muddy and wet. I beat the mud off as much as possible. Lumps of mud fell on the ground, but the cloth of my dress stayed moist and cold, my whole body shivered, but the thought of the difficult conversation I was about to have made me warm again.

I was afraid that I would offend Auntie with the things I was about to tell her, but I reminded myself that she would be offended and hurt regardless. Mother's arrival would be disappointing, because the image she had of her was not the reality. Would it then not be better for me to tell her in advance, so she could be prepared for what was to come?

I had made my decision and returned to the house, carrying the basket full of weeds on my arm. A tangle of roots, every little plant tangled up with another.

22

The truth. Is the truth cruel or justified, honest or cowardly? Should I burden Auntie with what I know? I want to tell her about all those unread letters, and sometimes a little voice inside me urges me on to tell her not only about that, but everything. Absolutely everything.

When I crossed the barn and headed for the kitchen the aroma of Auntie's baking welcomed me. It made my mouth water, but knowing that this cake was made for the person I feared most of all, spoiled my appetite. I kicked off my wooden shoes and they landed against the wall.

'Everything all right, Maria?'

Auntie's voice came from the kitchen and I knew I should step inside quickly or she'd come out to check on me, wondering what had caused the loud thump against the wall.

'I'm fine, just a moment. I'll be right there.'

I felt short of breath, but I wanted to enter the kitchen in a calm frame of mind. I had to come across reasonable and convincing, not as if I was driven by some sense of righteous piety. If I wanted to gain Auntie's support, I had to convince her not only with my words, but also with my attitude. It was important that she wouldn't doubt me. In my mind I rehearsed what I wanted to say, even though it wasn't much. There were just a few simple facts that I wanted to share with her, enough for her to know that it wasn't going to be a happy reunion with her sister.

I smoothed my hair with my fingers, straightened out a lock of hair that had escaped from my bun, and took a deep breath. Then I opened the door to the kitchen, and immediately forgot the words I had meant to say. On the table was the result of her love and trust, cooling off. It was a wonderful apple cake and I knew it would taste delicious. All for them.

What would happen if I would raise my hand and swipe the cake off the table, so it would end up broken and spoilt on the floor?

I looked at my feet. They were covered in thick woolen socks and I raised my toes one by one, then lowered them, just to distract myself from that traitorous cake. Auntie skillfully covered the cake with jam, a thick layer, and she looked up when she was finished.

'Would you like to try a piece, Maria?'

She already had the knife in her hand, and plates on the table. She seemed to be unaware of my reluctance, didn't seem to realize what she was doing.

'After all, we're not sure exactly what day they'll come, so we might as well enjoy a few pieces of this cake. If the cake is finished before they come, I'll just bake another.'

That was just like her. Not for a moment would she wonder to herself why she should go through so much trouble for her sister's visit. She just did. How could I possibly convince her?

'Would you mind if I prepared your room for their stay? You could share my room for the time being?'

I had not expected this at all and I froze, unable to respond. I stared at the cake while I thought of their bodies in my bed. My bed!

'No. No. I do mind. I don't want them to come, I don't want to see them, I don't want to hear anything about it!' I began to talk louder and louder until I furiously shouted words into the kitchen. They seemed to bounce off the windows, returning straight to me, tormenting me with their truth.

'NO!'

I lost all control, my foot stepped forward, my hand swung back and then forward again, my mouth shouting in fury. I swung my hand exactly where I wanted it to.

The cake pan clattered onto the floor, chunks of delicious smelling cake flew through the kitchen, against cupboards. Auntie shrieked in alarm and my hand returned to my side. I saw apple and cake in places where there shouldn't have been.

Everything fell quiet and my mouth closed shut in shocked silence.

What had I done? I saw how a lumpy mixture of apples and raisins slowly oozed down the pan rack, leaving a slippery trail behind, until it reached the edge and dropped onto the floor.

I sank down to the floor, picked up the cake pan and began to scoop the pieces of cake up with both hands. I picked up chunks and put them back into the pan. I crawled across the floor on my knees and found more apple and raisins, stuck on table legs, on cupboards, on seats. My tears fell on the floor and my dress rubbed them away as I shuffled across the floor. I pressed the pieces into the cake pan, tried to re-shape them, tried to fit them like puzzle pieces. My hands were sticky with sugar and jam, but I paid no attention to it, I kept trying to put the cake back together.

I didn't dare look up at Auntie.

I stayed on the floor, my head bent over the baking pan, my eyes gazed at the shapeless mess. I couldn't bake a new cake, I had never made one myself. The few times that I had helped Auntie in the kitchen I had done more damage than good, so there was nothing I could do for her.

I sat on the floor, defeated. Auntie would be furious with me. Any moment now she would give me an ear full, pick up her bible and read admonishing verses to me, put me in my place and punish me.

I wanted to shield myself from her fury and my fear, I wanted to cover my ears and eyes with my hands and slip out of the kitchen, but I knew I had to wait for her. She was the one who had been offended and I was to blame. This time there was no doubt whatsoever as to who was guilty and deserved punishment.

I was alerted by the scraping sound of a chair being moved. My muscles tensed as I waited in silence for what would happen. Two feet came in view and I could tell she sat down. Another moment and I would know what my punishment would be. I closed my eyes and waited.

In my mind I heard the Reverend's voice teaching me about the ten commandments, placing extra emphasis on the fifth commandment. A shiver went through my body. What would she say?

A deep sigh finally broke the silence that had lingered in the kitchen from the moment that I had thrown the cake off the table in anger. The sound of her sigh pierced the fear that surrounded me and I dared to slowly lift my head.

Auntie Be sat on a chair, her legs a little bit apart, her elbows on the table, her head in her hands. I saw how she brought a finger to her cheek and slowly scooped off a sticky lump of cake that had ended up there. She put the finger into her mouth and sucked it clean. She closed her eyes and didn't say a word until her mouth was empty.

'Delicious.'

No! It's not delicious. It can't be, it mustn't be.

'Don't say that.' I said with trembling voice.

'But child, this cake is delicious. You can say what you like, but I know how to bake a cake.'

'It's disgusting.' I forgot my fear for her wrath and thought of the Reverend and hated him.

'The cake may be in pieces, but it still tastes very good, believe me.' She reached with her hand and scooped up another chunk.

'I want to destroy him.' That was what I wanted, destroy him in full view of his god and his congregation, crush him, dump him down the cesspool, leave him to choke on his own stinking despair.

'This cake is already destroyed, Maria. Destroyed, but still tasty.'

'Filthy, will never be clean again.' We're virgins until our virginity is taken from us, after that there is no way back. Something is torn, forever, irreparable. Broken pieces are all that's left, filled with little bits of hope, until that hope is gone too and nothing is left at all. My anger and fear struggled, and words chased each other around inside my head like mad bees chasing out intruders. Then I finally opened my mouth.

'He always came to me. When mother was away. When mother was asleep.'

I sank back onto the floor and wrapped my arms around my knees. Slowly I rocked myself while silent tears rolled down my cheeks and fell down. They left salty circles on the red tiles. I left them, uncaring.

'I did call for her, really. At first out loud, but later in my head, I would cry out, but not even God heard me.'

I remembered large hands, heavy breathing.

'I deserved it, he said. "It's the will of God that I punish you," he said. He was cruel, he hurt me, and he turned me away when in the end…'

Mara!

Her calloused hands pulled me toward her and she sat down on the floor beside me. I kept rocking back and forth. Back and forth, back and forth.

'Oh, my child, oh, my child.'

'Mother did nothing. She didn't hear me. I think she didn't hear me. I don't know.' The words left my mouth faster and faster, now that all my worries came out in the open and I could hear them with my own ears as I spoke them out loud for the very first time.

'He is her father and he took her away from me, he took everything and gave nothing in return.'

Back and forth, back and forth. New tears fell on the tiles, new stains, salty spots on the floor. People would walk over them, the spots would be covered up by dirt and in the end they would be scrubbed away with a brush and soapy water. Nothing would remain of them.

'It started a long time ago already and sometimes it seemed that life had always been that way, as if I had not had a happier life before. But I knew that things used to be different, this farm used to be my home. I was happy here with Father and Mother, Grandpa and Grandma, and with you. Until he came and they married. And now he'll return. He wants to take me back to that house.'

'Oh, my child.'

'I don't want to give him any cake, don't want to give him a place to sleep, don't want to give him food to eat.'

Back and forth. My buttocks hurt, my back felt as if a heavy weight had been weighing down on it for days, but I couldn't stop rocking. My fingers had let go of my shoulders and I had taken hold of the hem of my skirt and pulled and twisted at it. The fabric bunched up between my fingers, and then I straightened it out again, just to start all over again.

'He can't have any cake.'

'I won't give him any cake, darling. I won't.'

I was silent. My heart seemed to return to its proper place, no longer high in my throat, choking the words before they left my mouth, but further down, in my chest. It hurt, everything hurt.

I was silent. What else was left to say? The pieces that constituted my life were lying about in this now dirty kitchen, apple, shame, cake, raisins, rape.

'I am so sorry, Maria. So sorry.'

Auntie stroked my back, tucked some loose strands of hair behind my ears and wiped a tear from my face. I looked at her and saw her cheeks were wet and I realized she also had left her tearful imprints on this floor. Her tears were blending with mine. I cried as I wiped them away with my hand, I tried to take them away, but all I did was make moist smudges on the floor.

We leaned against each other in silence, on the hard kitchen floor. Finally Auntie broke the silence. Instead of remaining quiet and moving on to regular daily tasks she asked the first question.

'When did it all start, Maria?'

I swallowed hard as I considered her question. If I closed my eyes, all I saw was the torment he put me through again and again, but when exactly had it started?

'I think it started when I... got older.' Did I have to tell her that he had come to me when I had had my period for the first time, at the moment that my body began to show the shapes of a woman? That he at first only touched my developing breasts, and that the rest all came later? Did it make any difference?

'Where was your mother?'

'Invisible.'

With that last word my tears could no longer be held back and I started to cry vehemently. With long, loud wails and a horrible noise. I sat on the floor with shaking shoulders. Speaking out loud of the doubts I had about my mother was harder than to tell her of what the Reverend had done. Auntie sat with me and held me, she shared my pain and her tears found their way down her rounded cheeks. When I calmed down she spoke again.

'I'll send hem away when they come.'

I nodded gratefully.

'I'll have to send her away too.' Auntie muttered and rose. My bones hurt from sitting on the floor, by eyes were sore from crying, my nose was plugged and my mouth dry from breathing. I realized that Auntie probably felt similar. Regardless, she stood up instantly.

'Come.'

She stretched her hands out to me to help me up. I hesitated. How could I possibly stand up and sit down on a chair, return to regular life as if nothing had happened?

'Come, child.'

I made a decision, ignored her outstretched arms, pushed off and stood up on my own, even though my knees creaked and my back protested. With my head hanging I walked to the table and sat down. I looked at the tablecloth and without thinking about it my fingers found three strands and started to twist them into a braid.

My secret was no longer mine alone and I didn't know if I would ever be able to look Auntie in the eye again. She squeezed me softly and I had the courage to glance up for a moment. Her eyes looked at me with such compassion, still filled with unshed tears. I quickly looked back at the tablecloth and pulled my hand back. Why had I told her?

Again she held her hand out to me, this time with a handkerchief, and I gratefully took it from her. My head pounded and my nose was plugged as if with a bad cold. Blowing my nose didn't bring much relief. There was so much left in my head, so much I hadn't told her yet.

I crumpled up the handkerchief and tucked it in the sleeve of my blouse. We sat at the kitchen table in silence, until Auntie spoke.

'I need to do something and I need your help with it.'

I nodded, of course, there was always work to be done on the farm and we had wasted enough time together already. I didn't know what time it was, but no doubt Auntie did and it probably was time to milk the cows, or to knead dough, or to clear the dung passage.

I pushed back my chair and got up, ready to help.

'What can I do?'

My voice was soft.

Auntie bent down and picked the cake pan from the floor. She held it against the edge of the table and wiped a few more crumbs in to the pan, then she gave it to me.

'Come along.'

Auntie headed for the door and stepped into her wooden shoes, I picked up mine in the barn and stepped into them as well. She wrapped a shawl around her shoulders and took the cake pan from me for a moment so I could grab my shawl. Then she returned the cake to me and opened the barn door.

I followed her across the yard toward the pig house and I followed her in. Why was I carrying a cake pan if we were going to feed the pigs?

The dog came running and jumped barking against the door of the pig house when it closed behind me. Undoubtedly he had smelled the cake and had hoped to beg for some of it.

'This is the only place for this cake,' said Auntie. She pointed at the sows, lying about lazily in the pen.

'I want you to do the honors.'

My hesitation was only short lived, then I turned over the cake pan, and I saw the pieces fall into the feeding trough. Immediately the animals got up and came our way, snorting. What had been a beautiful round cake only this afternoon, was now gobbled up within seconds by hungry pigs. We watched in silence.

When the last crumbs had disappeared, Auntie broke the silence.

'If he wants cake, he'll have to go and look for it here.'

I sniveled a watery smile. I imagined how the Reverend would stand here in his black suit, right in the middle of the pigs dung, groping with his hands in their trough, fighting for a few crumbs of dirty cake.

Together we returned the cake pan to the kitchen and had another cup of tea. It was strange, but we didn't talk anymore about the things I had told her earlier that afternoon. We just chatted about nothing in particular and divided the chores that were left to be done that day. I could tell though that Auntie had been shocked by the things I had revealed to her. With mounting astonishment I watched her scoop five spoons full of sugar into her cup.

I felt strange, my head felt heavy from crying and I felt a headache creeping up, but I also felt relieved that I no longer carried my secret alone, but now shared it with Auntie. We smiled at each other and when the teacups were empty and we got up to get back to work, Auntie hugged me without speaking a word.

Auntie and I had agreed that I would muck out the stables and it felt good to be physically active. Gradually my head cleared, even though my temples kept thumping as a result of my tearful outburst. As I worked I calmed down. It was odd, my secret was out in the open now, but, no, I didn't feel the humiliating shame that I had expected to feel.

Twice Auntie came to see me and asked if everything was all right, both times she had brought something nice to eat for me. Her compassion warmed me. The first time she brought some dried apple slices and the second time she brought a piece of sausage. I wasn't hungry, but I couldn't say no to her, so I took them and ate them while she watched. We didn't talk at all at those times, but we shared more than we ever had before since I had come to live here.

'Thank you very much.'

She nodded and left.

I continued scooping up muck with renewed energy and I filled the wheelbarrow with the soiled straw. I always enjoyed mucking out the stable. When I had cleared the floor, I could spread out clean straw and I loved the smell of it. Sometimes I'd lie down on the straw for a little while after I finished, and I'd close my eyes while I'd fold stalk after stalk into little pieces and toss them away. Sometimes a piece of straw would split, sometimes it would break, and then again others had some curious elasticity and seemed impossible to break.

This time also I laid down on the straw after I finished my work.

But this time I left my hands folded on my stomach and I stared up at the beamed roof over my head. I my mind I heard the words I had spoken and saw the tears I had spilled on the kitchen floor, Auntie who had come to sit beside me. Her arms around me, the shock I could see on her face.

For a moment I considered the pain Auntie must be feeling, finding out how wrong she had been about her brother-in-law and her sister. I knew she'd feel alone now, there was no other family, only me.

And Mara.

Would Auntie change her mind now that she knew my secret? Was it possible that Mara would be returned to me now?

I closed my eyes and thought of the tiny body I had cradled in my arms, her sweet face turned to me in unconditional trust. Where was she now? I could see her sleeping in a cradle, her face perfectly at peace. But all of a sudden there were two large hands of a man, they lifted her out of the cradle and carried her away. I wanted to run after her and take her back, but the black figure was larger and faster than me. Bewildered, I called out her name while I kept running, but when he turned round and I saw his face I fell to the ground, defenseless, and I knew I could never win.

With a start I sat up and looked around me. Mara. Straw. The Reverend. I heard the dog bark somewhere in the yard. I blinked my eyes and remembered that I was in the stables. There was no one else, no daughter, no Reverend.

I trembled as I rose and I smoothed out my hair as best I could. My fingers felt weak as I pulled straw out of my hair and off my clothes. Would I forever mingle my memories of Mara with those of the Reverend?

23

I try to slow down time and hold on to the days, but they keep slip-
ping through my fingers, mercilessly. With every passing day I feel
the distance between me and Mara grow. I know that Auntie is
alongside me now and tries to comfort me, but it doesn't help. Nothing
helps.

'Mara, I have to go to the village for a little while.'

'But it's almost evening.' Don't leave me alone, not now, not
after everything I've told you. Or is that why you're going? You
don't want to be in my company any longer than necessary?

'Go on then.' I looked out the window and avoided her eyes.

'Would you like me to stay?'

'No, not at all. On you go.' My voice trembled and still sounded
a bit hoarse after all the weeping from this afternoon. Auntie gave
me another searching look, but then she picked up her basket and
stepped outside.

'I'll be back very soon.'

'See you then.'

I walked after her and stopped in the yard to watch her go. She
walked with a steady pace and turned once to wave at me. Listlessly
I waved back, then I returned to the house. Lonely and deserted.

Now I was all alone with my thoughts. They circled around
Mara and the Reverend. I sat down in the kitchen with pen and

paper. I had decided to write the Reverend a letter. Certainly he knew where Mara was and I wanted to make him tell me, so I could find her back. Slowly I started to write. I wanted to write a civil letter and tell him politely what I would do if he wouldn't help me, but very quickly the words on the paper turned into terrible names and curses. My hatred for the Reverend seemed to leak out of my body just as the ink leaked out of the pen. Memories became images as real as life and I saw it all happen again before my eyes, but this time I was no longer silent. This time I screamed out all my impotence and anger at him.

Black scratches appeared on the paper. Virginal purity forever defiled. A baby was hated, loved, born and lost. I tore the paper, dipped the pen too far into the inkwell and it spilled over. I wrote furious stripes and illegible words.

'Maria, I'm back!'

With a jolt I was shaken out of my reveries as I heard Auntie's voice calling me across the barn. I looked up at what I had done and was stunned to find paper shredded to pieces, angry pen marks mixed with neat letters, all mingled into illegible smudges. The point of the pen had bent where I had pushed too hard and the tablecloth was soiled with ink marks.

I could feel my cheeks flush red and I quickly stood up, gathered up the pieces of paper and held them for a minute, not knowing what to do with them. Before Auntie came in I threw them into the fire. I didn't have time to do anything else. The pen and the ink told their own tale when Auntie opened the door and entered the kitchen.

Her eyebrows rose in surprise when she saw me, still standing close to the stove.

'There is ink on your cheek.'

I wiped a hand over my cheek, but didn't know where to wipe exactly. Auntie looked at the table. The pen was still there, so was the inkwell. Unused pages of writing paper were strewn about the table.

'Did you write a letter?'

I wanted to say yes, but the word got stuck in my throat, so I nodded.

'I've stained the tablecloth,' I finally managed to say. Auntie nodded and walked to the table. She gathered the pages into a neat pile and put the lid on the inkwell.

'The pen is also bent.'

She had noticed already, I thought, but I had to say it to her, I had to own up.

'We'll tidy this up and then we'll eat.'

Auntie was busy already and finally I managed to move and help her. I pulled the tablecloth off the table and folded it up. Monday we would wash it. Maybe the stains would come out.

Auntie put a new tablecloth on the table and quickly added plates. I took the bread, butter, sausage, cheese and jam, and we sat down to eat.

'I had forgotten all about the time, or I would have set the table already.'

'Don't worry about it, we'll just enjoy our meal. All is well.'

Obediently I fell silent and watched how Auntie folded her hands and closed her eyes. As we were used to, I waited quietly for Auntie to finish her prayer. To my amazement Auntie suddenly began to pray out loud, thanking God for his good care. I wanted to protest and walk away, close my ears until she finished, but I remained seated, frozen.

Her words reached my ears and quietly slipped in my head where they kept echoing in my mind, even when her voice had stopped. Care for Mara. Grant us wisdom and peace. Teach us forgiveness. Be our Father forever and ever.

'Enjoy your meal, Mara.'

Auntie nodded her head at me and served me first, then herself.

'I phoned them.'

I looked up at Auntie, startled out of my frozen state.

'When?'

'When I was in the village. I went to Reijer's house and used his phone.'

'What did the Reverend say?'

'He wouldn't hear of it, but I was adamant.' Auntie was silent, took a bit and chewed. Then she said: 'He wouldn't let me talk to Anna.'

No, of course not. He would never do that.

'And what now?'

'I don't know. Nothing, I think. We'll have to wait and trust in God.'

'Did you ask him about Mara?' I curled my toes underneath the table in nervous anticipation of her answer.

'I asked, but he wouldn't answer me.'

I curled my toes even tighter under my feet. So tight that suddenly a painful cramp shot from my pinky toe right through my whole foot. I quickly tried to stretch my foot again, but it was as if the cramp held my foot in a vise.

'Did you tell him anything?'

The palms of my hand were sweaty, the pain in my foot slowly left and I had to ask questions.

'Not too much. It's not my place to condemn him, Maria. I told him he is no longer welcome in my house, especially not as long as you live here.'

I took a bite to eat and considered her words. Would the Reverend be in fear after this phone call? My mind was blank as I finished my plate and helped Auntie to clear the table and wash the dishes.

24

I am more at peace and in a strange way also less depressed now that I have told Auntie my secret. The words that came from my mouth seemed to have carried away with them a heavy load. I have been relieved from that weight. Words were spoken and have been carried off by the wind, gone forever. Of course the memory remains, but it is as if it is covered in a fog, a thick blanket of fog that softens and shields. But maybe this feeling is only temporary? Still, I'm glad I've told Auntie everything. Every now and then we exchange a glance, and I know she understands. She really understands, even if she'll never know the pain or feel the fear.

I had put on the trousers that Auntie used when she cleared the dung passage. In the months before I gave birth she had forbidden me to help her with that chore because she believed the work was too heavy for a pregnant woman. After I had recuperated I told her that nothing could stop me now from helping and one day I had stepped onto the edge and started to scoop before she could do it herself. It had been heavy work indeed, and it was dirty work. The stink of urine mixed with cowpies was penetrating and made my eyes water.

The very first time I helped I had worn my skirt, and after three full scoops I had slipped and ended up with my leg right in the dung. My wooden shoe had slipped away in the thick layer of manure and my sock and the hem of my skirt were heavy with filth. I tried to crawl back onto the edge, but slipped again and fell on my knees right into the dung. The cows ignored me, but the stench made my stomach turn. Auntie must have heard my screams, for she came running and her eyes searched round, bewildered. When she saw me she started to laugh. But she immediately came toward me and extended her hand to me to help me up. I didn't dare to accept her help, my hands were too filthy, but I had no choice and Auntie encouraged me.

'Go ahead, we'll wash our hands in a minute.'

'I'm filthy.'

'It doesn't matter, come on.'

Finally I took her outstretched hand and she pulled me up and helped me onto the edge.

'Hold on to me.'

I put my hands on Auntie's shoulders and we shuffled carefully along the edge back to steadier ground. My wooden shoes were slippery and I squeezed Auntie's shoulders, afraid to slip again. The stench that hung about me was horrific and I didn't dare look at Auntie. She didn't seem to be bothered at all. She helped me strip and also brought the zinc tub to the kitchen. She filled a kettle with water to draw a bath for me. At first I wanted to refuse and suggest I wash myself with cold water, but the stench permeated everything and in the end I stepped into the kitchen. Despite the bath it took a week before the stench had fully disappeared from my nose.

Since that day I knew that Auntie had a pair of trousers in the barn, which she wore when the dung passage had to be cleared. The trousers allowed more movement, and when I missed my footing the trousers did not become heavy and difficult to handle. The first time I wore the trousers I felt strange, as if I no longer was a woman, but someone without a gender, for I wasn't a man either. But I got used to it quickly and enjoyed the freedom the trousers offered.

I whistled as I emptied the dung passage and filled the wheelbarrow with manure. Afterwards I would spread the manure over the field, a chore I enjoyed. I whistled a tune that had stuck in my head since Auntie had sung it that morning. I knew that it was a hymn, but I hadn't paid any attention to the words. Only the melody I remembered.

'Good morning, Maria.'

I started with a jolt and shakily straightened up. I almost lost my balance, but just managed to stabilize myself against the wall and in doing so avoided another dive into the dung.

'Reijer.'

'I didn't mean to startle you. You're whistling a nice song.'

I walked towards him and jumped off the edge.

'I like the melody.' In my mind I could hear him think that a woman like me was now also walking around in trousers and that things really couldn't get much worse with me. I felt my cheeks flush, but I refused to let him know how I felt.

'Do you have time to talk?'

'I'm almost done. Do you mind if I finish this off first?'

'Of course, I'll wait with your aunt in the kitchen.'

'Is she in the kitchen already?'

Reijer nodded.

'I'll come as soon as I'm done here.'

I quickly climbed back on the edge, scoop in hand. A few more scoops and I could go inside, but the knowledge that Reijer would be there, waiting to talk to me, did not spur me on. I wondered what he had come for and I wished I had told him that I was too busy to talk to him.

Finally I was finished scooping away the dung, and I wondered if I would quickly take the wheelbarrow outside to spread the manure over the field. But that would be too rude and I left the wheelbarrow behind. I hurriedly picked up my skirts and changed my clothes on the hay floor above the cows, where I was invisible to unexpected visitors. When I was ready I climbed down the steps and hung the trousers back on the hook. I washed my hands at the pump in the barn and then slowly headed for the kitchen. Maybe Reijer was in a rush and would leave soon.

I kicked off my wooden shoes and opened the door. I immediately was greeted by the aroma of freshly baked cookies and as I walked in I saw that Reijer was thoroughly enjoying them. He wasn't going to be leaving anytime soon.

'Here I am.'

'Come and have a seat. I baked cookies and the tea is ready.'

'Thank you.'

I sat down on the chair beside Auntie and in doing so kept some distance between me and Reijer, who sat at the head of the table. Soon a steaming mug of tea appeared on the table in front of me with a cookie on a small dish. I ate the cookie in silence.

Auntie was quiet too and Reijer seemed to be completely at ease in this silence. Not me. I wondered if Reijer would be able to see on my face the things I had told Auntie a few days earlier. I imagined that here in this kitchen he would suddenly receive a heavenly vision, revealing to him my past. He mustn't know a thing. But I realized that I no longer was the only one guarding my secret. I shot a quick glance at Auntie, but she looked the same as ever and calmly drank her tea. I quickly finished my own, then pushed my chair back to get up.

Auntie's voice stopped me.

'I was just talking to Reijer about your wish to raise Mara yourself, Maria.'

These words were so unexpected that my hands started to tremble. So she had spoken to him.

'I have tried to explain to him why I think you ought to have the chance to that, but…' Auntie looked at me, gave her shoulders a slight shrug. I could tell by her face that she hadn't said a word, she meant to leave that to me.

I looked Auntie in the eye and felt desperate. *How can I possibly tell him all that? Haven't I been humiliated enough? I don't want to share my secret with him. Just tell him I want Mara back. Shouldn't that be enough?*

'Mara is my daughter,' I said reluctantly. My voice sounded gruff.

'We already discussed that, and I was under the impression that your aunt, and possibly even you, agreed that it would be best for Mara to be in a family with two parents.' Reijer's voice was soft and polite. I knew he looked at me, but I refused to look at him. I picked with my fingers at the fringes of the tablecloth and took three strands to braid with.

'From what your aunt has told me, I understand that something has happened that has made her change her mind. She wants me to help you two, to find Mara.'

I pulled on the fringes, hard, the tablecloth moved and one of the strands broke off. Had Auntie really asked him that? Why had she chosen him to help us? Wasn't he a pastor, a traitor, a...

'I thought that Reijer might be able to tap into certain sources not open to us,' Auntie said. I quickly glanced up and saw her worried face.

'I know that your aunt is a wise woman.' Reijer nodded at Auntie as he spoke these words and then he returned his gaze to me. I kept a close eye on him from the corner of my eye. 'But I want only what is best for your child. I cannot cooperate with something that in my opinion is not for the best.'

His voice almost sounded apologetic and I looked up at him. His eyes were friendly and I noticed the deep wrinkles of concern on his forehead. It was so striking, the difference between his usually so cheerful face and the worried expression on his face now. I knew he wasn't going to be funny now. For a moment I could understand why his congregation was so fond of him. He was, as a rule, friendly and cheerful, but when problems arose, he seemed trustworthy, and maybe he was. Just maybe.

The kitchen fell silent and again I looked at the tablecloth. Twisting a braid was so simple, I could do it with my eyes closed. Three strands, twisted around each other, again and again. All three were the same, each took turns and together they formed a new string, stronger than each single one.

Auntie's opinion about me and Mara had changed since I had told her my secret a few days ago. It seemed that she now believed that I deserved to have my child. I thought she understood how the loss of Mara had shaken me, because I had finally found the courage to love my baby, and then I had to loose her. Everything had been against my will, conception and pregnancy, birth and disappearance. Nothing had gone the way I would have planned it, but the beautiful thing was that, regardless, my love for Mara had sprouted and blossomed. I knew that she had spoken with Mien again, and, even though she had not told me, I suspected that she had also tried other avenues. But all her attempts had come to nothing.

Did I really have to tell Reijer my secret now, in the hope of changing his mind? Why him? Would he be able to do what Auntie hadn't been able to?

'What can you do for us?'

'I can enquire with other pastors in the area. Your child probably has been baptized recently. A pastor would know if a child in his congregation wasn't born to the family but was adopted.'

I considered his words. What he said sounded reasonable.

'But what if she's living on the other side of the country?' My voice sounded small and high-pitched. The thought that Mara could be that far away choked and discouraged me.

'I can find out exactly where your father has been pastor.'

That also sounded reasonable and I leaned slightly forward as I realized that the chance that someone could help me find Mara was real and likelier than ever.

'Please help me then.'

Reijer extended his hand to me across the table and left it there with the palm of his hand open. I looked at it warily and knew what he expected of me. Trust.

My hands seemed to be glued stuck to the little braid. I looked at his hand, then at mine and wondered to myself if I could do it. Could I put my hand in his?

I started to tremble and sweat. My face turned hot and sweat dripped down my armpits. My breath came fast. My eyes darted back and forth between his hand and mine. I blinked quickly and reminded myself of how short the distance was, how simple a gesture it would be. I blinked again and saw a man's large hands behind my eyes.

My hand in his.

Could I do this for Mara?

Could I *not* do this for her?

Was it really a gesture of comfort and trust, or would I surrender myself to his authority if my hand touched his?

Would I be comforted or would I be desperately overpowered?

My hand was as heavy as a piece of lead, my arm wouldn't move,

I felt so hot. So very hot. I could hear Auntie's voice saying something to Reijer and I slowly saw the hand move away. I saw flashes of black. Pitch black.

'Everything is black.'

My voice sounded far off and inaudible. Then the light was gone and I fell.

When I awoke I was in bed.

'I sent Reijer away,' Auntie told me when I opened my eyes. 'I'm sorry I forced him to ask you about your past. I thought it would have been good for you to tell your story once more. Also because it might have convinced him of your love for Mara.'

'What happened?'

'You fainted.'

'I felt so hot.'

'Drink some of this.' Auntie held a cup of coffee up to me and I took a sip. She had added a liberal dose of brandy, I noticed. The taste was quite pleasant and I took another sip.

'I'll get up now.'

'Stay in bed a little longer. You're still so pale.'

I nodded and finished the rest of the coffee. Then I sat up and waited for the headrush to fade, then I stood.

'I'm fine now, really.'

Auntie went ahead of me and cast worried glances over her shoulder, checking to see if I was all right.

'I only cause you trouble,' I said.

'Don't ever think that, Maria, it is wonderful to have you here,' Auntie answered. I followed her quietly to the kitchen.

Regardless of Auntie's request, Reijer hadn't left, but was still waiting for us.

'I couldn't just up and leave,' he said as we walked in. He rose and grabbed his cap. 'I first wanted to know how you were, Maria.' His eyes looked concerned, but my eyes quickly moved down to the hands fumbling with the cap. Could it really be that difficult?

'I'll leave now, then you can rest.' He nodded at me and Auntie, and walked toward the door.

'No, wait.' I gasped for air and thought of Mara. 'Don't go yet.'

Reijer stopped hesitatingly, then turned around to face me again.

'Maria.' Auntie's voice seemed to hover in the kitchen, concerned and motherly.

'Please, sit down again.'

I was amazed at the sound of my own voice. I sounded firm and determined. Suddenly I could see Grandma, this small woman who could handle any farm worker with her legs firmly planted slightly apart and her arms folded over her chest. Her back straight, her shoulders square, and her voice full of authority. When she stood like that, nobody seemed to realize how small a figure she actually was and everyone obeyed her.

I straightened my back and walked to the table, pulled back a chair and repeated my invitation. I waited for Reijer to take a seat, and then I sat down myself. From the corner of my eye I noticed that Auntie wanted to pull out a chair as well. I made a quick decision, without really thinking it through.

'Would you mind if the two of us just talked together, Auntie?' I was afraid that I had hurt her with this request, but it suddenly seemed important to me to speak with Reijer in private. It wasn't right for her to stay. I smiled at her and nodded. She nodded in response and I felt she understood. Auntie went outside and we sat at the kitchen table in silence. The clock counted away the seconds, and I wasn't sure what to say. Reijer waited silently, it was up to me to open up the dialogue.

'Do it again,' I whispered finally, without looking at him.

'What do you mean?' he asked after a moment of silence.

I was surprised he asked, wasn't it crystal clear what he was supposed to do? Had he not just offered me his hand?

'Put your hand on the table.'

My ears thumped as I watched how he laid his hand down. I heard nothing but my own breathing as I slowly lifted my own hand and put it in his.

I felt warmth.

I closed my eyes, I could feel the pain.

I felt a solid warmth.

I opened my eyes and saw that he had curled his fingers around my hand. He didn't squeeze, he just held it.

I wanted to pull, run and scream.

I did none of those. Instead, I left my hand in his.

'This is very difficult for me,' I finally said.

'I don't understand.'

Slowly I pulled my hand back and looked at it. Nothing strange had happened, nothing frightful. Neither had anything overwhelmingly awesome happened. Putting my hand into the hand of another person wasn't earth shattering at all, and it also didn't bring me any peace or new insights. I felt disappointed and slumped against the back of my chair.

I started to talk very softly. The words came out in a different order than a few days ago when I had told everything to Auntie, but the content was the same. I shivered and my arms were covered in goose bumps as the memories came alive before me once again. It didn't matter that Reijer could hear the words that I whispered. It was just me and my memories, and I wanted to speak the words out loud so I could beat the past with the truth.

I fell silent for a moment to collect my thoughts, then I took a deep breath before I continued where I left off. I have no idea for how long I talked, time seemed to stand still, yet at the same time it seemed to hurry on so fast I couldn't keep up. Finally I finished and spoke the last word. A silence fell over the kitchen and it spun thin threads, connecting me and Reijer, in the same way as Auntie and I were connected by invisible threads. Once again there was someone who knew, again I had to await their judgment or forgiveness. Or possibly their pity, but pity is not what I wanted.

I shivered, how could I possibly have told everything to a pastor! Wouldn't a pastor of all people be ready with his verdict and condemn me? I fiercely started to gnaw at the skin around my nails.

'I don't know what to say, Maria,' Reijer said in the end.

I kept gnawing and waited for his judgment.

'Can't you look at me?' His voice was soft and I thought I had misheard his words.

'Please, Maria?'

He wanted me to look him in the eye, and see his judgment there? Suddenly I thought of Mara and I knew I had done it for her. She was the reason that I had told him everything and it was for her that I would have to raise my head.

In his eyes I saw compassion.

No reproach at all. No blame. No condemnation.

Compassion.

'What he did was wrong, Maria.'

My shoulders sagged as I looked away and replied. 'I let him do what he wanted.'

'You had no choice. He was the one who did wrong. I am ashamed…' Reijer's voice halted and he swallowed hard.

'I admire your courage, Maria.'

I didn't respond. I didn't have that much courage.

We sat in silence together until Auntie returned to the kitchen and looked at us both with understanding. Then she poured the coffee and passed around more cookies. I quickly ate and drank it all and then I got up to disappear from the kitchen.

'I'm sorry, Reijer, Auntie.'

I left the kitchen, stepped into my wooden shoes and went outside. I took a deep breath and I noticed that my whole body was shaking. Again a part of my past had fallen away from me. The load felt lighter, and yet heavier at the same time, because now there was another person who knew it all. Another person I would never be able to look square in the eyes. Another person who's trust I wasn't sure I could depend on.

His words resounded in my head. They were calming, but I didn't dare trust them. Maybe he would stand on the pulpit this Sunday and preach on this sinfulness living among them.

My thoughts flitted around between everything he might be and everything I had come to know about him lately. Hope and fear struggled inside me. Could he find Mara for me? Would he do that, would he be willing to do that?

25

*Auntie had done all she could to try and find Mara. She went to
see Mien to discuss it with her and she even phoned the Reverend. All that without success, and there were no other options
left to her. How ironic it is that now my only hope is found in another
pastor.*

*Hope and despair are strange companions. Yet, they are with me
daily. When will one of them win and destroy the other?*

'You should come with me to the market sometime, Maria.' It was
Thursday, and, as was her routine, Auntie was going to go to the
market. She went every week, not only to buy groceries, but also to
sell her eggs and butter, and to catch up on the local news. All the
farmers from the surrounding areas came to the market so a lot of
gossip was exchanged. It was also the day that she picked up her
mail. In the past months she had send off quite a few of my letters
and also brought a few back for me. She had never asked me who it
was that I wrote to, and even though it wasn't really a secret, I had
never told her.

Before, it would of course have been unthinkable that I would
have gone with her, but now... I looked down, at my flat stomach
and I knew it no longer prevented me from being seen in public. I
was simply a niece, visiting her aunt. But the thought of all those
people walking around at the market made me shudder and I was

about to decline when Auntie started to talk again.

'It would be good for you to be around people again. Do come along, Maria.'

'What am I to going do there? Everyone will be asking questions...'

'I'll tell them the truth, that you're my niece and that you're staying with me. A few of the women will remember you, Maria.'

'Even worse, then they'll remember Mother too and ask questions about her.'

'You can't live in isolation forever, not even if you stay here. But I won't force you.' Auntie turned around and walked outside, across the yard to the wagon that was already waiting for her.

Her words resounded in my head and in my mind I saw Mother before me. Mother, who only stepped outside the door to go to church. Who had me do all the groceries for her so she wouldn't have to go into the street. Mother, who would only be in the kitchen, caring for him, obeying him, forgetting about me.

Would I become just like her?

I ran outside and called out as loud as I could.

'Wait!'

My shawl flapped behind me and I gave it a tug to wrap it tightly around my shoulders. Auntie Be reigned in the horse and the wagon came to a halt. I kept running until I reached her.

'I'm coming.'

Auntie patted the seat beside her. I clumsily clambered on and sat down beside her. Then she clucked her tongue and urged the horse on.

'You are a brave woman, Maria.'

Yes, I was so brave, my legs and hands trembled, I gasped for air – and not just because I ran that short distance. The sweat on my hands was not the sweat of labor, but the sweat of fear. I was so brave that I wanted nothing more than to jump off the wagon and run back home, safely, unseen.

But I remained seated.

It had been so long that I was amongst people that I felt overwhelmed by all the noise that came at me. The rattling of the wagon's wheels on the cobblestones was only the beginning. When we had left the wagon behind and joined the lively bustle in the streets, voices of men, women and children came at me from all sides.

At first I felt a strange fear and I wanted to cover my ears with my hands and run away, but slowly the noises became like long lost friends. The silence on the farm had been good for me, but it occurred to me only now that I had actually really been lonely there. All these months I hadn't spoken to anyone besides Auntie Be and Reijer. And Mien.

The first place we went to was the church in the center of the village. That's where the butter and egg market was located and we had to take care of business there first. The overhang that was built against the side of the church was large enough to offer space to several farmers from the area to sell their eggs and butter. Auntie found her spot and placed her egg basket in front of her. I had a basket that was filled with butter and I placed it beside the eggs. Very quickly customers arrived and I realized these were all regulars. It wasn't long before we had sold everything. Auntie exchanged a few words with the farmer beside us and then she took me around the church to the other side where the market was. Auntie pulled me along to a stand with brightly colored fabrics. She started to pull out rolls and asked me which fabrics I liked. I pointed at two different rolls and Auntie began to barter with the salesman. I suddenly understood that she meant to buy the fabric for me so I pulled on her sleeve.

'Auntie, I don't need anything.'

'I would like to give you something.'

We were interrupted by the salesman who asked if he could help someone else in the meantime. Auntie shook her head and took the fabric before I could protest anymore. I stood there, silent, and watched how the salesman cut the fabric and then tore it off the roll. Auntie took it from him and put it into her basket, then she took my arm and pulled me along onto the market.

We slowly made our way past the stalls and I soaked up all the sounds and smells. I even started to believe that it was good I had joined society again.

'Hello Be, how are you?'

A woman's voice spoke behind us and Auntie turned. I turned with her and the first thing I noticed was that the woman was huge. I immediately remembered her from when I was young, then too I had been terribly impressed by her enormous size.

'And who is that you have with you, it looks like…'

'This is Maria, my niece,' Auntie Be said.

'Maria? Oh my goodness, Maria! You're the spitting image of your mother, child.' The woman held her hand to me and I shook it politely. My hand completely disappeared into hers.

'Do you remember me? Aaf van Tree.'

I nodded and the woman continued her inquiry.

'How is your mother, is she here too? Didn't you move somewhere south, somewhere along the coast?'

'Maria is visiting me for a little while,' Auntie said when I didn't answer. I could only think of one thing. I was so afraid of the question that was bound to come soon. I held my breath and curled my toes inside my wooden shoes.

But Aaf van Tree didn't ask any more questions. Instead she said goodbye and excused herself because she had more errands to run. Then she walked briskly toward the cheese stall.

I gave a sigh of relief and relaxed my toes.

'What will you say when someone asks why I'm here and for how long?'

'The truth. I'll tell them that you're staying with me and that we are having a wonderful time together.'

'But there'll be more questions.'

'We'll see, but don't worry about things that haven't happened yet.'

I didn't respond, but I also didn't agree with Auntie. As we waited for our turn at the cheese stall I tried to unobtrusively look at the faces around me. I had no doubt that we would run into more of Auntie's acquaintances.

All of a sudden my eyes caught sight of a passing baby carriage. I turned round and tried to look inside it but could only see the lace ruffles of a white baby bonnet. I stepped away from Auntie and followed the woman pushing the carriage. I simply had to see inside.

My wooden shoes clattered on the cobblestones, I bumped into people and apologized several times. Finally I caught up with the young woman and could look inside her carriage.

The baby was adorable, had round red cheeks, a dimple on the chin and a little tuft of hair poked out from underneath the bonnet. Blond. Bright blue eyes.

It wasn't Mara.

Defeated I stood still right in the middle of the path between the stalls. The woman hadn't noticed anything and quietly kept going, further and further away from me. Would I ever walk across this market with Mara close by me in my own baby carriage?

People bumped into me as they walked across the market, but I paid no attention to them and just stood there. Then Auntie grabbed me and pulled me to a bench at the edge of the square.

'What was that all about, Maria?'

I still felt numb and it took a while before the meaning of her words penetrated to my mind. Finally I answered.

'I thought it was Mara.'

Auntie shook her head and clucked her tongue. She said nothing and I wondered if she maybe had not understood me. We sat on the bench together in silence and stared at the people at the market.

In the end Auntie broke the silence. 'We'd better move on now.' She nodded at me and stood up.

'I don't think you're going to find Mara here, Maria.'

Her words sounded kind enough, but they felt like a reproach. I was silent and followed her obediently. The only place we still had to go to was the sidewalk outside the baker's. That was the place where the postmen had their spot on market day. Auntie and I would pick up the mail and then go home. We had no reason to stay any longer after that. My first excursion into society had become a strange mixture of pleasure and desperation.

Besides the weekly there were also a few letters, but I didn't look when Auntie accepted the post from the three postmen who were having an enjoyable time together on the little sidewalk in the sun. Auntie chatted with them for a while, but I kept myself out of the conversation. I looked around me at all the bustle on the market and wondered if I would recognize anyone from when I was young if I saw them now. All of a sudden my attention was drawn to the two linden trees that lined the main shopping street. I looked up the trunks and smiled faintly when I noticed a large hole in the shape of a heart.

Auntie was finished, said goodbye to the postmen and linked arms with me. I nodded at the men and followed Auntie back to our wagon.

'Was it that terrible, Maria? I really thought it would have been good for you,' Auntie said as we were on our way back home.

I thought about her question, but I had no answer. It really hadn't been that terrible, and yet my behavior had been surly. Once again the difference between me and Auntie had been confirmed, once again I had disappointed her.

'I'm going for a walk.'

She nodded and I waited for her to go into the house. She didn't, so I started to walk anyway. When, after a little while, I looked over my shoulder, I noticed she was still there, following me with her eyes, shielding her eyes with her hand. Like a soldier on guard. Would she still be there when I returned?

I left the farm and found myself a way through the bushes so I could reach the sandy path alongside. Dragging my wooden shoes across the sand I walked slowly, aimlessly. My steps created small dust clouds and the dust clung to my dress and my skin. I rubbed it off, but it only helped temporarily.

Why had I gone to the market? Had I thought from the start that I would find Mara there? Would I for the rest of my life continue to look for her amongst strangers, always wondering in which baby carriage my child would be? It had been strange to be in the village. I could still hear the noise of the wagons wheels on the cobblestones, the buzz of all the voices, feel the crowds bumping into me. It was like a living wall that separated me from my child.

I wasn't used to people anymore and now, being alone with plenty of room about, I stretched my arms out wide. I turned round on the path and kept my head high, up towards the sunny sky. I could tell that the quietness here calmed me down. I spun round faster until I felt like a spinning top. The wind pulled at my clothes and blew off all the dust.

I opened my mouth to shout out loud, but that seemed too strange, so no sound crossed my lips. I stood still and waited for the world to settle down around me. Then I continued walking and suddenly I knew where I was going.

Since the day that I almost drowned in my despair I hadn't returned there. It wasn't far and now that I had a goal I walked on with determination. Soon I reached the water and looked over the smooth, almost black surface. I crouched down and touched the water with my hand. The movement of my fingers made the sand swirl up and turned the water murky.

I sat down and took off my wooden shoes and socks. I put my feet in the water and my toes played with the sand. The cold of the water felt comfortable and I remembered the steps I had made, the weight of my dress. I closed my eyes and suddenly remembered the water plants that had carried me.

No, not carried. They had pulled and almost strangled me. Reijer had saved me.

And still I found it so difficult to trust him.

How could I ever learn to deal with the presence of strangers? I couldn't treat every person as an untrustworthy villain now, could I?

I lifted my left foot and the water dripped down. The water had not been a solution, despite the apparent simplicity of it. I stood up, with my feet still in the water and I could feel the water lap at the hem of my dress. Then I bent down and fished a rock from the water.

I threw the rock away from me with all the strength I possessed and this time my voice did work.

I screamed, 'No!' Let that rock sink to the bottom, not me. I still had hope. Maybe Reijer could return Mara to me. It gave me a sense of satisfaction to hear the rock splash into the water, and I looked for another rock, bigger this time and threw it far away as well. I waded through the water in search of rocks and sticks to throw. I would never again surrender myself to these depths. I didn't know what to do about my future yet, but not that.

Finally I turned my back to the water and stepped onto the dry sand. My dress was soaked up to my knees and I bundled the fabric together in a knot between my legs so I could walk unhindered. I picked up my socks and wooden shoes and walked to a patch of grass. I sat down and wiped the sand off my feet with my socks. I stood up, ready to walk back home, barefoot in my wooden shoes.

Then suddenly I caught a movement from the corner of my eye, and I looked up.

'Auntie?'

Slowly she approached.

'I was so afraid you'd try again…' She nodded at the water, and I understood.

'It's all just so difficult. The market. The people.' I miss Mara.

'You'll learn, and I'll help you.'

Yes, I could learn. I had to. I had to be ready for when she'd come home. I had to be ready for my daughter.

Auntie gave me her arm and together we walked home.

I still had some work left to do in the garden, so I picked up the hoe and a basket for the weeds. To my great surprise someone was already at work, someone had already done a big part the weeding for me.

'Reijer?'

He smiled as he got up.

'I thought I'd better make myself useful while I waited,' he said and pointed at the basket full of weeds at his feet while he playfully swung a clump of grass on top of his head.

I smiled and approached him slowly. I stopped when three steppingstones separated me from Reijer. My embarrassment had slowly dissipated over the last few days, but now it seemed to have returned in full force.

Reijer shook his head and caught the clump of grass, then flung it into the basket as if it were a ball. Then his face turned serious and he looked at me.

'I've done a lot of thinking these last few days. You have taught me something extraordinary, Maria.'

I wrapped my arms around me, expectantly, wondering what he meant. Reijer stepped one steppingstone closer to me. He tried to catch my eye, but I turned away, too shy to face him.

'The love you have shown for a child that was conceived under such circumstances, has taught me a lot. You've touched me, Maria.'

I remained silent. What could I possibly say in response to such undeserved words of praise? I tried for so long to hate Mara. Slowly I stepped back, bringing some distance back between us.

'Don't run, Maria.' Reijer reached out to me, but didn't come closer.

'Tell me why you came.' Please let it be good tidings, I'm feeling so weak. My burden is so heavy and I need air, but all there is, is this heavy weight making it hard to breath freely.

'I found her.'

There was a roaring sound in my ears and I almost lost my balance. What? What did he say?

'I found her.'

I looked up at him and found air to breath. I took a deep breath and felt so free. The heavy weight fell off me and I smiled.

'Where is she?'

'I've brought the details for you.' He put his hand in his pocket and pulled out a piece of paper. He looked at me expectantly, questioningly. But instead of allowing him to come closer to me, I made two big steps toward him.

Reijer handed me the paper and I unfolded it. I read the information he had gathered. My fingers trembled and I almost dropped the paper. I held on to the paper with all my strength, never would I let go of it, never.

Then I screamed a high-pitched scream. I threw my head back and shrieked out loud to the heavens. I raised my arms to the sky and jumped as high as I could.

I screamed till I had no breath left in me.

Then I laughed and Reijer laughed with me. I turned around and started to run toward the farmhouse, I stopped for a moment, motioning Reijer to come along. Full of excitement I suddenly veered left as I remembered that Auntie was with the pigs. I had to run to the pig house, not the farmhouse.

I screamed again and jumped aimlessly up in the air before continuing to run. My skirts flapped about my ankles and I pulled them up so I could run faster. Every now and then I checked over my shoulder and saw that Reijer was still following me, at a slower pace but with a big smile on his face.

The door to the pig house opened up and Auntie emerged with a concerned expression on her face. She shielded her eyes with her hand and walked briskly towards me.

'What's the matter, I heard screaming…'

'Auntie, look! Look!' I pressed the paper into her hands and looked at her with anticipation. She hesitated, then started to read. I saw a smile appear on her face and I clapped in my hands. Again I started to jump and shriek for joy.

Auntie laughed with me and pulled me close to her. She held me tight and patted my shoulder affectionately.

'Wonderful, my child. Just wonderful, wonderful.'

26

Justice hurts more than I had expected. There is no satisfaction in hurting another person. It's a torment to my soul. Have I become like him by taking from someone what they love?

We had traveled by train to the little town and only had to enquire once before we found the house. It wasn't far from the station. It was a simple, but neatly kept working-class cottage. I tried to picture the people who lived there, so happy with the child they had wanted for so long. And today I came to claim that child, birth certificate in hand to prove I had the right to take my child back. But inside I felt horrible as I considered that I would do to another woman what had been done to me. After all, how could someone not love Mara?

The cottage was in a poor area of town. It was well looked after, but no more than that. For a moment we stood in silence together, then I put my arm through Auntie's again and we walked together up the short walk to the front door.

I pulled the bell forcefully and we could hear it peel somewhere inside the house. It remained silent and I threw a sideways glance at Auntie. We hadn't announced our visit, it was possible that no one was home. That meant we had made the whole journey for nothing and had to try again another day.

Once again I rang the bell, harder this time and I pulled several times in a row, quickly. Now there was movement inside. I heard footsteps behind the door and the soft voice of a woman, though I couldn't make out what she said. Then the door was opened.

'Hello, good afternoon.' Her eyebrows arched enquiringly, but she had a friendly smile.

'Good afternoon.' I took a deep breath and all of a sudden forgot all the words I had meant to speak. The woman in front of me was no more than ten years older than me, she had a friendly, round face and the smile around her mouth seemed to be quite at home there. I noticed little laugh wrinkles around her eyes and knew she had cheerful disposition.

'What can I do for you?' She still sounded friendly, but it occurred to me that she must be wondering what these two silent women were doing at her doorstep. I still couldn't utter a word though. My nerves were on edge and I broke out into a clammy sweat thinking of what I had come to tell this woman.

Auntie started to speak before the silence became unbearable.

'Are you Mrs. Van Doorn?'

'Yes, I am.'

'In that case we would appreciate it if we could come inside for a moment. There is something we need to discuss with you.' Boldly Auntie moved a step forward and the woman unwittingly opened the door a bit wider to let us in. Auntie went ahead and I followed.

The hall was small and narrow, but the tiles on the floor were clean and the worn out carpet on the stairs also was clean.

We stood all three, uncomfortably, in the little hall. Mrs. Van Doorn had placed her hands on her hips.

'Before I invite you in any further, I'd first like to know what your business is.'

'It's about the child you have,' Auntie spoke since I remained speechless.

The woman gasped for air and I saw that she wavered unsteadily for a moment. She stared from me to Auntie and back to me again. Then she leaned against the wall and even in the poorly lit hallway I could see that the blood had drained from her face. Slowly she opened the door to the living room and let us in.

'Come in.' Her voice was no more than a whisper and I could

hear the pain and fear in it. I stepped over the threshold and felt such a lowlife.

'Please, have a seat.' She pointed both of us to a chair and I sat down on the edge of mine.

The woman sat down across from us. I could she her hands were trembling and her face was still ashen.

'What have you come for?'

For my child, to take her home.

The words had seemed so obvious and simple when I had practiced them at home. Every time I had spoken them out loud I had felt happier. Now however, there was a large lump in my throat, stopping me from speaking even a word. It was hard to breath.

Auntie fumbled in her bag and eventually pulled out a piece of paper. I knew it was the birth certificate. Without a word she handed it to Mrs. Van Doorn.

'No. No.'

The piece of paper rustled in her trembling hands.

'No.'

I half expected her to rip the paper up in anger, making it impossible for justice to take its course.

'She was taken from me without my knowledge.' These weren't the words I had prepared, but my mouth spoke them before I thought about it. 'I miss her day and night. She's a part of me, my heart is no longer complete.'

'No.'

Yes.

I could see the pain I caused this woman by coming here with my request. And, even though the words weren't said out loud, all three of us knew how this was going to end. For a split second I considered getting up to leave without looking back, without her. I knew this woman loved my daughter, I could see it in her eyes, I could hear it in her voice, I could feel the absolute anguish that filled her whole being.

'What did you call her?'

'Janneke.'

Janneke.

'I called her Mara.'

'Mara. Bitterness. Sweet bitterness.'

She slowly rose from her seat and warily looked at us.

'What is it you wanted to do?'

'I want to take her home.'

'She is ours. We've waited so long…' The woman started to cry and I could feel her pain deep inside me. Auntie put her arm around my shoulders, which made the pain and sadness I felt for Mrs. Van Doorn even worse. She had to go through this alone, her husband was probably at work.

'I won't give her away.' She seemed to have made a firm decision and resolutely stood up straight. 'She's my daughter. I won't give her to you. Out with you two, out!'

I gently shook my head, though I understood her completely. 'She's my daughter.'

'Out!' She pointed with a trembling finger and there was nothing left of the smile that had been on her face earlier. She was now a mother fighting for her child.

Auntie rummaged in her bag again and pulled out another piece of paper.

'Maybe you should read this. Maria has every right to claim her child. She is the biological mother and nothing can change that. I'm sorry.' The sheet of paper was a description of my legal rights. The woman could protest all she wanted, but I was fully allowed to take Mara with me. No matter how difficult it was to do that now.

Despite her anger the woman took the paper and read it. I saw her shoulders slump. I saw how reality hit her and undermined her ability to fight. She was powerless and she knew it.

'Can't you wait one more day? Or two, or maybe a week?'

Auntie shook her head pointedly and I was grateful to her, for I would have promised this woman anything to ease her pain.

The piece of paper fell from the woman's hand and fluttered onto the floor. She turned round to the door that we had entered through. I looked at Auntie, confused, and wanted to get up and follow the woman, but Auntie nodded at me and put a finger against her lips.

The woman disappeared and I could hear her shuffling footsteps on the stairs. My thoughts and memories whirled through my head and contradicted each other.

Whore. You have no right to this child.

But she's my daughter, my own flesh and blood. I carried her, I gave birth to her and fed her. I love her.

Look at what you're doing to this woman.

Do I have to suffer for the sake of a woman I don't know?

You are a whore. This woman is innocent, she finally has a child to love.

And what about me?

What about me?

The woman returned to the room carrying a small bundle in her arms. Her eyes and cheeks were red from crying.

'Can you at least wait until my husband is home? He will want to say goodbye to her.'

I hardly heard her question, for my attention was focused on Mara who was so close to me all of a sudden. I jumped up and walked toward the woman, prepared to take the child from her. When I stopped in front of her I understood her pain and struggle, but then she put Mara in my arms. The warm little bundle against me felt so familiar and at the same time it didn't. She had grown a lot in these three long months, but I could see her eyes and knew without a doubt that this was my daughter. Then she started to flail her arms about and her face turned sad. Before I realized what had happened she started to cry. I clucked my tongue and made soft noises, but it didn't seem to mean anything to her.

With desperation I quickly glanced at Auntie and suddenly I heard that voice again. *She's better off elsewhere, Maria. What makes you think you could care for her.* From the corner of my eye I saw Mrs. Van Doorn step forward with her hands outstretched, as if she meant to take Mara over from me. I quickly turned away from her and bent over Mara, ignoring the words in my head. With my nose I stroked her cheek and kept muttering words of endearment. Slowly the crying got softer and her arms and legs relaxed. I lifted her up and held her against my shoulder, her head resting in the palm of my hand. Still sobbing a bit she lay against me, close to my heart.

Auntie and I awaited the return of Mr. van Doorn. I had returned Mara to the arms of the young woman who had been her mother, and I watched how she said goodbye to my child. It hurt to see it, but I had to be tough for Mara's sake. Never would I abandon her.

It was heartwrenching when later that afternoon the husband came home and burst into an impotent rage when he learned what we had come for. The farewell was bitter and I felt justly hated. What should have been a day of triumph had ended up as a bitter sweet reunion.

Everything had changed. The cradle stood once again in my bedroom and every time I walked past and saw my daughter lying there I took such delight in seeing her, and I smiled. I often would lean over the cradle as she slept and I'd talk to her. I always told her I loved her, and I would sing nursery rhymes that I remembered from when I was young.

When Mara was awake her eyes would attentively follow my every move, and I hoped she knew that I was her mother. That I was more to her than just the woman who looked after her. I was looking forward to the day that she would call me 'Mother', but in the meantime I thoroughly enjoyed every minute we had together.

Reijer came to visit and I thanked him. He spoke little, but I could see the contentment in his eyes. When he sat down I put Mara in his arms and he rocked her gently. Her little mouth quivered for a moment and I was worried she'd start to cry, but the sound of his deep voice calmed her.

'She's beautiful, Maria,' he said finally as he returned my daughter to me. 'A miracle of God's creating love.'

I took her from him without a word, but his words resounded in my head for the rest of the day. God and miracles. Fairytales and reality.

27

It was market day again and Auntie asked me if I wanted to come, but I said no. When she had left I thought about her offer and it slowly dawned on me what it would have cost her if I had gone with her.

I thought back to the week before when I had come along with her on market day. The people we had met, the conversations Auntie had had with her friends. Some of them she had known for years and some of them knew me too. They knew who I was and they knew I was unmarried, only sixteen years old.

Auntie's reputation would be ruined if it became known that I had a child. Nobody would consider the circumstances or keep in mind that she had only helped me through a difficult time. And I was convinced that Auntie would never lie about it. If I were to appear in public with her, she would speak the truth to everyone. She would freely tell that I was her niece and Mara her great-niece.

I imagined us walking together over the market, with Mara in a baby carriage. Auntie would do all her errands and she'd discuss fabrics with me, but the salesman would only bother with her to receive his money. He wouldn't give her the time of day for a friendly chat. The postmen would hand her a bundle of mail, but at the same time continue their conversation and not bother to even look at her. I imagined how Auntie would greet and talk to her friends. How they might just contain their contempt for as long as their conversation with Auntie lasted, but as soon as we would walk on I would be able to hear their hushed remarks.

The shame, the shame, the shame.

Eternal, unforgivable and impossible to cover up.

How could I do this to Auntie, to be ridiculed and treated with contempt in her own hometown? She had lived here all her life, had grown up on this farm and was part of this small community. If I stayed here, everything would change for her.

I heard the wagon return and I went out to the yard to welcome Auntie back and to help her with the wagon. She cheerfully waved at me when she saw me and I saw that her cheeks had a healthy fresh colour.

'Hello, Maria!' Her voice sounded happy and I smiled.

'Hello, Auntie. You must have had a nice time at the market?'

She nodded and climbed down from the wagon. The dog came running and bounced excitedly around her feet. She gently pushed him back with her leg.

'Next week you really ought to come with me, Mara. Or Sunday, then you can come to church with me. But that can come later.' Auntie took my arm. 'Come along, I've got something for you.'

She pulled me to the little bench beside the front door and put her basket down. She waited for me to sit down and then started to rummage through her basket. She pulled out a small parcel. It was wrapped in newspaper and tied up with string and a big bow. I warily took the parcel from her.

'What is this for?'

'Have a look.'

I slowly pulled the string and folded the newspaper away. In my lap were two tiny, white wooden shoes.

'I bought the smallest size they had,' said Auntie.

I took one of the tiny wooden shoes and held it in my hand. I thought of Mara's little feet and couldn't believe that these wooden shoes would ever fit her. Her feet were still so very dainty and small, quite unsuited for clunky wooden shoes. Yet I knew that one day she would be big enough and I would put these wooden shoes on her feet and watch her walk around on them.

'They're so cute, Auntie!'

'Can you see her already, walking in the yard?' Auntie smiled at me and I nodded eagerly in agreement.

Only much later, when I, with a smile on my face, put the tiny wooden shoes on my bedside table, I thought about it again. My smile disappeared and I felt a lump in my throat. Staying here would change Auntie's life. It would result in things I didn't want to be responsible for. Until now it had been fairly easy to keep myself hidden on the farm, but that was partially because I had arrived in winter when most of life was lived indoors. At this time of year there were all sorts of activities that took place outside, and Mara would also grow up fast. It was impossible to continue to keep myself in hiding.

I got changed into my nightgown and checked up on Mara in her cradle one more time. She was fast asleep. Her cheeks were rosy and her breathing was regular and deep. I knew she would sleep soundly all night. I kissed her forehead and whispered that I loved her. Then I went to bed myself and pulled the blankets up to my chin. For a moment I glanced at the little wooden shoes on the bedside table, then I blew out the oil lamp and it was dark. I was alone with my thoughts.

For several days I thought about my options and every time I ended up with the same conclusion, knowing full well that the path I chose would be a difficult one. When Reijer came I explained my predicament to him, but he really wasn't much help, at least I didn't think so. He didn't agree with me and thought that I should give Auntie the chance to decide for herself. He said that in fact, she actually had done that already. I didn't understand and also didn't agree with him.

'Do you think that the members of your church will be so broadminded that there won't be any talk?' I asked him.

He was silent for a moment and then shook his head. 'I'm afraid they won't be. At least, not all of them,' he added quickly.

'So Auntie will be humiliated if I stay.'

'Maybe you're wrong.'

'I can't do that to her.'

'Last Sunday I preached on the adulterous woman. Do you

know that story?' I nodded and felt my stomach cringe at the thought that he was going to tell me now what he should have told me a long time ago already. With my head down I waited for his words of admonishment.

'That story is in the end not about what the woman has done, but about what Jesus offers her. He offers her forgiveness.'

Good for her.

'But that's not all, He also shows the people who were watching that they have no right to judge another person without first looking at themselves.'

'How many of your church members have understood that lesson, you think?'

Reijer shrugged his shoulders despondently. I knew enough.

28

I know that I'll be welcome and that has made it easier to come to my decision. Did I tell you yet that Reijer doesn't agree with me? He says that by doing this I'm making the decision for Auntie, but I just want to protect her from hurtful remarks made by her friends. I'm very happy with the place you've got for me. It won't be long now until I come, since I know everything has been prepared. I'll tell Auntie about my decision as soon as possible. After I've done that I'll need a few days, possibly a week to organize things here. I expect it won't be very easy travelling with Mara, but I'm very much looking forward to show her to you.

Everything was ready. Now the only thing left to do was tell Auntie about it. When I had given Mara her last feeding for the day and had put her to bed, I went to the kitchen to talk to Auntie.

'Auntie, I have something to tell you.' My voice sounded tense and I knew Auntie noticed it too.

'Let me put on some tea first, child, then I'll join you.' She put her hand on mine and gave it a gentle squeeze. Then she put the water on to boil and searched the cupboards. I saw her take out a large green tin and I smiled. I knew that it was the cookie tin.

When the water was boiling I got up and poured tea for the two of us. Auntie filled a plate with cookies and put it on the table. There were six cookies, four too many my mother would have said, but I knew by now that Auntie would always have an abundance of food on her table.

'It's bad news you have for me, isn't it, Maria?'

I was taken aback by the quiver in her voice and I realized that Auntie was afraid of what I was going to say. Of course I knew my decision would also spell loneliness for her, but had she not been living on her own for years already? I swallowed hard as I started to tell my lie. I was relieved when I noticed how Auntie listened attentively and nodded a few times.

'I will miss you,' she said in the end, 'but it's only for two weeks.' She took a cookie from the plate and took a bite. I felt sick as I watched her, but I also took a cookie so she wouldn't suspect anything.

'When will you leave?'

'As soon as everything is organized. I can phone them and tell them when I'm coming.'

'That's good. We should make a list of things for you to bring along. We'll have to make sure that Mara won't lack a thing, won't we?' She winked at me and took another cookie.

I chewed my cookie without tasting any of it. It hadn't lied to her for nothing. It would be easier for her to think that I was only leaving for a short while. But it still hurt.

'Do you really have to go, Maria? I know, of course you do.' Auntie's voice sounded sad and she pulled me close. I hugged her and kissed her on the cheek.

'I'll be back, Auntie, I'll be back, but I have to do this first.'

She nodded, but I saw doubt in her eyes. She was afraid to remain behind alone, a fear I knew and understood. I took her hand and looked her in the eyes.

'I'll be back, Auntie. Really.' The blatant lie crossed my lips without any difficulty. There's nothing I wanted more than return to her, but it was impossible.

'I know, sweetheart.'

But I still could sense her doubt. I felt for her but I was determined to see things through.

'I looked up which train you're going to need for Amsterdam.'

'Platform one,' I said.

Auntie nodded and led the way. She pushed the baby carriage and I carried a suitcase with some of the necessary items. It wasn't going to be easy for me to transfer everything from one train to the next each time, but this time I wasn't as afraid of the journey. The baby carriage had to be stored in the baggage car so I lifted Mara from the carriage and put her in a wrap that I carried around my neck and shoulder. Auntie helped me on the train and walked with me to find a good seat for me. Finally I sat down and Auntie bent down to hug me one more time.

'Goodbye, and have a safe journey.'

'Thank you for everything, Auntie.'

Her warm embrace disappeared and I could hear her footsteps in the train. Then she stood outside on the platform again, waving at me through the window. I could see her strength as she smiled despite the sadness she felt. I followed her example and smiled and waved.

Then the train moved and all that was left for me was to sit out the journey. And enjoy my child.

As I recalled from my previous journey, the trip from Velp to Arnhem was only a short one. It seemed that the train had only just come to full speed when it started to slow down again, and soon we entered the station.

I waited for the train to come to a complete stop before I rose from my seat. I remembered how the train would jerk with sudden movements as it slowed down to a stop, and I didn't want to risk injuring Mara in a sudden fall. I was one of the last persons off the train, but the passengers on the platform were waiting patiently to board. One gentleman in a nice suit offered me his hand and helped me off the train. Only much later did it dawn on me that I had accepted his hand without any hesitation.

'Careful now, Ma'am.'

I smiled and he touched his hat.

'Thank you.'

He nodded and stepped onto the train that I had just left.

Slowly I walked across the platform and for a moment I felt the old panic of not knowing what to do, but again someone came to my rescue.

'Ma'am, is this your baby carriage and luggage?' A porter motioned me and I took a breath of relief. Mara started to stir a bit in the somewhat constricting wrap, but she was still asleep. I knew it wouldn't be long before she would wake up. I could feel the sweat trickle down my back, but I straightened up and hurried to join the porter who patiently stood there beside the baby carriage.

'No need to hurry, Ma'am. There's no rush.'

'I have to catch the train for Utrecht, sir, and I haven't a clue…'

I looked around, searching for a clock, but the only clock I saw wasn't working, both hour and second hand hung down limply like the broken wings of a bird.

'You've got some time still, don't worry. Shall I walk with you?'

I wanted to decline, but decided to accept his offer. Auntie had given me a bit of money and I would use some of that to pay him for his services.

Just at that moment Mara started to whimper softly and I knew that very soon she would be demanding to be fed.

'You just look after your little one, Ma'am, then I'll take care of your luggage.' The man tapped his cap and led the way to platform three where my next train would depart from.

I lifted Mara a little bit out of the wrap and held her snuggled against my shoulder as I followed the man.

By the time the train started to move I had changed Mara and was ready to give her a bottle. Thanks to the kind porter I hadn't needed to worry about a thing. He had loaded everything on the train for me and made sure I got a good seat with enough space and privacy to tend to Mara. I thanked him profusely and gave him some of the money.

He shook his head and placed his hands on his hips.

'Children are a gift from God and we ought to treat them as such, with special care,' he said. 'So also the mothers who care for them as only they can.'

He made a smacking sound with his mouth and continued: 'And I know what I'm talking about, 'cause my dear wife shows me this daily.'

'Then please take this money for your children,' I said. To my relief, he accepted the money in the end. He leaned over Mara for a
moment and stroked her cheek softly with his large hand. Then he
touched his cap and got off the train in a few large steps.

Finally we were on our way and I watched as Mara eagerly
sucked her bottle. The first few days when she was back I had cried
with each bottle I gave her. I cried because my own body was no
longer able to feed her, but Mara didn't seem to mind and after a
few days I learned to enjoy watching the movements of her mouth
and her contented lip smacking as her bottle was finished.

The train's motion made Mara sleepy. I could tell that while she
relaxed her head weighed down with drowsiness much quicker
than normal. I bundled her up again in the shawl that I had
wrapped around my shoulder and I relished to just hold her close
to me while I watched her eyes shut slowly.

When she finally slept, I also closed my eyes and dozed off.

'What a lovely little baby you have there.'

The voice of an old woman woke me up. I blinked my eyes,
wondering if I had travelled back in time and that the nun was
traveling with me, but when I looked closely I noticed that it was
an elegantly dressed older woman who sat across from me.

'It's such a tiny one, I could hardly tell you were holding a baby
at all. Is it a boy or a girl?'

'It's a girl.'

'What's her name, if you don't mind my asking?'

I hesitated for a moment. What if the woman continued asking
questions about Mara's name? What if she would look for more information than I was willing to share? Still, I answered her.

'Her name is Mara.'

'What a beautiful name.'

The woman leaned forward and looked closely at the face of my
daughter, which just peeked out of the wrap.

'She's beautiful.'

I nodded and didn't know what to say. I hoped the woman
would stop talking before she discovered I was holding an illegiti-
mate child. Just thinking of it, I could almost see her attitude
change to disapproval.

'My daughters are all older, married and no longer at home, just like you.' She nodded at me and smiled. 'I've got four grand children already, all boys.'

She was silent and seemed to expect a response, but my tongue was frozen and I was unable to speak any words at all.

'I used to long for a boy so badly, but my girls...' The woman closed her eyes for a moment and I saw how her lips curved up while she recalled a precious memory.

'My girls were better than all the boys in the world. You enjoy your daughter, Ma'am. Enjoy her for as long as she is young. Before you know it, she'll be grown up and find a husband. Now she is still all yours.'

The woman smiled at me, then looked away out of the window.

'This is my stop, have a safe remainder of your journey, Ma'am.' She gave me a nod, then walked slowly down the aisle to the exit.

I looked down into Mara's blue eyes, which were suddenly open, and I couldn't help smiling. This woman had seen my daughter and sung praises of her beauty. It had never occurred to her at all to call Mara a bastard!

I reached Utrecht much quicker than I had thought possible. Again I had to transfer, this time to Amsterdam. I was very busy trying to find my luggage and the right platform, so I had little time to worry about the imminent meeting. It wasn't long before I sat down in the train. Tired of dragging around all my luggage I closed my eyes and quickly dozed off. When I opened my eyes, much later, I saw that it had started to rain and I remembered my first train journey. How my life had seemed hopeless, and how much had happened these past few months. I knew that I had changed.

I got off the train at Amsterdam-Central Station and felt somewhat daunted by the enormous crowds of people assembled there, but I was here, together with my daughter and there was nothing else for it but to find myself a way through the bustle. By pushing the baby carriage I practically created a path for myself and I was soon outside. There I asked someone to help me find my tram. The tram dropped me off close to my destination and I took my time walking through the now sunny streets. A few times I asked for directions to people on the street, and every one of them was friendly and helpful. I pictured myself living and working in this city. Would I enjoy it after growing so comfortable with all that space at the farm? There was hardly any growth here and I already missed the smell of the cows, the dog's excited barks and the chickens running around my feet when I fed them. Was my future here in this city? I looked inside the baby carriage and Mara looked back at me with her big round eyes. She smiled at me and I smiled back. I tickled her under her chin and continued walking. Within five minutes I had reached my destination. I stood in front of a tall stone building and the letters above the door told me that I was at the right address. I smiled. Finally I would see her again, my praying nun. I thought of her last letter to me which at first had angered me, but after a while had touched me.

Since the day that the Good Lord, in one of his mysterious ways, made our paths cross, I have felt compelled to pray for you. Time and time again he reminded me, even when I sometimes forgot to. You and your daughter are always welcome here.

I took one last deep breath, took hold of the heavy doorknocker and let it drop against the wooden door. A loud noise resounded in the space behind the door, but I couldn't hear anything else. I was just about to lift the knocker up again when the door opened up without a sound. A nun looked at me. She looked extremely small beside the massive door, but her face was friendly and she gazed at me inquiringly. I showed Olivia's letter and introduced myself.

'Sister Olivia invited me.'

The woman nodded and opened the door further. I stepped inside, into a large hallway. Immediately left of the door was an alcove with a large cross bearing a suffering Savior. Strange, how I fled from one house of God, to find peace in another.

29

The time I spent in the convent with sister Olivia was in many ways a time of healing and rest. She took me into town and showed me the most beautiful sights. We walked through streets and looked at tall, old canal houses that leaned against each other.

'Like a bunch of old ladies on a bench,' sister Olivia said, and I smiled.

She also took me to see the nursery that was run by the nuns. It was a large house where the nuns looked after little children all day while the mothers went to work. It was only after several visits that I understood it concerned fatherless children. Not only children whose fathers had died, but also children like Mara. Their mothers were women like me. When we were at the nursery I helped out as much as I could, so there was little opportunity to talk to sister Olivia, but when we were in the convent we had plenty of time for talking.

The old nun seemed to understand me. Her letters had shown me that already, and now I noticed it again. We talked a lot and I shared with her more than I had ever shared with anyone. She listened and understood, sometimes she cried.

One day she showed me a bundle of papers and gave it to me.

'Go and read these again,' she said and walked away. When I looked at the papers I saw that they were all the letters I had sent her these past months. She had neatly ordered the letters by date, the oldest at the top and I began to read. After I had read everything I sat still for a long time, staring ahead of me. Only when there was a persistent knocking on the door I was jolted out of my contemplations.

'Come in.'

'I just wanted to see how you were doing,' sister Olivia explained. She peeked around the edge of the door without coming in.

'Come on in, please.'

She stepped inside the room and closed the door behind her. I rose from the only chair in the room and sat down on the bed, but instead of choosing the chair, Sister Olivia sat down beside me on the bed.

'How are you feeling?'

'Strange. I'm feeling strange.'

'I had half expected you to feel sad.'

Sad? Well, I was, but not just that. Reading my own writing also had a kind of a cleansing effect. I felt the same way as I had the day when I told Auntie Be my secret for the first time. I felt relief. Nothing was like it had been anymore, so much had changed and I felt happy. I felt happier now than I had then.

'It hasn't all been bad.'

'Not?'

'I've got Mara.'

'Yes, you've got Mara.'

The nun didn't speak for a long while, but sat with me in silence. Finally she spoke again.

'I think there's one more thing you need to do before you return to your aunt.'

I swallowed hard and interrupted her.

'I'm not going back to Auntie Be.'

'You're not?'

'I wanted to ask you, maybe...'

'You are not suited for a nun's habit, Maria,' Sister Olivia said after she had listened to my stumbling words.

'That's not what I mean.'

'What is it you mean then?'

'I want to find a job, and a place to live.'

'In Amsterdam?'

I nodded and cast a hopeful glance at her. The nun looked straight ahead, I couldn't make out her expression.

'We'll talk about this more some other time,' she said. 'I wanted to ask you something else, something much more important.' Now she looked at me. 'It seems to me that there's one thing left for you to do, maybe even two, though it may be a difficult thing to do.'

She was silent and I saw how she inhaled deeply, as if she was nervous.

'Have you ever considered telling your mother everything?'

The question came as a total surprise and I gasped.

'What!'

She didn't answer, but remained silent.

Tell everything to Mother? Of course I had thought of that, often. So often I had almost told her, so often I had practiced the words in my mind before I went to her to tell it all, but I always kept my mouth closed in the end.

'It's too difficult.' I said finally.

'Maybe you could write it down.'

Sister Olivia stood up, put her hand on my head, a gesture I had become used to these last few days. She mumbled a short and inaudible prayer, and went to the door.

'Think about it.'

I didn't answer.

It turned out to be the hardest thing I had ever done. Harder than guarding my secret, harder than carrying the shame of my pregnancy alone, harder than going through childbirth. I told myself that it really shouldn't be that difficult. Had I not gone through it all, and hadn't everything turned out all right in the end? All this misery had given me Mara.

Still, I couldn't write a word.

I sat at the table with the empty sheet of paper in front of me. It was the very first sheet. I was so scared, I hadn't written a word yet, not even the salutation. I finally found some courage when I reminded myself of the fact that I had, very consciously, decided to do this. Sister Olivia was right, this was one of the last things I had to do to properly deal with the past. Slowly I started to write, first the date, then the salutation. I couldn't get beyond a simple 'Mother', but it would have to do.

As the minutes passed, I thought about the things I would have to write. What was important, what wasn't? Slowly words came together in my mind and I started to write. First with some hesitation, but then, more and more confidently I entrusted the words to the paper. It was important that Mother knew I had had a good childhood, that she had given me that. I remembered all sorts of incidents and choose one that had often given me comfort in difficult times. I wrote about how we would go for picnics together after picking wildflowers, just the two of us, no one else. And how we would give the flowers to Grandma when we came home in the evening and how Grandma would display them in a vase like a prized possession.

My hands were trembling as I wrote the first paragraph. My fingers were moist and the pen slipped from my hand and it made an ugly mark on the paper. I put the pen down and kicked hard against the table leg, frustrated that I had ruined the letter. Here I was finally getting somewhere and then I let the pen slip. Why could nothing just work out for once? I wiped the sweat off my forehead and dried my hands on my skirt. I decided to leave the mark there. First I had to finish the letter. I could always decide later to copy it.

I started on the second paragraph and realized that I had to write down things I would rather ignore. But I had faced up to them before, when I talked about them to Auntie and later to Reijer, so I could do it again.

My pen scratched over the paper, sometimes the tip would catch and make a stain, but I kept writing. Every word I wrote uncovered a new wound. Writing everything down seemed to open up the wounds, but even though it hurt, it made the infection flow away. Maybe I really needed to do this if I wanted to heal?

I didn't need many words to describe my physical pain. I found it much harder to think about my mother's betrayal. Why had she never been there, why did she never hear anything, had she not known? Had she really not known about it?

Should I accuse her of negligence, or had she really been un-aware of what had been going on in her home? I decided not to write down this question, but ended the letter with a different question.

If you love me, please be honest with me. All I ask of you is to be honest with me.

Maria.

The end of the letter came so sudden that I sat still for a while, with my pen hovering above the paper, ready to continue. But there was nothing left to write and finally I laid the pen down on the table and picked up the page and waved it back and forth for the ink to dry. Then I folded it and slipped it into an envelope. I wanted to stand up and check on Mara, but my legs trembled and were so weak I didn't have the strength for it for several minutes.

'I wrote the letter.' I proudly held up the envelope for Sister Olivia to see.

'That's good, that's very good.'

'I'll post it tomorrow.'

'You mean you're going to let the postman deliver it?'

Sister Olivia looked at me as if she didn't understand what I had just said.

'Yes.'

'You told me once that your mother doesn't read any of the mail that gets delivered.'

My mouth fell open and slowly closed again. No, she was right, Mother didn't read any mail. Everything first passed through his hands and then it was destroyed. In all the years not one of Auntie's letters had been opened by Mother. She also wouldn't open mine.

Defeated I let my hand drop, still holding on to the envelope. As if the letter suddenly was too heavy, my fingers lost their hold on it and the envelope floated to the floor.

'She won't read the letter at all.'

'You're going to have to bring the letter yourself.'

I crouched down and picked the envelope up from the floor.

'How can I? I can't go back. He'll grab me and hold me, he'll destroy me again, claim his authority over me.'

'He is not all-powerful, Maria. Only God is.'

'The Reverend is his servant.'

Instead of responding to this, Sister Olivia brought up a different topic.

'A little while ago you mentioned a job and a place to live. Unfortunately I won't be able to help you to find those.'

I blinked my eyes and at first I didn't understand what she was talking about. My mind was still on the manse and the Reverend. A few seconds later I understood what she had said. My shoulders slumped.

'What a shame,' I said hoarsely.

'I'm convinced that your place is on the farm, with your aunt, so I can't help you.'

'You mean, you won't help me.'

'I can't.'

I closed my eyes and shrugged my shoulders, I turned round and wanted to walk away from her, but she was quicker and put her hands on my shoulders.

'Your place is with Auntie Be, that's where your home is.'

30

For days Sister Olivia urged me to return to the farm. She didn't mention my letter to Mother anymore.

'It's not right for you to leave your aunt alone, that is not what she wants.'

'You don't know her, I don't want to expose her to the shame.'

Again and again I repeated my opinion, until the day I was handed a letter from Auntie Be. *The other day I told my friends about you and your daughter. I didn't want you to have to deal with the burden of telling people the truth of your situation when you come back home. The whole community will know now that you have a daughter. But what they also know is that you will always be welcome with me and that I won't stand for any malicious talk.*

Auntie had cut the ground from under me and now all her friends knew of my shame. Shocked, I let the letter drop onto my lap and it was a few minutes before I was able to continue reading.

The attitude of people in town has been better than I had dared hope for. Maybe it has something to do with one of Reijer's recent sermons. He preached on the adulterous woman and pointed out to us that not anyone of us is to judge another person, only our Lord can. I don't know if Reijer had you in mind when he made this sermon, but I sure thought of you when I heard it.

When I had finished reading the letter, I showed it to Sister

Olivia. She read it carefully and then she smiled at me.

'What did I tell you? Your aunt is doing everything she can to get you back on the farm with her. I can quite understand her, I must say.'

I nodded, but said nothing.

Auntie's letter was on my mind for days and I remembered the moments we had shared. My reluctant reservations, especially in the beginning. Auntie's persistence and her calloused hand that hand placed my own hand on my belly. Her help with the cradle. Her betrayal that turned out not to be a betrayal at all. Time and time again I thought of the farm and knew it was my home. I was a farm girl and loved life on a farm. Now that I lived in Amsterdam I knew I missed not only Auntie Be, but also the pastures and the woods. I missed the quiet life and I knew I could not make my home here in Amsterdam. Not just because Sister Olivia wouldn't help me, but also because my heart was elsewhere.

I thought things over thoroughly and struggled in silence with my question.

Could I do this to Auntie Be?

Her letter said yes.

Sister Olivia said yes.

As for myself, there was nothing I wanted more than to return to the farm.

A few days later I made up my mind and I told Sister Olivia.

She embraced me and assured me that it was the right decision. I wrote a letter to Auntie Be and told her that I was coming back. I said goodbye to the mothers and children in the nursery and I thanked all the nuns for their friendly hospitality during my visit to Sister Olivia. They all embraced me and kissed Mara on her little forehead. She had stolen their hearts.

The day of my departure approached and Sister Olivia accompanied me to the station. She pushed the baby carriage with Mara in it. She cooed and smiled at my daughter and my heart melted as I watched.

We reached the large train station and were swallowed up by the throng of people entering through the doors. I suddenly told the nun about my other decision.

'I'm not going straight to Velp.'

'You're not?'

'No, I have to go to Vlissingen first.' And further.

The nun stood still and let go of the baby carriage to hug me.

'You're doing the right thing, child. You're doing the right thing.'

Sister Olivia bought a platform ticket so she could walk with me all the way to the train and I bought a single ticket for Vlissingen. On the platform we hugged one more time and I swallowed hard, realizing that this could very well be the last time I would see the old nun.

'You've got a beautiful daughter, Maria. Cherish her and fight for her, keep fighting for her.'

'I will,' I whispered. Quickly I turned away and got on the train. I found a window seat so I could wave her goodbye.

She stood on the platform, alone. Her hands were folded together, an old woman with a friendly smile and an abundance of love. We looked at each other and I lifted Mara up so Sister Olivia could see her.

'Is this seat taken?' A voice distracted me and I turned to face the woman who had spoken to me.

'No, not at all.'

Again I searched for Sister Olivia's eyes and I noticed how small she was. She stood there so lonely, like an insignificant beacon, while more and more people rushed past her to catch their train. A few men walked up together and their little group split as they passed the nun, three on one side and two on the other. One of the men tripped and swung his arms about in an attempt to catch his balance, and in doing so he touched the upper body of Sister Olivia.

The emotions I saw racing across her face touched me deeply and I recognized them immediately. I saw in those few seconds the fear, the despair and the misery. I saw how she made herself even smaller and wrapped her arms about her, how she created more distance between her and the men by doing a step back, and all of a sudden I understood.

I wanted to get up and go to her, tell her that I understood, thank her for how she had helped me despite her own pain, a pain she apparently still carried with her after all these years. But before I could do anything, the train pulled out. I waved at Sister Olivia, who seemed to have composed herself and waved back, and I held Mara close while I remembered the words Sister Olivia had spoken to me a long time ago. *It was an escape. Nothing but an escape.*

One more time our eyes met and I nodded at her to let her know I understood. She put her hand up and waved.

The train accelerated and soon she was gone.

I leaned my head back and thought about the letter I had written and wondered if it was enough, or too much, or not enough al all. How could I know what I should write her? Would Mother understand what I had entrusted to the paper, or would she condemn me and burn the letter?

Words and sentences flashed through my head. *I don't know how to tell her or where I should start.* Of course I had made an attempt with the letter, but was it enough? Should I have asked Sister Olivia for help?

Did you know about it, Mother, or is all of this news to you and are you shocked by the cold truth? What would Mother do if she read my letter and would read an accusation into it? I was afraid she would disown me and I would loose her forever. It was very possible that today was the last time I would see the woman who had given birth to me, weaned me, raised me, loved me, and deserted me.

Why did you marry that man? Did he make you happy? Has anything good come of it? Why, why, why? I have so many questions, but see no answers. Can you give me answers? Will you?

It was so hard to believe that Mother and Auntie were sisters. Auntie Be, who always faced her problems head on, but at the same time knew exactly when to remain silent. She always seemed to know exactly which words would heal and when silence was best. I could not remember ever seeing evidence of this tactfulness in my mother. She was silent. In everything. Through everything. And with her silence she closed her eyes and ears for what went on under her own roof.

Oh, Mother, what happened to the woman I once knew? The memories that had slowly come back to me during my stay at the farm seemed to be not mine but someone else's. Skipping through the meadows, picking wildflowers. Singing 'ring around the rosie', falling down and tickling each other with sprigs of grass. Was that truly my past, or was it all just something I once read in a book, was it all a false memory?

Auntie told me about how things were when I was young, so I know things used to be different. Is there a chance we can go back in time? Where did it go wrong? I would love to blame the Reverend for all that has gone wrong in my life, but there must have been other reasons. Had it all started the day my father died with the flue? Or later, when Mother agreed to a new marriage, a new home, a new life? Was it her silence or my own silence that had undermined everything? Maybe you will give me some answers. *You can always write me a letter at the farm, I'll be waiting to hear from you every day.* Auntie as well. She was ready to wrap her arms around Mother and forgive her everything. She would never abandon her sister, even though the story I had told her had hurt her very badly.

I wanted to tell you one more thing…

Forgiveness. Was it more than just a fancy word? My pen had wavered when I had slowly written the words down. The ink had leaked and left stains. The tip of my pen had got caught on the paper and another ink stain had made one of the words illegible. I had had to force myself to start over, to leave the last few lines as they were and to write the words down one by one, without hesitation. It had taken so much effort, but when the words were there, black on white, I had felt triumphant, as if I had just fought and won a heavy battle.

Mother, I want to forgive you, even if you didn't know anything about it at all, for it hurts when I think of how things could have been. If you believe in Auntie Be's God, than please pray to Him. One more line I had added to my letter. After that I had picked up the page and waved it about to dry the ink. With slow, thoughtful movements I had folded the page in three, and put it into the envelope. I had written the address neatly on the outside of the envelope, but had not added a return address. I also hadn't closed the envelope.

Even now, while I carried the envelope in my skirt pocket, it was still open.

From Amsterdam to Rotterdam to Roosendaal. The journey was long and uneventful. I nodded politely at the other passengers, but didn't start any conversations. The regular motion of the wheels on the train track felt comforting and every now and then I would doze off. At other times I would play with Mara and somehow manage to change her diaper in my cramped surroundings. In Roosendaal I transferred to the train for Vlissingen and I found a quiet spot, away from other passengers. I was glad to find the train fairly empty.

As I sat down, I took the letter from my skirt pocket and it crunched between my fingers. I rubbed my thumb and index finger over the paper. Just a while longer and I could give it to Mother. While the train came closer and closer to my temporary destination, my fingers kept rubbing and rubbing the envelope. I knew I was rubbing a smooth spot onto the paper, and it got softer and thinner, but I couldn't stop myself. This letter was my last hope, my last attempt at finding my mother back.

31

When I stood on firm ground again I pushed the baby carriage to the first manned ticket booth I could find. My suitcase was balancing precariously on the carriage and it took some skillful maneuvering to reach the booth without incident. I was glad that Mara kept looking up contentedly and didn't seem to notice how flustered I was. Although the journey so far had gone much better than I had dared hope for, I was still a novice at it, and in the train I had been wondering for a long time what to do about the final part of my journey. In the end I decided that it would be best to stay the night in Vlissingen and finish the last part of the journey the next day. Of course this meant that I had to find lodgings for the night and I shuddered at the thought of everything that could go wrong.

I had reached the ticket booth and saw an older man with alert eyes, quite a different man from the sleepy fellow who had spoken to me so impatiently on my initial journey.

'Good afternoon, sir.'

'Ma'am.'

'I would like to stay the night in Vlissingen and was wondering if you could recommend a place.'

The man blinked a few times and then he smiled.

'My sister has some rooms for rent. I'm sure you could stay with her.'

It almost seemed too good to be true, but I felt exhausted and I nodded gratefully.

'Can you tell me how to find her house?'

He nodded and started to tell me, but my head was in a whirl and I had lost track long before he finished his explanation.

'Hold on, I'll write it down for you.'

He took pen and paper and started to write quickly.

'If you hurry, you may still be in time to join them for a warm meal.'

He handed me the paper and I looked at the drawing he had made and the directions he had written down.

'Thank you, sir, thank you very much.'

'Not at all, ma'am. You think you'll be able to find it with that?'

I nodded and thanked him once again. Then I stepped aside to make room for the next person. I glanced back and saw the man at the booth give me a quick wave.

Holding on to the slip of paper, I followed the signs to the exit of the train station. This time I felt less lost in the large hall with its enormous doors on each side. Maybe because I was more mature now. I also pushed a sizable baby carriage with a suitcase on top so I was something for other passengers to reckon with. But I'm sure it was more than that, it was something within myself.

I walked outside through the center doors. The little map in my hand told me I had to turn right and immediately right again. According to the man's brief directions I should reach his sister's house within five minutes. I slowly continued and carefully checked each street name to see if I followed the directions correctly. It was indeed not far and even at my leisurely pace I reached my destination, Fish Lane, very soon. Number twenty-four turned out to be a well kept house with a sign hanging at the front announcing that there were rooms available. I couldn't help giving a sigh of relief when I found out that the man at the station hadn't just spun me a tale.

I left the baby carriage for a moment and climbed the two steps to the front door and rung the bell. Then I quickly returned to join Mara on the sidewalk.

I didn't have to wait long for the door to open, and a smiling, middle aged woman wearing an apron appeared at the door.

For a moment she looked surprised to find nobody at the doorstep, but then she saw me and walked up to me with a friendly smile, her hand outstretched in greeting.

'My name is Dina Crabbe, how do you do?'

I introduced myself and told her I was looking for a place to stay for the night.

'Of course, of course. Here, let me help you first with the carriage.'

She pulled the suitcase off and disappeared into the house. She returned, and together we lifted the carriage up the little steps into the house.

'I was just about to put dinner on the table, so if you'd care to join us first, we'll have a look at your room after.'

I nodded, overwhelmed, and followed her into the cozy dining room where a table for six was prepared. Three of the seats were already taken by three children. They rose as one from their seats to shake my hand. My hostess nodded approvingly and the children sat down again.

'Have a seat, ma'am. I'll be right back.'

Not quite sure, I chose one of the chairs and pulled the carriage at an angle behind me. Then I sat down and folded my hands in my lap. I felt ill at ease, having disturbed this family as they were just about to have their dinner. The children were silent as well and I felt such relief when the woman returned. With a thump she heaved a heavy pan on the table and took her apron off before she sat down. I noticed that one of the seats was still empty, but the woman paid no attention to it and took the plate in front of me.

'It's nothing fancy, but it's wholesome,' she said, before she returned the plate to me. There was a steaming lump of food in front of me that looked nothing like the food I'd been eating the last number of months. In fact, it reminded me of the food my mother made, so for a few moments I stared at it in silence. In the meantime the woman filled the children's plates and finally she helped herself.

I still sat staring at my food when the children already started to eat. The woman put a spoonful in her mouth as well, then suddenly looked at me and put her spoon down.

'Quiet children. Our guest would first like to say grace before her meal I think, don't you?'

She looked at me inquiringly and I realized that she had mistaken my hesitation for a need to pray. The children now stared at me too and I felt my face flush red. I quickly bowed my head and closed my eyes. What a hypocrite I was.

I don't know why, but for some reason the mealtime prayer that I used to say as a child came back to me, and when I opened my eyes I realized that I had actually prayed.

Somewhat confused I started to eat and I answered my hostess's questions without really thinking. I didn't taste anything of the food. Halfway through dinner the doorbell rang and Mrs. Crabbe returned with the man from the train station.

'I kept wondering to myself if you had been able to find it all right and I just wanted to make sure,' he said. In his hands he held a cap, and he crunched it up into a small wad and then unfolded it again. It reminded me of Reijer.

'I'm glad to see you're enjoying your dinner.'

'My brother is like a walking advertisement for me,' Mrs. Crabbe said while she pulled back the chair with the empty plate in front of it and the man sat down.

'Are you joining us for dinner?'

'No, thank you, the Missus is expecting me.'

I listened in silence to their conversation, and suddenly and idea came to me. I felt very forward when I opened my mouth, but I asked my question anyway.

'Sir, tomorrow I need to cross the Westerschelde. Do you know of anyone I could sail with?'

He was quiet and thoughtfully rubbed a finger over his nose.

'I might know of someone…' Again his finger rubbed back and forth. 'What time did you want to sail?'

I shrugged my shoulders and said: 'It doesn't matter to me, any time will do.'

'I think that for a fee you'll be able to sail with Piet Kannegieter.'

I saw Mrs. Crabbe nod her head enthusiastically at the mention of that name and I looked questioningly from her back to her brother.

'He's going through some tough times now, but if you're willing to pay him…?'

In my mind I calculated how much money was left of the money my aunt had given me, and I knew there must be plenty left. Despite my protests, she had given me a whole purse full.

'Of course I'll pay him.'

'In that case I'll talk to him tonight.'

'That would be wonderful, sir.'

'You let me know what time you'd like to go and I'll arrange things with Piet.'

I could hardly believe how easily things were arranged. These folk were so kind, so I gratefully accepted their help. It was arranged that tomorrow morning at seven o'clock I would depart from the harbour.

After dinner the woman showed me to my room. It was a tidy room and I felt so blessed to have met the man at the station and that he had sent me here.

I withdrew for the night with Mara and went to bed early. Despite all the excitement of the day I fell asleep quickly, all my worries for the coming day disappeared into the background and I had a peaceful and restful night.

32

In the morning, Mrs. Crabbe woke me up and when I came downstairs she had breakfast prepared for me. I tried to eat some of it, but I felt my stomach protest with the tension I felt. Today I would return to the manse.

'Come child, eat some more,' Mrs. Crabbe said.

'It's delicious, really.' My words weren't convincing and I knew my hostess could tell.

'I don't want to put my nose where it doesn't belong, but if you ask me, a young mother ought to take good care of herself. But you know what, I'll wrap up a few sandwiches for you, for along the way. I'm sure your appetite will return when you're on the water.'

'Thank you very much.'

It struck me that Mrs. Crabbe no longer addressed me with 'ma'am', but I felt more comfortable now that she treated me as what I was, a girl, with a child.

'If you like, you can use the kitchen to wash the bottle and prepare a new supply of milk.'

'Thank you.'

I pushed my chair back and followed my hostess to the kitchen where I quickly washed everything and warmed up fresh milk for the thermos. I also prepared a bottle for Mara so I could feed her. I was finished soon and just as I came down with my suitcase, the door opened up and Mrs. Crabbe's brother entered.

'Are you ready?'

'Yes, I just have to bring the baby carriage outside.'

'Let me do that for you.'

While he brought my belongings outside, I settled my bill with Mrs. Crabbe and said farewell to her. She hugged me as if we were old friends and before I could say a word she bent over Mara to give her a kiss.

'A beautiful girl you have. Enjoy her. They grow up so quickly.'

I nodded and followed her to the door, the baby carriage stood ready with my suitcase on top. I decided to keep Mara in the wrap and I stepped onto the sidewalk.

The crossing was uneventful. Piet Kannegieter was a friendly and talkative man. He chatted to me about this, that and the other thing. I found out that he, like so many others these days, had lost his job last week, and that he now took on any little job to earn some cash. His two sons, who had always worked with him on the boat, had left for the city in the hope to find work there, but he himself was too old to try that.

I felt sorry for him, and when we docked I made him a proposition.

'If you've got time and are willing to wait for me, I'll pay you three times the fare.'

He shook his head and scratched his head underneath his cap.

'I can't accept that, ma'am.'

'How else will I be able to return?'

'Aren't you planning on staying here then?'

'No, I hope to be done here in an hour or so.'

He thought for a minute, then nodded.

'All right, but I can't accept the amount you're offering. Let's make it double the fare.'

'That's good.'

I held out my hand to him and he gave it a firm shake. I still meant to pay him the amount I first offered anyway. I had no need for the money and would gladly let him have it.

'Would you mind if I left my luggage on board?'

'Not at all. I'll wait here, and as soon as you've returned, we'll depart.'

'Thank you.'

It was time for me to step off my floating little island. Piet Kannegieter quickly jumped down on the quay and held out his hand for me. Gratefully I accepted his help. From now on I'd be on my own. No, not entirely. I looked down at Mara's face and she stared up at me from inside the wrap. Mother's grandchild.

Slowly I started to walk. At this time of day there wasn't much activity in the harbor, and the few men I saw were so engrossed in their work, they paid no attention to me. It was the beginning of a new and warm spring day, but despite the warm temperature it was cloudy and I half expected it to rain yet. I wished it would start pouring with rain right then and there so the chances of running into familiar faces would be that much smaller.

One more time I checked my skirt's pocket. The envelope was still there, safe and dry. Before I left this morning I had quickly put a pencil in my pocket as well. I still wasn't sure if I had said everything I needed to say in the letter and I was still in doubt over some of the words and phrases I had used. Not that I could do much about it anymore at this point in time.

There wasn't a soul in sight in Harbor Street, but I knew it was very likely that I would run into someone I knew. In order to reach the manse, I had to walk through Hooghe Breet Street, the main street where most of the shops in town were located. People would see me and recognize me. Of course I had known all the time that this moment would come, but now that it truly was here I felt strong waves of doubt come over me. I looked back over my shoulder at the boat that had just brought me here. I couldn't see Piet Kannegieter, but I knew he was around and I only needed to walk back if I wanted to disappear. Nobody had seen me and nobody would miss me.

I looked ahead of me again and gasped a startled breath when I almost bumped into someone. I caught myself just in time, then we both stood still.

'I'm sorry, I wasn't paying attention.' I first checked up on Mara, then I looked up at the woman.

Helène.

Memories flashed through my head and formed a terrible tale of judgment and rejection. I shivered as I realized how similar our lives now were. Deep within I knew what the future had in store for me, and now I looked that future in the eye.

She looked back at me and blinked a few times.

'I am truly sorry,' I said and I put my hand on the sleeve of her coat. Did she understand that I meant more than just my inattentiveness? Should I explain? I stood with my mouth half open and couldn't find the words, and the silence hung between us like an invisible web that connected us but also separated us. Then, with a jerk, she pulled her arm free and my hand fell.

'Don't you think you should go and walk on the other side of the street?' she sneered at me.

I lowered my head with shame and shook 'no'. When I raised my head I no longer wanted to be a coward.

'No, I'm going to keep walking on this side. And I offer you my apologies. For everything.' The last two words came out in a soft whisper, but I knew she had heard me.

She looked at me thoughtfully and then her eyes glanced down at Mara. Her face softened.

'Once I was just like you, pastor's daughter.'

She gently stroked Mara's head. Then she slipped away without another word.

Silent and numb I stood still. Her words echoed in my head. I closed my eyes and remembered the first time we had met. Mother had frightened me and pulled me along. I had obeyed Mother despite the fact that the woman had been kind to me that day on the market. I had let myself be frightened and taken in by tales about fallen women and bastards. Obediently I had avoided Helène at every occasion. I had even, with some other children, thrown chestnuts at her and her little son.

I looked into Mara's innocent face and thought of Helène's poor son whom I had always hated for no reason. Was this the kind of life that lay ahead for my child? Would her mother's shame brand her for the rest of her life?

I looked at my daughter and saw her open up her eyes. She

smiled, blinked and stretched her arms and legs. She was a beautiful child. Many people during my journey had assured me of it and I could see it for myself. There was no reason for me to feel embarrassed for her, nor was there any reason for her to feel ashamed of me. I pulled her up out of the wrap, then folded the cloth around her. Holding Mara close to me, against my shoulder, clearly visible for all to see, I continued walking with determination. I walked faster and faster, and my feet automatically found their way to the manse. I took the corner into Hooghe Breet Street. I started to get out of breath and I could feel sweat trickling down my back. It wasn't far to the manse now, but I knew it was impossible to pass through unnoticed. Someone would recognize me and they would immediatley see Mara too, and in the next instant they would condemn us both.

I closed my eyes for several moments, but kept walking, hoping that I wouldn't run into anyone, that I would be invisible. My hope was dashed very soon when I heard footsteps approaching. I kept focussing on Mara, still hoping I could go on undisturbed, but even before I heard a voice speak, I heard an oh, so familiar cough, and I knew who was standing there in front of me.

'Is it really you, Maria?' Her exaggerated squeal of surprise seemed to echo through the street and I wished for the ground to open up and swallow me, but there was nothing for it, I had to face her.

'Good day, Mrs. Kleut.' I looked straight at her, determined to remain dignified, and I noticed how her steelly blue eyes started to gleam with indignation. She openend her mouth to speak, but she remained speechless with her mouth hanging open like that of a fish gasping for air on land.

'Shouldn't you be at your shop counter, Mrs. Kleut? It's not like you to be walking about town at this time of day. I won't keep you any longer.' I smiled at her and then turned my gaze back to my daughter.

'Come along girl. We've got business to attend to today. Goodbye Ma'am.'

I ignored her and quickly walked on, my nose in the air with pride. No longer did I let my shoulders hang. Everyone was allowed to know I was here, with my daughter.

From the corner of my eye I could see that several little groups of people gathered in the street. Behind me I could hear Mrs. Kleut's shrill voice and I knew she would have assembled a little crowd around her and was giving them the full details of her encounter with me. She'd say that, yes, it really was me, Maria, the pastor's daughter. And that - oh, but keep this hush-hush! – I carried a child in my arms. She would talk in a hushed voice, yet loud enough so everyone who wanted to could hear every word.

I ignored it all and walked past the little white church I hated so much. The small ornamental ship over the entrance door still looked so ridiculously small, but I quickly looked ahead of me again. I could see the manse, diagonally behind the church.

I took a deep breath and stood still with my eyes closed. My hand once more checked my pocket to make sure I still had the envelope. My fingers curled around it. I knew the letter must by now look crumpled and creased, I had held it in my hand so often. Only a few more yards separated me from my mother. I hesitated as I was about to step onto the path leading to the house. There was a very small chance that the Reverend would be home, but I was fairly sure he wouldn't be. Wednesday mornings were always dedicated to home visits. I stood, contemplating what to do, when I felt a raindrop on my cheek, and then another, followed by more.

Without more a-do I opened the little gate and followed the path to the backdoor. Even if the Reverend was home, it wasn't likely that he would see me here. The study was at the front of the house, beside the frontdoor, and Mother's domain was the kitchen at the back of the house. That's where I was most likely to find her. Mara suddenly seemed to weigh much more than usual and my feet also felt heavy. I almost tripped when my foot got caught behind one of the uneven stones in the path.

I had reached the backdoor.

The wind had started to blow and the rain was coming down hard now and it blew against the window. Wet streaks washed the windows and made it impossible for me to see what was going on inside. I tried to keep Mara sheltered from the rain by leaning over her while I ran the last few yards. Out of habit I simply pushed open the backdoor, without knocking. And there I stood in the warm kitchen.

I was gasping for air and needed a few moments to catch my breath. Then I looked up.

Mother was sitting at the kitchen table with some mending in her hands. She stared up at me in shocked surprise. Her mouth fell open. Her hands fell limply on the table and the thimble rolled away, it just stopped at the edge of the table.

I could only hear the sound of my hurried breathing. I turned and closed the door, locking the rain out. Now I my ears picked up another sound, that of the rain hitting the window. Slowly my senses returned and I could smell the familiar aroma of Mother's kitchen, I could feel Mara's little body, still weighing me down. Water had soaked through my clothes and I shivered.

'Maria?' Her voice was no more than a whisper and I wondered if I had heard her correctly.

Before I could respond, Mara stirred and made a loud wail that echoed around the kitchen. I realized how strange it was for me to stand there, in the house where I was raised, in the same room as my mother, but with my back against the door, on the mat, like an uninvited guest.

'Mother.'

'What are you doing here, you're not supposed to be here, not with that child.'

Her words were like the sharp knife stabs. Her voice was indifferent and there was rejection in her eyes.

'Mara. Her name is Mara.' I held on to the daughter I had fought for, and I didn't know what else to say.

'You're not supposed to be here, he won't stand for it. Not with the child.' Her eyes seemed to look straight through me, her lips moved and shaped the words but she didn't seem to be really talking to me.

I pulled the letter from my skirt pocket. The envelope was rumpled, and to make it even worse, two wet drops fell down my face onto it the paper.

'This letter... It is for you. I came to deliver it to you.'

'Letters are delivered by the postman.'

'It would mean so much to me if you would read this letter, Mother.'

Her eyes seemed to glance at the envelope in my hand, but I wasn't sure. She still gazed in that odd, remote way.

'Don't give the letter to the Reverend, Mother. Read it for yourself. That's all I ask.'

Mother still hadn't moved. She sat stiffly on her kitchen chair and didn't seem to have any inclination to hug me.

'Auntie Be sends you her love,' I whispered.

I wiped my feet on the doormat, walked three steps into the kitchen and placed the envelope on the table. I quickly grabbed the pencil from my pocket. I turned the envelope over and hastily wrote with clear letters a short sentence on the back. I had trouble breathing and droplets of sweat were on my forehead. This was my last chance, the only thing left for me to do. I returned the pencil to my pocket and stepped back.

'Please read this, Momma.'

Those were the words I had written. My voice halted, I tripped and turned around. I opened the door and stepped into the rain. Momma, that is what I used to call her. My Momma. How long had it been since I last called her that? And now, all of a sudden that word had found it's way back into that cold kitchen.

I gasped for air and my side ached, yet another pain. The rain beat down on my head and body, and I wrapped my arms protectively around Mara's little body. I was pretty sure she was still dry, but it wouldn't be long for the rain to soak through the fabric and make her wet and cold. It was time to leave. I turned back slowly. I wanted to see her one more time and wave to her, the lonely woman at the kitchen table. But when I turned I was amazed to find her face pressed against the window, so close to me I could touch her.

The heavens wept for her with raindrops streaking down her face behind the window, distorting her features. Unsure, I lifted my hand to wave. I searched her face for a sign of life and I softly whispered one more time 'Momma'.

Then I walked away with hanging shoulders. After about 10 yards I turned again to look at her. I was hoping for something, but

I didn't know what. I think I stood there for at east a minute before I finally turned away to continue walking. At the little gate I turned one last time. The rain was like a curtain between us and I couldn't see much more than a now slowly moving shadow. She pressed her hand against the glass in a desperate gesture. To hold on to me? Or to ward me off?

I didn't run into anyone on my short walk back to Harbor Street. I was half running, half walking, and I jumped over some large puddles that had formed. My biggest concern was that the blanket around Mara wouldn't stay dry. Just as I was about to step on board, a loud voice called out.

'Maria!'

His voice made me stop. Within me was a turmoil of words and memories. I took a deep breath and counted slowly to five, then I climbed on board, ignoring him.

'Mr. Kannegieter!' My voice sounded weak and couldn't even be heard over the sound of the rain, so I called again. Then I saw Piet Kannegieter's head appear from the forecastle and he hurried towards me, leaning his head and shoulders forward because of the rain.

'Are we ready to go?'

'There's just one more thing I need to take care of. Would you mind holding on to my daughter for a moment, and keep her dry in the forecastle?' I pleaded while I held Mara out to him. Piet Kannegieter nodded gravely and asked me no more. His hands were large but gentle as he took Mara from me.

'I'll take good care of the little one.'

'Thank you.' I watched them go and didn't turn till I had seen them disappear into the forecastle.

I stepped onto the quay with my gaze steady on the Reverend. He was still a small distance away when I stood still. The Reverend stopped and we both stood there like two fighters in a ring, measuring each other up. With my chin up I met his gaze squarely, unwavering. I searched his face for signs of his God-given authority. My eyes swept several times over his black hair, the angry frown on his forehead, the black eyes and thin lips.

I couldn't find a trace of the power that once had revolted me and that I had been unable to withstand. Instead I saw a man dressed in black, with wet and unkempt hair, and with a raindrop hanging of his nose that dripped down and kept returning.

My own clothes were also getting drenched by the constant downpour, and I could feel the cold fabric stick to me. But it wasn't as cold as his fury. I watched him in silence. But the silence didn't last. He put another step forward, lifted his finger in the air and started to shout.

'You filthy whore! You disgusting wench! You have ruined my life by coming here with that… that…' He halted and stammered. Even though I couldn't see it in the rain, I knew that spittle was flying out of his mouth. 'That thing!'

Thing.

'Mara. Her name is Mara!' My cry was lifted and carried off by the wind into the village, but he didn't listen and continued his tirade.

'You have ruined my life! Elder Kleut came to tell me that you were in the village with… with… that bastard! You deserve to be punished. I should punish you. It is your duty to honor your father and your mother. Maria, remember the fifth commandment.' He wagged his finger back and forth, then made a fist and raised it to heaven to add force to his words.

Unwanted images that were linked to those words returned to me and I wavered unsteadily. What could I do? How could I stand up to him? He was always there, bigger and stronger. So powerful.

I closed my eyes and took a deep breath. I opened up my eyes and looked at him again. The blood raced through my veins and, despite my cold wet clothes, I felt hot. Not today. Not ever again.

I thought of Mother. How she had sat there so lonely on her kitchen chair, ignorant of the pain she had caused me. How she didn't know my child. These thoughts of the present mingled with memories, both good and bad ones. She would stay here with this man, forever yielding to him and obey his wishes, but not me. Not anymore.

'God will punish you, and I will be the one who will first administer you his punishment.'

He moved forward and I felt the urge to step back in fear, but I didn't. I stood firm. The God he served was not the same God as Auntie Be's. If one of those gods existed, I wanted to put my hope in Auntie Be's God. With my eyes closed I called out to him in a silent prayer. I held my faced lifted up to the dark skies while raindrops ran down my cheeks like tears.

'Stop ignoring me!'

The holy silence was shattered by that pitiful servant. I cherished another moment of silence, still ignoring his words. The rain suddenly stopped and I wiped the last few drops from my face.

'It's over, Reverend.'

I turned around and left him standing there. I climbed on board and walked to the forecastle without looking back. I wanted to hold my daughter. For now and forever.

Epilogue

'Come along now.' Piet Kannegieter beckoned me and I walked toward him unsteadily.

'I'll start the engine and you sit down here.' He helped me in and immediately picked up a warm woolen blanket, which he wrapped around me.

I reached out my arms and whispered her name. Kannegieter handed Mara to me and I held her close. I pressed my nose to her hair and her neck. I smelled her scent and I thanked God. I held her in my arm and gave her something to drink. It felt so comforting to feel the warm weight of her body against me. I watched intently while she drank and I saw how she closed her eyes and drank greedily, unaware of the world around her. She simply entrusted herself to the safety of my arms.

I had done everything I had set out to do here. Now it was up to Mother to decide what to do next. I could only hope and pray.

While Mara drank hungrily, I stood up carefully and wrapped my cloak around the both of us. I had to go outside, I had to look back one more time. Carefully, so as not to disturb Mara, I climbed up the little steps and stepped onto the deck. Kannegieter was standing at the helm and noticed me immediately. He nodded at me but said nothing.

I passed behind him and held on to the rail on the after deck. All that remained of the village were some blurred outlines. Only one clearly visible building seemed to say farewell to me in the distance. The white steeple of God's house. I stood there until I couldn't see anything anymore. Even after that I remained on the after deck for a long time. Mara started to coo and flail her arms about as if she was trying to catch the droplets of water that sprayed about, or the wind, or life?

I was on my way home, with my daughter.

Once more I had traveled many miles and again I was on the train between Arnhem and Velp. This time I was on my own, without a nun to help me. There was a chance that I would have to spend the night in Velp, since I hadn't had an opportunity to notify Auntie of my arrival time. I wasn't concerned about it though, I knew I was almost there.

The train slowed down and I started to walk toward the exit. I held on tight until the train had fully stopped. The doors slid open and I was the first passenger on the platform. I immediately walked along the train toward the baggage car. A few men were already busy unloading the baggage and I tapped my feet impatiently while I waited for the baby carriage and my suitcase.

'Maria!'

I turned and my eyes swept over the crowds.

'Maria!'

She was here!

'Auntie Be!'

I started to run forgetting all about my luggage. People made room for me as I ran and we soon reached each other.

'There you are!'

Auntie grabbed my hands and smiled at me happily.

'Why are you here today? How did you come here?'

'I waited for you.'

We still stood facing each other, hands clasped together, yet slightly removed. Then I stepped forward and hugged Auntie.

I was home.